Praise for

A *Kirkus Reviews* Most Anticipated Book of Spring 2025

★ "A wise, emotionally rich tale of a young man finding his way through family trauma."
—*Kirkus Reviews* (**starred review**)

"*Cope Field* is a commanding novel in which a troubled student learns difficult truths about his family and chooses a new path forward."
—*Foreword Reviews*

"An intense, emotional, heartfelt read, *Cope Field* by T. L. Simpson perfectly captures the complicated feelings of adolescence when you know your problems are bigger than you but you don't know what to do about it yet. Craw channels all of his anger into his 95 mph heater, while Hannah turns up the volume on her punk music, but somehow they see each other in a way nobody else does. Populated with memorable characters like Craw's hilarious younger brother Big Time and his generous-but-volatile father who has the whole town fooled, *Cope Field* immersed me in this world of the Ozarks and pick-up trucks and grass fields and plain speaking. I read the whole book like I'd watch any baseball game—with my heart in my throat, waiting for the ones I'm rooting for to triumph in the end."
—**Alicia Thompson,** *USA Today* **bestselling author of** *The Art of Catching Feelings*

"Simpson's sophomore novel steps up alongside *Strong Like You* to define a new age of sports literature. With a cast of complex and heart-wrenching characters, raw insight into the triumphs and tragedies of teenage masculinity, a no-pulled-punches look at life in the Ozarks, and a voice so authentic you could call it poetry, *Cope Field* strikes hard until the nail-biting finish. A must-have for all the angry kids trying to find their way through."
—**Matteo L. Cerilli, author of** *Lockjaw*

"Simpson's frank, unflinching portrait of two defiant teens struggling to transcend brutal violence is a crackling alchemy of baseball and punk rock that shook me, made me cheer, and kept me up all night. A rare, relentless, gorgeous gem of a novel, recommended for anyone who's ever had something to fight."
—**Sarah Lariviere, author of** *Time Travel for Love and Profit*

"Timely and timeless, *Cope Field* is a viscerally impactful story about much more than baseball. I couldn't put this book down."
—**Sara Farizan, author of** *Here to Stay*

"*Cope Field* is an absolute triumph. Simpson's sophomore book is a beautiful, heart-wrenching story of a young man who loves big in spite of his pain. The most honest thing I've read in a long time, this story is about the courage it takes to proverbially kill your heroes and find your voice. And while it tore me apart, Simpson's prose also put me back together with hope and the possibility for healing. A must-read."

—Erica Ivy Rodgers, author of *Lady of Steel and Straw*

"I loved Crawford's story and the lengths he goes through to protect the people he loves. Heartbreaking, relatable, and punk rock to its core, *Cope Field* is a grand slam of a book."

—Anthony Nerada, author of Indie Next Pick *Skater Boy*

"Simpson has a knack for delivering entertaining reads that take on important issues teens and young adults grapple with. *Cope Field* is a gripping and timely read."

—Jeff Wooten, author of *Kill Call*

"*Cope Field* is a home run. A gripping modern classic, full of so much heart and grit and punk rock tenacity, each word refuses to leave you dry-eyed. T. L. Simpson simply doesn't miss."

—Freya Finch, author of *Rise*

"With a voice that grabs hold of you and doesn't let go until its gut-wrenching final page, Simpson weaves a heartbreaking tale of the complicated nature of love, loss, and family. A beautiful, important novel."

—MK Pagano, author of *Girls Who Burn*

"*Cope Field* will punch you in the gut, break your heart, and somehow put it back together again. T. L. Simpson writes an unflinching story about one teen boy's reckoning with his anger issues and the insidious truth hidden behind his father's perfect public image. It deserves to be an instant classic."

—Trish Lundy, author of *The One That Got Away with Murder*

"T. L. Simpson shines a bright light on a subject too often relegated to the shadows. A baseball book about so much more than baseball. Riveting."

—Carl Deuker, author of *Golden Arm*

"T. L. Simpson writes with a dynamic balance of yesterday, today, and where we're headed as an audience in his sublime literary hands. *Cope Field* provides the reader with a stunning view from a box seat, close enough to the action to both revel and win."

—Paul Volponi, bestselling author of *Black and White*, *The Final Four*, *Rikers High*, and *Top Prospect*

COPE FIELD

T.L. SIMPSON

Mendota Heights, Minnesota

Cope Field © 2025 by T. L. Simpson. All rights reserved. No part of this book may be used or reproduced in any manner whatsoever, including internet usage, without written permission from Flux, except in the case of brief quotations embodied in critical articles and reviews.

First Edition
First Printing, 2025

Book design by Karli Hughes
Cover design by Andrew Selbitschka
Cover and interior illustrations by T. L. Simpson

Flux, an imprint of North Star Editions, Inc.

This is a work of fiction. Names, characters, places, and incidents are either the product of the author's imagination or are used fictitiously, and any resemblance to actual persons living or dead, business establishments, events, or locales is entirely coincidental.

Library of Congress Cataloging-in-Publication Data
Names: Simpson, T. L., author.
Title: Cope field / T. L. Simpson.
Description: Mendota Heights, Minnesota: Flux, 2025. | Audience term: Teenagers | Audience: Grades 10–12.
Identifiers: LCCN 2024047088 (print) | LCCN 2024047089 (ebook) | ISBN 9781635831054 (paperback) | ISBN 9781635831061 (ebook)
Subjects: CYAC: Anger--Fiction. | Community service (Punishment)--Fiction. | Child abuse--Fiction. | Friendship--Fiction. | LCGFT: Novels.
Classification: LCC PZ7.1.S5655 Co 2025 (print) | LCC PZ7.1.S5655 (ebook) | DDC [Fic]--dc23
LC record available at https://lccn.loc.gov/2024047088
LC ebook record available at https://lccn.loc.gov/2024047089

Flux
North Star Editions, Inc.
2297 Waters Drive
Mendota Heights, MN 55120
www.fluxnow.com

Printed in Canada

for melissa

Everything buzzes.

My elbows.

My hands.

Pops woulda yelled at me. Woulda said, "Every time, Craw. Every damn time. Your swing is off. Your stance is off. Everything about you is off."

He'd have said that if he wasn't on the floor.

Blood leaking from his mouth and nose, him cursing and gargling his own juices.

One thing he taught me.

Do the right thing.

Do the hard thing.

But looking at him, I'm not so sure. He always says baseball is about timing. I guess he's right. My timing was off. You hit too low on the bat, those vibrations move through your body. Electrocute your bones. Hit too high? Same thing. There's a sweet spot. Dead center of the barrel. Right where you want to be. Wouldn't have buzzed if I had done it right. But looking down at him, looking at Big Time crying across the room...

I can't say it matters much.

It seems like my timing was just about perfect. Pops tries to get up. One hand on the ground. Blood falling on the artificial turf like drops of rain. Bright red against green. Christmas colors. Then he falls again, rolls to his back, and looks up at me. "Jesus, Craw," he says. "Call 911."

part one
cope field

crawford cope thinks baseball matters

AMERICAN IDIOT
GREEN DAY

Pops holds Big Time's hand as we cross the parking lot. He looks back at me. Clean-shaven. Wearing a suit and a pair of aviator glasses. I can't even see his stitches. Hidden in his tangled brown hair, which he wears swept back. He says, "Smile some, Craw. It's going to be alright."

And I believe him. Because one thing about Pops is this. No matter what happens, he will take care of it. He'll make sure everything keeps moving. Pops is the glue that keeps us together. And he always has been.

He kept us together when Momma left.

He'll keep us together now.

"Don't worry. I'm fine," I tell him.

Big Time says, "Can we get pizza after this?"

Pops tells him we can. We can get as many pizzas as he wants. Because it's not a bad day. It's a good day. It's the kind of day we will celebrate after. So where do you want pizza from, Big Time? How much pizza you think a little guy like you can eat?

Big Time smiles and says he can eat all the pizza. "Every pizza there ever was."

Pops looks back at me again. Saying with his eyes, *Can you believe this kid?* He smiles, like nothing ever happened between us. But I can feel it. I can't forget. God knows I have tried, but I cannot. Been two months and all this stuff been swirling around inside me like the contents of a toilet bowl. Nothing I can sort out. Nothing I'd *want* to sort out, either. I was glad at first, but now I am mixed up and all over the place. What kind of person hits their own father with a baseball bat?

Crawford Cope. That's who.

Pops holds the door to the courthouse open for me. We walk toward the courtroom. Inside, there is nobody except a Judge. Who winks at Pops and says, "How you been, old-timer?"

"Been real good, Brucie Boy."

Seems like Pops is buds with every person we meet. He grew up in Quiet County. Then we moved back here once baseball was done with him, right before Momma run off and we never saw her again. They just about built a statue of the man up at Hosanna, which is where half the county goes to school, even though it's a good hour to get there for some of us. Hosanna isn't much of nothing to begin with. A blip on the map. Blink, and you'll miss it. But they have a baseball team. The Hosanna Patriots. Colors: red, white, and blue.

You can't find anyone around here who don't know about Hunter Cope, the boy from the backwoods of Arkansas who made it through to The League.

The Judge laughs and says, "Hey, my nephew just started playing baseball. When should I start teaching him the right way to swing the bat? He just goes up to the tee and thunks it off. Like, it gets some distance. But not much. Just a little. Kind of funny—all these kids with no clue what to do. Kids in right field running all the way to first base trying to get the ball. Hell, I even seen the runner go chasin' after the ball one time."

They both laugh. Pops says, "That'll happen."

"So when's too young? And are you giving lessons?"

"Start 'em off early, I say. Ask my boy here. He was hitting nukes by the time he was six. And no to lessons. Family secret."

The Judge looks down the bench at me. Head to toe. Like he is sizing me up. "I believe it," he says, matter-of-fact. Like, don't question it. He *is* a Judge, you know. "You look just like your father. I bet you hear that all the time."

I sure do. About every single day of my life.

Big Time says, "I hit a shot over the fence. First game ever."

"Oh?" the Judge says.

"That's why they call me Big Time."

"Well, aren't you something."

The lawyers come in. They sit down where they are supposed to sit. One says hello to me. Asks about baseball. Asks about workouts. Says his son complains they are too long. Says he wishes he could get him to give a damn. "All he wants to do is play Xbox all year. Then he gets out in the heat and feels sick to his stomach. I said to him, 'Of course you feel sick, Luis. You're soft.' But he don't listen to me."

I just say "Oh" to that.

"He's a freshman. Luis Iglesias? You know him."

"I know him a little."

"Yeah? What you think? He a good catcher?"

"He just got moved up to varsity."

"So you haven't played with him yet?"

"Not a lot," I say. But I'm looking past him at Big Time.

Pops says, "Can I talk with Craw outside a minute? Before we start?"

The Judge says he can. So he leads me back out of the courtroom. Leaves Big Time behind, sitting on a bench, watching some YouTube video on his tablet about outer space, no doubt. In the hallway, Pops looks this way and that. Then he looks me straight in the eye, one hand on my shoulder.

"It's going to be fine," he says.

I don't say nothing. I find it's best to keep my mouth shut most of the time. To keep this swirling toilet bowl locked up inside my skull. Open my mouth just a little and it can all come out at once. Then what?

Don't nobody want that.

"Listen," Pops says. "Don't say nothing to the Judge. You have the right to remain silent and all that, you know? Don't say a thing. This ain't like a jury trial. You're still a kid. And everybody in that room is on your side. Nobody wants to see you throw away your future."

I break eye contact. Look at my shoes. Jordans. Crisp and clean.

Pops pulls me into a hug. "Most of all, *I* don't want to see you throw your future away," he whispers. "I'm on your side, Craw. I promise. Even after everything you done to me."

"I hear you." It comes out soft. Like a mumble.

"You think you're the only one who ever lost his cool and done something stupid? Believe me, I been where you are a hundred times. I've lost my cool in ways you can't even imagine. You just got some anger problems you gotta get under control. But don't worry. Me and the Judge go back a ways. And I done talked to him about everything. He agrees with me. Everything is gonna get better from here. You just gotta put in the work, Craw. It's just like baseball. You got some work to do. That's all."

My soul is leaving my body. Watching this whole scene from far away. A little ghostie up in the rafters. Like *bon voyage*.

Pops takes my chin in his hand, directs my eyes to his. "Hey," he says. "I know you feel bad about what happened. But I don't. You got to forgive yourself because it's all in the past, and all we can do is try and be right from here on."

I nod my head yes.

"We are family," he says. "And there is not one thing more important than family." He gets quiet, thinking. Then he scruffs my hair like I am a child. His hand goes to my cheek. Gives me a little slap. Not hard. But hard enough to snap my soul back into place.

He's right.

There is nothing more important than family. When Momma left us, I learned the hard way how it feels when a family breaks up. There is no way I am visiting that pain on Big Time. Pops does his best to be both Mom and Dad. Failing sometimes. But getting it right sometimes, too. We coulda fallen apart back then. But he kept us going. And how did I repay him?

I busted his head open with a baseball bat.

Because I can't control myself.

Because my fuse might be long, but it runs hot. And when I have had enough, I don't have the means to stop myself from acting stupid. I guess that is what they mean when they say I got anger management problems. All folks get mad sometimes. Not all of them grab a weapon and hurt somebody.

"You know what happens if you lose your cool in front of the Judge?" Pops says.

One of the lawyers opens the door. Behind him, I can see Big Time sitting on that bench. He is laughing so hard at whatever video he is watching. Headphones on. Oblivious to how loud he is being.

"Nothin' good, Pops," I say.

He nods. Gives me a soft smile. "Nothin' good at all."

Big Time glances over his shoulder. Sees me. He gives me a grin and a thumbs-up. Still oblivious. God, I love that kid.

The lawyer leans out the door and says, "The Judge is ready to start."

I FOUGHT THE LAW
THE CLASH

Everything goes down exactly like Pops said. I keep my mouth shut. He does all the talking. And the Judge seems to know everything already.

Everybody is in agreement. Crawford's a good kid. A great kid. An asset to the community. Not to mention an important member of this year's baseball team, given he pitches in the 90s. Given he controls the ball when he pitches. Given nobody in the state can hit off him. And none of that is even considerin' his presence at the plate.

The Hosanna Patriots need him this year.

Oh, and he's just a fantastic young man, we all agree. A fantastic young feller who needs a little bit of help with his anger problems.

And we're gonna win state again. Just like we did back when Hunter was slinging for us.

"Isn't that right, Craw?" Judge says to me. "We gonna win state?"

I nod. Feels rotten inside, moving my head like that. Up and down. Lying without speaking. Judge leans across the bench, eyes me for a long time. He says, "Before we move on, is there anything you want to say to me? Something you might *need* to say to me. Something I might oughta know before I decide on this case?"

I do have words inside me. Raging around like wildfire. Burning up my insides. I wish I could siphon them out. Breathe fire like some kinda dragon on this entire room.

Then Pops raises his eyebrows, shakes his head one time. So subtle, nobody sees it but me.

It's like water on fire. Leaves me smoldering.

Leaves me silent.

Because he's right. This is the anger problem, I guess. Eating me alive. It's what got me here. So I gotta choke it down.

Big Time's face is buried in his screen. He still has no clue we are standing on the edge of something. Teeter one way, and our lives change forever. Teeter the other, and it's just me. Shoulderin' a boulder up a hill. Forever.

I lock eyes with the Judge. Make sure he knows I am serious. "There's nothing," I say.

Judge nods slow. He writes something on a piece of paper. "Take this," he says.

He reaches down. Hands it to me. There's an address written across the top.

"Be there every Saturday at eight in the morning," Judge says. "Until whatever time they turn you loose."

"What is it?"

"Craw, I'm sentencing you to three hundred hours community service. You've got some anger issues to work through. It's okay. We all got something we gotta work on. And you can cool your head working with Roger out in Jerusalem."

"Working on what?" I ask.

He and Pops share a look. No clue what that look is about. But I don't think on it too long. Everything is happening too fast.

"You'll find out when you get there. Keep your head down. Nose to the grindstone. Do the work, then get back to your life. Get back to baseball." He smiles at me. Warm. And real. He means it. I can tell. "You're going places, Craw. Swinging for the fences. Let this here be nothing more than a bump in the road."

I don't say a word. I can't. My mouth won't move. Like everything in my head is locked behind my teeth, and I don't got the key.

Pops nudges me.

He nudges me again.

Finally, I get some words out. "Yes, sir," I say. "Just a bump in the road." It feels like I pulled those words up my throat on a string of glass. Like it took all I had to spit them out. And I am shredded raw from the inside out because of them. I got to work on this. I got to fix whatever wire went loose inside my brain and made me act this way.

Yes, sir.

Bump in the road.

FAMILY VALUES
FIFTEEN

Pops is in one of his spendy moods. Must be feeling good after everything. He keeps his promise to buy Big Time as much pizza as he can handle. Drives us north into Missouri, where we eat at a pizza buffet and Pops downs a whole pitcher of beer.

Big Time peters out after two plates, and Pops says, "Had enough, have ya?"

Big Time lifts his shirt and pats his belly.

"Thought you said you could eat every pizza that ever was?"

"Well, Pops, that's what you call a figure of speech."

That gets a laugh from me. Big Time is always saying things too big for his britches. Things a kid like that oughta not know about. I guess he's learning something from those YouTube videos. One time he went on a ten-minute rant explaining to me quasi-stars or black holes or some such thing I can't even remember. I sure as hell didn't learn about figures of speech or black holes from the Ninja Turtle cartoons I watched growing up.

On our way out of the pizza buffet, this older man stops us. He's like, *Oh my God*, sticking a hand toward Pops. "You're Hunter Cope."

"That's me," Pops says, standing up tall. Because he lives for this kinda moment. Especially when we are outside Quiet County, where every person you come across knows every little thing about him. Being recognized like this in a whole different state is a nice reminder that Pops' name still carries some weight. Folks still know who he is.

The old man asks if we can wait right here. "Sorry. I don't want to intrude. It's just, I don't got nothin' for you to sign. Can I run out to my car? Can you wait here? Are you busy?"

Pops tells him we aren't. The man comes back with a dirty envelope from the electric company and an ink pen that looks like it's been rolling around on the floorboard of his truck for a hundred thousand years. A real relic, that thing. He passes them to Pops and says, "All I got, sorry."

"S'alright, Pard. Who am I making this out to?"

"William Freedman. Are these your boys?"

"Yep."

"They play ball?"

"Sure do," Big Time says, puffing out his chest. "Goin' pro, just like Pops."

"What about the big'n? He sure looks like a ball player to me."

I don't say a word.

Pops writes,

To William, thank you for the support. Go Royals!

Then his little loopy signature:

Hunter Cope #12

"He plays. I assure you the apple don't fall far from this tree."

The old guy laughs. "Maybe I oughta have you two sign this thing, too. You never know." He passes it to Big Time first, who writes in all capital letters: SUTTON "BIG TIME" COPE. Then he gives it to me. I write crawford cope. Small box letters. As perfect as I can make them. Like they came from the clanging keys of an old typewriter. The old man looks at the sigs and says, "Thank y'all both. I won't hold you up no more."

Back in the truck, I watch that old fella walking with the envelope. He looks down at our names etched on that dirty slip of paper, then he holds it to his chest like it's a prized possession. That old guy's smile is huge. And it puts a smile on me, too.

What Pops did matters to people.

Maybe it's just a dumb game. But it matters.

Pops cranks on the radio and sings along to country music. He glances over his shoulder and smiles at me. Big Time joins in with him, and they warble like a pair of coyotes at the moon. Before long, I let my guard down enough to join in. And we sing together. Like the three worst Opry guests of all time. Ugly and beautiful all at once. And it's like—why wouldn't I fight to save this? To do whatever is asked of me to keep us three together. Three boys with one heart beating in the hills of the Ozarks. Three who overcame so much hurt. Who have so much left to give each other. My eyes sting with tears thinking about it.

Cope Field

Pops takes us to a retro arcade, where you pay five dollars and can play all these old-school video games. The kind you used to have to drop a quarter into. But they got that little feature switched off. You can play as much as you want for as long as you want for five bucks. After that, he takes us to a sports store and buys me a new baseball bat. Five hundred dollars right there. Plus a new pair of Jordans, which I didn't need, but I got a little collection growing anyway. I wear 'em out of the store, feeling pretty fly if I am being honest. After that, we head to an electronics store, where Pops eyeballs a seventy-two-inch television.

Big Time says, "What do I get?"

So far, nothing but pizza.

"What do you want, Big Time?" Pops says.

Big Time taps his chin. Then he waves for us to follow. Me and Pops look at each other like, *What in the hell is this?* He leads us to where they got all these tablets on display. "Now, listen," Big Time says.

We listen.

"I don't wanna hurt your feelings, because I know that tablet I've got was a Christmas gift a couple years back."

"Okay," Pops says, amused.

"But it's old now. And the new iPad is out. And it can play better games. Plus, it gots a real good camera, because I was thinking I might could make some baseball videos. You know, like teaching folks the right way to swing and stuff. So this ain't what you might call a *want*. It's more of what you might call a *need*."

"Baseball videos, huh?" Pops says.

I can feel the grin on my face. Like, this is us. This is our family. And I guess the relief is starting to wash over me a bit. That my stupid mistake wasn't stupid enough to destroy us. Us three are still together. Still up to no good. Still listening to Big Time run his mouth forever.

"I do need it, Pops. I lay awake at night thinking about it."

Pops cracks up. He calls over an associate. Big Time does this wild dance in the aisle, and that little dance gets me belly laughing. The kid just defaults to happy, even when we are not buying expensive toys. I wish I could remember how to do that. Wish I could dance in the middle of the electronics store and not worry about what the whole world thinks of me.

"Anything for my boys," Pops says.

And looking at Big Time, looking at Pops, I really believe things might be different now. I am gonna be better. And the way forward for Big Time is gonna be smooth. If that's true, then maybe it's worth having gone through what I have gone through.

I hang my hat on that one.

Getting better.

Working hard.

Staying together.

All worth it for Big Time.

CLEAR THE AIR
OFF WITH THEIR HEADS

It's quiet in the house. I got the lights low in my bedroom. And because I am full-on dedicated, I go ahead and find some tea light candles in the kitchen, scatter them around my room, and light them. I sit in the center of my bed with my legs crisscrossed and look around at all my baseball trophies. Then at this old poster of Nolan Ryan on the wall. He's got blood all over his face. A smear on the front of his jersey. You can't see his eyes for the brim of his hat, and he's fingering a ball hidden in his glove.

Pops says there are all kinds of life lessons in baseball. And I think I am getting near to one right now. Ryan's all bloody because he got stroked by a line drive by Bo Jackson. Thing is, he went ahead and got Jackson out, stayed in the game, and pitched seven innings.

That is grit.

That is mind over matter.

Ryan may be the greatest pitcher who ever lived. With stats that will probably never be touched. And that is because of moments like that. Moments where others woulda let the pressure get in their brain and tear them apart. Nolan stayed strong. And I got to do that, too. I got to figure out a way to get past these anger issues. Or they will destroy me before I can even get started.

I reach across the bed and find the VR headset Pops got me for Christmas two years ago. Then I pull up YouTube. I type in: *dealing with anger issues.*

It's all doctors talking and being boring.

But one of them says to try meditation. So I type in: *anger management meditation.*

I click on the first video. The VR headset makes it 3D. It is like I am floating over the ocean. The water cresting in little white caps far below. I can hear the wind. The sound of the waves. And somewhere distant, this low and droning music. A voice whispers to me: "*Of course you are angry. You have every right to be angry.*"

I look around.

Nothing but ocean.

"*But you have hurt others with your anger. Haven't you? You wouldn't be here if you hadn't.*"

I've watched these 3D videos before. Pretty neat, I guess.

But this one has me feeling some kind of way.

I slide the visor up and glance around the room, I guess making sure I haven't floated away.

"*Listen to my voice. Listen to the waves. Look around you. Or close your eyes. I will speak, and you will listen. And we will root out the source of your anger together. Only by understanding our hurts can we truly overcome them.*"

I slide the headset back into place.

I am a skeptic. But willing to try anything at this point.

"*Think back to the last time you were angry enough that you hurt someone. It could be you said something you didn't mean. You may have lashed out. You may have physically hurt someone. Go back to that moment. I know it is hard, but it is very important.*"

I close my eyes.

The fake wind roars in my ears.

I see Pops standing over Big Time. The bat on the artificial turf between them.

I'm scared.

I see my hand reaching for the bat—

The door to my room flies open, snapping me out of my memory. I yank off the headset. See Big Time standing in the doorway. He screws up his face and gestures to all the tea light candles. "What in the hell are you doing?"

I toss the headset onto the bed behind me and snuff out all the candles real fast. "Nothing. Go away, you idiot."

"You're real weird, bud."

"Will you get out of here already?"

"I'd love to, but Pops wants to practice. So meet us at the indoor field in five. Pops said to bring that new bat he bought you."

When he's gone, I sit there a moment longer. Anxiety building up in my stomach. Because that dungeon is tied up in what happened between me and Pops. And my heart wants to think all is forgiven. But I know I am going to have to earn it.

3 STRIKES
URBAN OUTFIELDERS

I break in the new bat all evening inside the indoor practice facility behind our house. Pops built it after Momma ran off. Because why not? He always wanted one to train me up in. And she never let him spend that kind of money when I was small, saying all the time it'd spoil me. Telling him, "If he's got the talent to make it, he's got it with or without an indoor facility in the backyard."

Which. Maybe not all the way true. Baseball is about routine. It's muscle memory. It's working at the same thing over and over and over again until you can do it without thinking. But the sentiment is nice, I guess.

Now she's not here to stop him.

It's not like he built the facility from the ground up. There was an old workshop back there, which he converted. Put down fake grass inside. Nets for batting cages. Space to play catch. A pitching machine. All kinds of odds and ends that must have some use, but we never touch. It's got enough space for an entire travel ball team, but me and Big Time have it all to ourselves. I like to call it the Baseball Dungeon because you sure as hell can get trapped out here.

Pops can still throw in the high 80s, even after two Tommy John surgeries. It's enough to warm up on. Good practice for most of the arms I'll face at the high school level. Plus, he can throw 'em tricky, so I get good looks at sliders and curves. When his arm wears out, he puts me on the pitching machine. Cranks that baby up to 90.

"See what you can do," he says.

Big Time sits on the other side of the net. Crisscross applesauce. His elbows on his knees. Chin in his hands. He's wearing a pair of wraparound pro-rassler-looking visor glasses even though we're inside. "Rip it," he says.

I crack the first one straight at the pitching machine. Pops ducks behind the net, laughing. "That's a shot." He hits a few more buttons and says, "Ninety-five." Then he loads another ball, which I hit to the back of the netting. "Another shot," Pops says. He hits some buttons. "One hundred."

"Rip it, rip it, rip it!" Big Time says. Sounding like an old bullfrog on a log. He stands up, starts pumping his fist. Pops loads the ball. Fires it.

My eyes key in. My body goes automatic. I don't think even one bit of this. Yet my body does it. Muscle memory worked in deep by ten million repetitions. Step up to the plate. Load the hands. Explode the hip. Squish the bug. Drive the knob. Extend. Follow through. Chest to the sky.

Boom.

After Pops says I am done, he puts Big Time at the plate. Starts him at 40 miles per hour, same speed as the pitching machines in rec league. Then he has me come in and throw a few so Big Time can see them off the hand. Big Time talks a big game about his swing. And he's got reason to. Kid can hit with the best of them. But he's got a wild arm. If you play catch with him, you will spend half the time chasing balls you had no chance at. It's ridiculous. You can walk him through it a thousand times, saying, "Snakes out" or "The ball follows your glove" or all the other ten million things folks come up with to explain how to throw a baseball, and he will keep right on hucking them over your head. Pops likes to say, "This ain't catch. This is chase." On account of him having to chase the ball half the time.

After Big Time's done at the plate, we fetch our gloves and play catch. And it don't take long before the ball is bouncing off the wall with a metallic *smack*, Pops chasing after and cursing under his breath. First few are fine. Then Pops says, "You side-arm that ball one more time, I am going to bust your ass."

I grit my teeth. Heat bubbling in my stomach.

The next throw is high. Pops jumps but can't jump high enough. The ball thuds off the wall. Pops snatches it with his glove, spins, and hurls the thing back at Big Time with the kinda force he mighta used throwing to first on a tight play. I see the whole thing in slow motion. Big Time's eyes widen. His face goes white. That ball zips through the air like a bullet, shredding space and time, the sound like a firecracker going off when Big Time snags it out of the air with his glove, less than a foot away from his face. He stands looking at it, like he can't believe he caught it.

Cope Field

Pops says, "Throw it like that."

Big Time bursts into tears.

We are done.

I throw my glove on the ground. Anger roils up in me. I wish at that moment I'd finished that stupid VR meditation video. Maybe it had some advice for staying cool in moments like this. I march straight toward Pops.

Pops stands proud. Shoulders back. Hands at his sides. Welcoming anything. "What?" he says. "You got something for me, Craw? Ain't we working on ourselves now? You want me to report back to the Judge you done messed up again, after all that leniency he showed you?"

Big Time hollers, "Don't. Please... don't!"

And that catches something inside me. He is talking to *me*.

I don't say nothing besides, "Come on, Sutton. Let's go on up to the house. We done enough practice today."

Outside, the sky is devoid of clouds. Stars like you have never seen stars. Across the way, all these fireflies blinking in and out of the dark. More than could be counted by me or anyone else. I can't breathe. Can't catch my breath. We stand there watching. Feeling the cool breeze. Listening to the locusts sing. Birds in conversation someplace far off. The moon low, red and giant in the sky. Big Time says, "He is just trying to make us better."

I sigh. Sorta shut down inside. "I know."

Maybe this wouldn't keep happening if I was a better son. Maybe if I was more in control. Maybe if I didn't jump straight to the worst. Maybe if I didn't have a million confusing feelings swirling around inside me at all times...

I got too many maybes. Not enough concretes.

That is my problem.

I look down at Sutton. His eyes brown like Momma's. Hair red like hers, too. Lookin' at him has me feeling some kinda way. Because the older he gets, the more he looks like her. This child cannot even remember the woman who birthed him. And he don't know that about once per week, I sit down at the computer and punch her name into a search engine. Stare at it for a long time.

But I never hit enter. I can't.

I cannot will my finger to press the button. To populate results. To see what's become of her.

Because what if she has a good life now? What if she's happy? What if she got pictures of herself up on Facebook?

A new husband.

New kids.

Big smiles across their faces.

Love in their hearts.

How could she be happy without us?

How could she make it somewhere better without taking us with her?

I don't want to know because I am not sure my heart can take it.

Then there's this other part. One I have never said out loud to anyone. This deep, insidious feeling in my stomach.

It is my fault she left.

One half my brain knows this can't be true. The other half insists it is. And the insistent half is the louder half by far. I am chewing on that thought at almost all times. On some level. Deep down under everything. Eating around its edges. Or maybe it's eating me. Either way. Something is getting chewed on.

Pops steps outside behind us. He puts his hands on the small of his back and stretches. He says, "I'm sorry, boys."

Me and Big Time look at each other.

Pops says, "I love you both."

"Love you, too, Pa," Big Time says.

"I know I'm intense sometimes. But I promise y'all, I am only trying to make y'all better. Trying to help you along. And one day, you will look back on this and you'll see it. And you'll be glad I done all the things I done to help you."

"I'm glad about it now," Big Time says. "I just got scared in there. That's all. But you saw I caught it. I caught that thing. Didn't I catch it, Pops? We all saw I did."

Pops laughs. "You sure did. I wouldn't have thrown it like that if I didn't know you could catch it." He picks up Big Time, throws him over a shoulder, and starts walking. Their shape punches a silhouette in the moon. "You know, boys, since your momma's gone, it's us versus the world."

I can't speak one single thing that's inside my brain.

Not one thing.

HOMESICK
A DAY TO REMEMBER

A memory:

Me as a little boy. Momma on the porch watching me and Pops play catch in the front yard. She is reading a book with this muscled man with no shirt on the front cover. But she stops reading and puts the book broken-spine across her knee. Sutton, all chubby and squishy, sleeps in a car seat at her feet, which she rocks gently with one toe. There are blue Christmas lights strung up on the trim of the house, still on even though it is daytime.

"Momma, hey Momma, watch."

That's me. Hollering because I want to show her how I can dive for the ball and catch it like the outfielders do on television. Pops saying, "You're a pitcher, Craw. You ain't gonna be catching many pop-ups you gotta dive for."

I am ten. We have only lived in Quiet County for a little while now.

I just want to show off for my momma. But Pops is not having it. He puts his hands on his hips. Says, "Craw, let's go around back. Get some tee work in."

"Come on. Just one time," I say.

Pops rubs the inside of his elbow. "My arm's hurtin', Craw. I don't wanna throw it no more."

But that means nothing to me. Pops is invincible in my mind.

I get to fussing and carrying on until Pops tells me I better hush it if I don't want my butt busted. In my memory, he is smiling. Got love in his heart when he says it. Like he won't really do it.

But my memories are hazy. Sometimes wrong, I think. Because looking back, we all knew this was serious. We *had* to have known. The three of us, knowing this threat had been leveled at a child and reacting like it was ordinary.

Because for us...

It was.

Momma says, "Aw, Hunter, let him try one time. You got one more in you, don't you? Hunter I know always has one more pitch in him."

"Waste of time."

"He'll remember it." She said this a lot. *He'll remember it.* Because Momma was adopted by an older couple, folks who died before I was even born. She never knew her own parents. Or if she had any sisters or brothers or aunts or cousins. When Momma thought back on her childhood, she didn't remember Christmas mornings, Thanksgiving dinners, arguments, goofin' off, or any of the normal family stuff. One time, she told me she had a big empty space in her heart where her family should have been. She said I put my little hand on her cheek and said, "Don't worry, Momma, I can live in there. I'll grow great big so I can fill it up!"

This was her favorite story to tell. I must have heard it ten thousand times. Making memories meant something extra to her.

Pops scratches the back of his head. "Alright, fine."

I grin great big and hurry across the yard. I get in my ready stance, and Pops launches the ball in the air as high as he can. High and short, so I have to run up under it and dive to make the catch.

I take off running, keeping my eye on the ball. And just like they do on the television, I jump, glove out, belly first, and snag the ball just before it touches grass. I skid a few yards, then roll to my feet, huge smile on my face.

Momma gives me a standing ovation.

Pops says, "We done?"

I feel the smile melt off my face. Or maybe my memories added that part in later. Who knows? But I remember Momma's smile for sure. It stays on. And that smile is seared in my memory. The amber sunlight in a crescent along her face, sparkling in her brown eyes and auburn hair. "Best do what he says, Crawford. You're gonna be a star one day. I know it."

It is the last thing she ever says to me.

SANDLOT PARTY
ISOTOPES

Zero clue where I'm meant to do community service. I plug the address into my phone, and it shows up as a field in the middle of Jerusalem. And that's not a sarcastic way of me saying it's far away—although it *is*. The place really is called Jerusalem.

Not big enough for a baseball team, that much I can tell you. Not big enough for a school of any kind, either. Pops says it's unincorporated. Which I think means it isn't a real town. Just folks living together. Calling themselves a town without having to get any real government involved. That is my guess. Do not hold me to it.

Big Time follows me to my truck. He walks to the passenger door and opens it.

"What are you doing?" I ask him.

"Going with you."

"You can't."

"Why not?"

"It's community service."

"So?"

"So you aren't allowed."

"Why not?"

I invoke his real name. Let him know I'm serious. "Because, *Sutton*, I don't want you to come." The last thing I need is to spend an entire day breaking my back in the spring heat while Big Time yacks my ear off about the solar system or black holes or whatever. Besides, I don't even know if he's allowed.

"You know what? I don't want to come actually," Big Time says, climbing back out of the truck, stretching to reach the ground thanks to the lift kit. "I think I'll float around the pool some. Eat some ice cream sammiches. Play on the PlayStation." He points a finger gun at me. "I'll think about ya, though."

T. L. Simpson

I watch him walk past the front of the truck. He meanders on the porch, clearly hoping for me to change my mind. When he sees it as a lost cause, he throws me two finger guns and says, "Peace," before dipping back through the front door and into the air-conditioning.

It's a long drive. Nothing but cow fields and rotted trailer homes and American flags; little kids running around in the yard, barefoot and diapered, playing hard; mommas looking on from the porch, cell phone in one hand, vape in the other. The road sort of blurs out. My brain goes on its own little journey, wandering down pathways of thought I keep asking it to stay away from. But there's no stopping it.

Take this, for example.

Through the trees right now, there are these golden beams of light. The sun rising up from twilight, igniting the skyline in oozing orange and yellow. Like there is distant fire in the sky. It is a painting. Pure beauty. The kind of thing that'll make you gasp and wonder about what hand put down that image and why. For my eyes? In this moment? Out of all the moments that ever were, here I am. Was I meant to see this? To participate by observation? And if I was, does that mean I am meant to endure all the rest, too?

I might could ponder on that for quite some time. But my brain has its own ideas.

Thinks about Pops instead.

About bottles of pills scattered around the bathroom. Momma yelling at him. Telling him to look at what he's become. *You've got everything, Hunter. Everything! A home. A wife. Two beautiful boys who love you. Why can't you see it?* Him standing to strike her. But stopping himself. Then falling to the ground weeping.

I think about my ulnar collateral ligament, of all things. My ulnar nerve. Tommy Johns. Slinging pitches. Eighty. Ninety. Hell, would sure like to hit 100 one day. An arm isn't meant to move like that. But mine will. On God, mine will.

I can see Pops' eyes. The way they were when he was gone. And by gone, I mean stoned.

Empty. Staring ahead. Unfeeling. Like there were no nerves in his whole body. That is a part of Pops that don't a single soul but me and Momma know about. How he got hooked on the pills after his surgeries. How he couldn't stop. How he about went crazy. How he changed into something he never was before.

Cope Field

It has been a long time since I've seen him like that. But I won't lie. It was a bad time.

And maybe Momma was right to leave him.

But she didn't just leave him. She left all of us. And the Pops she left behind was in a bad place. But Hunter Cope did what he was famous for back when he played baseball. He rose to the occasion. When it mattered the most, he got it right. He cleaned up. Got help. Got better. And he done that because he loved me and Big Time so much. It was Pops who stayed around, Pops who changed all of Big Time's smelly diapers, Pops who fed us, who drove us to school. All while getting himself clean.

They say I got anger problems. And I guess I do.

Pops had his cross to bear. And I got mine. Nothing to do but shoulder through it. Get to the other side. Come out better for it. Better for our family. For Big Time. Because it's like Pops is always saying to us, especially when we are at each other's throats: "Family is all you got in the end, so you better protect it."

My GPS says, *You have arrived at your destination.*

I look around.

A field. Just like the map showed. A giant, empty field.

WOMANARCHIST
BAD COP/BAD COP

I'm early, so I wait in the truck. I said the field was empty, but that is not all the way true. There are two little buildings across the way, some distance apart but kinda catty-corner to each other. Next to one of them, an old empty flagpole. No flag. All the grass is grown high. And the whole thing is bordered by trees. I can't get much of a signal, so I sit there staring straight ahead, thumbing through channels on the radio, getting nothing but gospel music and static.

Someone knocks on my window.

There's a girl standing there. For a second, our eyes lock, and I have this moment where I feel I have slipped out of time and space, like I am hanging on inside a little bubble. It's like that sunrise. Of all the moments, here's this one. And here's me . . . here for it. Most times when you hear about folks getting transfixed by eyes, they're talking green. They're talking blue. They are talking some oddball color. But this girl has the plainest eyes you can imagine. Hazel. The color of yellow that's been yellow for too long. Like old mustard. Why this grabs me, I do not know.

She waves.

I crack the window. "Hello."

"Community service?" This girl has electric blue hair that's bright pink on the ends. You can see where she's dyed it and dyed it again because the color changes brown near where the strands go into her head. She smiles. One tooth crooked, jutting out a little too far. A piercing in each cheek, little silver balls glistening against her brown skin. Her shirt says DREAM WARRIORS and has these anime girls standing in all different poses, each of them wearing what looks like fancy sailor costumes. She's got a messenger bag slung across her shoulder, covered in buttons and patches. All kinds of things. Too many to read right now.

Cope Field

She waves a hand, fingernails chewed and painted black. "Hello?"

"Community service, yeah," I say.

"Me, too. Don't worry, you're in the right place."

I get out of the car. I'm at least six inches taller than she is. She looks me over, head to toe.

"Well, howdy, Cowboy." Which I guess is a reference to my boots and wranglers. "What's your name?"

"Craw."

"Like Crawdaddy?"

"No."

"Kidding. I know who you are."

"You do?"

"Of course I do. Crawford Cope. Son of the great Hunter Cope. Best ball player to ever come out the holler. And with two sons following in his footsteps. The pride of Quiet County." She says this with no small degree of disdain in her voice, putting on a too-thick, fake Southern accent when she says *holler*. "You don't grow up here without hearing the stories. So I guess that leads me to my next question. What did Crawford Cope, son of a living legend, with more money than could be spent in a hundred lifetimes over, do to land himself in community service? My guess, something that'd land another kid in juvie. But, you know, the world works differently for kids like you."

"What is that supposed to mean?"

"It means spill the tea. How'd you get here?"

"I drove."

"Funny. But for real."

"Why would I tell you anything about me?"

"Because I wanna know."

I'm realizing I've seen this girl before. She goes to my school but is one of those people on the periphery of everything. An NPC. We are not a big class, and I could not even tell you her name, so that tells you right there how far on the edge she is.

Another truck crests the horizon. It drives slow toward us, then pulls off the road and parks in the grass. An older man steps out, hitches his pants up by the buckle, and walks to the other side of the truck. He opens the passenger door and roots around, then he walks toward the flagpole with a triangular-folded American flag. We watch him fumble with it, then attach it to the flagpole. He works the pulley, and the flag unfurls in the wind as it reaches the top. I swear to God Almighty I hear a bald eagle scream.

He looks up at the flag for a minute, then he turns his attention to us. He's got a belly so huge his shirt can't quite tuck in around the waist, and the buttons look like they might give up the ghost any second. He spits tobacco in the grass and says, "Crawford Cope?"

"Yes, sir."

His eyes move to the girl. "And Hannah Flores."

"That's me."

"Well, I'm Roger Hendrix, and my understanding is we are to get to know each other pretty good over the next few months."

Hannah folds her arms across her chest, chewing gum. "Can you just tell us what we are doing out here so we can get it done and go home?"

He smiles. I get this feeling Roger is the kind of guy who don't let much phase him. Here's this snotty teenager, some girl who probably got arrested with weed in her locker, giving him lip, thinking she's got a handle on everything, when really she don't. Roger has the authority of the state of Arkansas behind him, which may not be worth much in the scheme of all things, but it is worth a great deal here in this field.

He says, "I got you here for as long as I need you here."

She don't say a word. So he goes on telling us that here in a few hours, a flatbed truck with donated chain-link fencing, fence posts, buckets of paint, and other things we might need will be showing up. But before that, we gotta knock all this grass down. "I got a mower in the back of the truck. Y'all can divvy this up however you want. While one of you mows, the other needs to sweep out them dugouts. I'll get a power washer up here another day."

"Dugouts?" I say, a little surprised. Then I look a second harder, and it's like, *Oh, duh, those are dugouts.* This *field* is an old baseball diamond.

"Yes, sir. Ask your daddy. Surprised he ain't tell you all about it."

Hannah's eyes say, *What in the hell is he talking about?* But I don't know what to tell her. I don't got a single answer floating around inside my skull.

Roger says, "Did nobody tell you, Craw? This field gonna be called Cope Field. When it's finished, I mean. A field for all the little boys and girls out here to practice on. Maybe host some travel ball tournaments? A real *if you build it, they will come* situation. You got a chance to give back to the community here. A chance to give back to the game of baseball. That's hardly punishment, you ask me."

I keep my mouth closed.

Hannah says, "That's fantastic. If only there were any little kids living out here."

Roger says, "It really is."

He don't detect sarcasm real good. Or else he don't care.

GIRL'S NOT GRAY
AFI

This girl is testing me, I swear to God. All day she calls me Crawdaddy. She says, "Craw," emphasis on "*daddy*." Then throws her head back laughing. Some other times, she calls me Cowboy. But never Craw. If she comes close to Craw at all, it is always my whole-ass name. *Crawford.* Like Momma woulda yelled at me from the front porch when I was in trouble, back when she was still with us.

Next, she'll be dropping my middle name.

Crawford Lee! You get your rear in here and clean that room.

Not like I'd tell her my middle name.

Roger has this huge zero-turn mower, which I am more than happy to drive around the field, knocking down grass. While I'm doing that, Hannah disappears into one of the dugouts, I assume so she can sweep them out like we were told.

So, I zoom around. The sun's warm on my shoulders. It ain't so bad. Pop in my earbuds, crank some tunes, and it's hardly even work. I'd do this all day.

There's no back fencing. No way to know where the outfield ends except by my good estimation from having been on more than one youth baseball diamond in my life. There's no backstop, either. But I carve out what I think looks right. Roger hollers we'll have to mow the side yards, too, because they'll be installing bleachers after they pour down some concrete. "Gonna get us a bush hog out here, rip down them trees over yonder."

I am sure I have cleared enough for a baseball field. So, I ask him why.

He says, "That'll be extra parking."

Extra parking? Just how many people are they expecting to use this field out here in the middle of fuck-you Arkansas, where it takes an hour or more to reach from any direction? Now that is some kind of nonsense right there, and with my name on it. I ask him what in the actual hell. And he just laughs.

"Ask your daddy," he says.

Since I got the mower off, I take the opportunity to find out where Hannah's at.

Still in the dugout, Roger says. So, I walk over.

She is sitting on the bench, no broom in sight. She's got a spiral notebook open in her lap, the kind with blank white pages for drawing. She snaps it closed when I walk through the door. But I catch a glimpse. The unhinged ramblings of a crazy woman mixed up together with some bug-eyed anime drawings. The kind of thing only an NPC like Hannah would fill a notebook with.

She looks up at me. "Problem, Crawdaddy?"

I point at the mower. "Your turn."

I walk to Roger's truck to fetch the broom. When I get back, she's got that notebook open again. Drawing.

"What are you doing?" I ask, hardly able to believe the audacity.

"Drawing."

"No shit?"

It's like, *What in the hell?* So I do the only logical thing. I start sweeping. Frantic style. Hurling dirt out the door of the dugout. Little clouds raising around my feet. Dirt everywhere, really. She says, "Stop that."

But I don't.

I do it *harder*.

Then she coughs and is like, "Will you stop it?"

And I'm like, *What?* Without words. Just *what* with my eyes only.

"You're getting dirt on my Chucks."

"Well, you better get out of here then."

"You know what? You are exactly who I thought you were."

I keep sweeping without saying anything. I am interested to hear where this is going. Who did this girl think I was? I have a few guesses.

"I saw you in the truck there, and I thought, oh great, now I got to spend all my Saturdays with Crawford Cope. But then I thought, No, Hannah. You don't *really* know him. Who cares if he's popular? Who cares if he's some ruggedly handsome Calvin Klein model-looking jock? So WHAT if he's the antithesis of everything you believe in? Give him a chance. Don't write people off. 'Cause believe me, I know *all* about being written off. So I come over and knock on your window and say hello. Trying to be a good person. Trying to do the right thing. But no. I shoulda listened to my gut."

"Are you trying to say you think I'm handsome?"

Her cheeks go bright red. "Me? No. But I am sure normal girls are into your—" She gestures at all of me with her hands. "Your whole vibe."

"What vibe is that?"

"Asshole vibe."

"Well, shoot, Hannah. That hurts. You don't even wanna know what I thought of you."

"Oh? And what's that?"

"I didn't think of you at all."

"Okay, Crawdaddy. Fine. Believe me when I say your opinion doesn't matter."

She walks back to the mower. Roger shows her how to start the thing up. Gives her basic driving instructions. And I'm thinking that's the end of it. Figure I done enough assholin' to get her to stop talking to me. Which is all I really wanted to begin with. If I'm gonna be stuck out here doing community service on some stupid field named after Pops, then I'm going to do it listening to the dulcet tones of Wiz Khalifa, not some turbo Goth weirdo.

But when she's done mowing, Roger hands us two plastic trash bags and tells us to walk up and down the highway. "Pick up any garbage you see."

So we walk down the road without speaking, stopping sometimes to pick up cigarette butts or plastic bags or old, yellowed soda bottles. And I am thinking there is not a spot of beauty in this whole damn world men won't defile in some way or another. I won't ever forget going down to the creek with Big Time a summer ago only to find about thirty-five empty beer cans, a hot dog wrapper, plus a bloated dirty diaper floating right in the middle of the water. That creek is our spot. And some folks come and don't give one shit about it. And here, on the highway, they go on throwing stuff from their cars as they drive past. Out of their life. And into mine.

After a while, Hannah, who I guess can't handle the silence, starts telling me her entire life story. Including—no, *especially*—the parts most folks would be embarrassed to talk about.

"SRO turned my locker and found a baggy of what he called a 'green leafy substance,'" she says. "Thing is, it was just some parsley I

Cope Field

brought to school to sell to that cheerleader, LeAnne Wilson, because she's dumb as hell and doesn't know any better. Easy way to make fifty bucks. Believe me, I am straight edge, so any kind of drugs are a nonstarter for me. And the SRO knew it wasn't weed. He's seen plenty of weed in his life, I am sure. Yet, here I am."

Whole time I am keeping my mouth shut because Hannah has *too much* to say. Like she says every thought that comes to her brain. Even after I was mean to her. All I can think about is Big Time floating around in our pool back home. Probably having himself the quietest time ever. Full-on relax mode. Probably eating all the damn ice cream sandwiches and not saving any for me. Meanwhile, I'm stuck here listening to this girl tell me every little thing about her. Listening to her life, it's like damn. Okay. There is a reason Pops don't want me talking about our private life much. They call it a *private life* for a reason. Nobody gots to know every little thing about you. I swear to God. My cheeks turn bright red listening to her, but she don't seem to notice.

She tells me her momma got accused of prostitution a few years back, and there musta been some truth to it since they convicted her. Hannah says everybody at school found out.

"You don't come back from that," she says. "Socially, I mean. They sent Momma to the state pen for being a whore, and evidently she made a lot of money from it, not that I saw a red cent ever. Here I am in a shirt I had to steal from Walmart and ripped-up jeans handed down to me from a cousin. While she's making bank off gross dudes and keeping it all to herself. And of course, I'm now a whore by association."

I drop my trash bag on the grass. "Why are you telling me all this?"

"I'm just talking. Why don't you try it sometime? How about you start by telling me what Mr. Do-No-Wrong with his squeaky-clean reputation did to end up with community service?"

I ignore her.

I actually remember when her momma got arrested, although I am just now connecting Hannah to it. I remember how it was a big joke around the school. And how some folks didn't believe it really happened, but Roby Jacobs, who was a senior outfielder on the team but now works at a chicken plant a few counties over, told me he was at the gas station where she got arrested. Said she hopped a fence to the elementary school across the road and the cops had to tackle her. Drug her out in handcuffs, her hollering and screaming every obscenity

39

you can come up with the whole way. Whole generation of kids got educated that day, he said.

I feel a little bad on that one. Really.

Because I know all about disappearing mommas.

MERRY CHRISTMAS (I DON'T WANT TO FIGHT TONIGHT)
RAMONES

A memory:

I'm in bed, unable to sleep, and still thinking about catching that pop fly for Momma earlier. She'd been so proud of me. And afterward, Pops had me work off the tee until my whole body was begging for a break.

A good day of work, he said.

Now, hoot owls and crickets are making noise outside my window. And our old yellow lab, Lady, still used to city living, is not having it. Poor pup is all over the house. Toenails clicking on hardwood. She's at the windows. Sniffin' and whinin'.

I sit up in my bed. Thinking, *If Lady barks, then there's a reason to get scared. If she don't bark, then it's just my imagination.*

A long time passes.

And I hear voices. Low tones. Pops, maybe. Then Lady goes ballistic. I shoot out of bed and look through the window, across the moonlit field and down to the highway, which borders the outer edge of our property on the far side of a gated fence. There are Christmas lights on the edge of our house, blue-colored. White lights blinking on the fence by the road. Lady rushes through the yard, and Pops comes out on the porch hollering for her to be quiet. He catches the dog by the collar and tugs her inside. Whole time I am watching unknown through the window.

The door shuts. The front porch light goes off.

But Lady keeps on barking.

So I keep on watching. My little wild eyes darting around. For a long time, nothing happens. I can hear my own heart thudding in my ears. Can hear Lady carrying on somewhere else in the house. Pops telling her to shut up. His voice getting more and more frustrated.

Something moves past the window, and I near jump out of my skin.

I clap my hand over my mouth to keep from screaming.

A man stands there, in plain view, looking up at the front porch.

He's tall. Bone skinny. His skin unnaturally pale in the blue Christmas lights. I watch him a long time. From where he's standing, I can only see the back of his bald head. But I can see this part clearly: The man has a big, ugly tattoo right on the back of his dome. The kind only an insane person would put right on their head. A skull with bulging eyes, a snake hanging out its mouth. Droplets of black blood oozing down from its fangs. The stuff of nightmares.

I slide out of bed. Inch my way across the floor on my belly. Scared to death that when I open the door, the hallway light will spill across the window, catch this man's attention. Draw his eyes and that horrible snake in my direction.

I crack the door.

The hallway light is off. So I slip through. Our dog sounds far away. Like Pops locked her up.

"Momma," I call out.

No answer.

"Pops?"

Sutton's nursery is down the hall. I glance toward the living room, where I can see the glow of the Christmas tree. Then I hurry toward Sutton's room. Touch the doorknob.

A voice stops me. "Go back in your room, Craw."

Pops.

He stands at the end of the hallway. A silhouette punched out of the light filtering from the room beyond. His fists are balled up at his sides. I cannot see his face.

"Pops..." I whisper. "There's someone out there."

"I know. I will handle it. You hide under your bed. Don't come out for nobody except me."

"What about Sutton?"

"Don't worry about him. I'll come get you soon."

I do what he says, not knowing what else to do. It is hard to say how long I wait for him. In my memories, it is hours, curled up on the carpet under my bed. Praying to God the next voice I hear belongs to Pops. Or Momma.

Pops comes eventually. He sits on the bed and calls out my name.

When I come out, he's holding Sutton, swaddled up against his chest.

Sutton makes little baby squeaks.

"There's no easy way to say it, so I'm just gonna say it," Pops says. "Momma's gone. She took off. And I don't think she is coming back."

Hearing that wrinkles up my insides. How can that be? Momma loves me. She told me so many times. Why would she leave us? "I don't... understand."

"She left with that man you saw. Some kind of thing they planned, I reckon. I don't know. All that's important for you to know is she's gone. And she ain't coming back. But you will be okay because you got me to care for you. Alright?" His voice is far off. Distant. Like he is talking to someone else, and I am eavesdropping.

I don't say nothing.

"There's something else," Pops says. "There'll be some policemen come here soon. Because I done made a missing person's report. Said she been kidnapped. Because don't nobody come up here and run off with my wife. Thing is, Craw, the cops might ask you questions. But I don't want you to tell them what you seen. You leave that burden to me, okay? I don't want you getting stuck in the middle of something between grown-ups."

My mind leaves my body. But I manage to nod my head.

"Good boy, Craw," Pops said. "Your momma tried to destroy this family. Her and him together. I won't let that happen. But I need you to trust me. Need you to keep quiet. Let the grown-ups work this out. Okay? Don't breathe one single word of this to anyone. Ever."

Yes. Yes, Pops. I will not say a word.

WHO I AM HATES WHO I'VE BEEN
RELIANT K

I float over the ocean.

The voice speaks to me. "*We are angry because of internal pressures, but we are triggered by external ones. Remember, our fight-or-flight response is an important tool that helps us survive, but sometimes our reactions are overreactions.*"

The wind blows in my ears.

We are moving.

Over waves. Over a little archipelago of sand dunes. We cross over the shore. Over a little village, over tiny moving cars. We soar out over a dense forest of massive pines.

"*Breathe deeply from your diaphragm. Picture your breath coming up from your stomach. Speak to yourself. Tell yourself out loud, 'Be calm.' Repeat it to yourself as we continue…*"

I think of Pops the other day in the dungeon, when he threw the ball too hard at Big Time. I think of Big Time, snapping it out of the air just in time, bursting into tears. I think of how moments after, even though he cried, he made a big show of how proud he was of himself for catching it.

But all I can think after that is:

What if it had hit him?

And I am filled with anger.

"Be calm," I whisper. "Be calm."

BLEACHER CREATURE GIRL
ISOTOPES

I'm in the bullpen cycling through my pitches with Luis Iglesias, our freshman catcher. You don't see a lot of freshmen playing varsity, which says something about him. I remember his daddy called him soft back in court. But he is not. He's a gritty kid. But not the kind of grit that hurts to rub against. I didn't know him before the season started since most freshmen play junior varsity. But two weeks ago, Coach Rodriguez moved him up, had us start working together. You get to know your catcher fast when you're a pitcher. And it was clear to me right away, Luis was going to take over the starting role before long.

Here's how tough he is.

In one practice, he missed one of my heaters. The ball smacked him straight in the faceguard. Got stuck there in the visor. He toppled over backward, and I thought for one second he might have been knocked clean out. I ran over there, and this absolute maniac was staring up at the sky, his mouth agape. Eyes looking someplace distant.

I leaned down with my hands on my knees. "You alright?" I asked him.

"Dios mío," he whispered. "Craw, I saw Jesus."

I helped him to his knees. Then I helped him to his feet. The ball was still stuck there. He had to take his helmet off to pop it free. He held it up and asked Coach Rodriguez if he could keep it.

"What for?" Coach asked.

"So I can show my kids the ball Crawford Cope nearly killed me with before he was a famous MLB pitcher."

"You want me to sign it?" I said, 100 percent joking.

"Hell yes I do."

And this kid pulled an ink pen out of his back pocket. Like what for? In case you get hit with a ball and need to get it autographed?

Who keeps a pen in their pocket during baseball practice? So, I signed this stupid ball. *sorry bout the time i nearly killed you. hugs and or kisses. love, crawford "craw" cope.*

Luis smiled bigger than you'd believe.

Now, he's calling all his favorite pitches. He likes my slider 'cause it hooks outside the strike zone. High school batters will chase that all day. Then, if they wise up, you can mow 'em down with a heater. The last thing you wanna do against my heater is be looking for a slider. You'll be out before you can blink.

"You're a fuckin' beast, Craw," Luis says, after a while.

"Hell yes I am," I say.

"We are winning state this year. On your arm alone."

"Naw, don't nobody win state on a single arm."

But that's not true. In high school, that is not true at all.

Luis says, "Craw, when you go pro, tell 'em to take me with you."

Pops, who likes to hang on the netting during warm-ups and distribute advice, shakes his head and laughs. "They gonna call him up right outta high school. You'll just be a sophomore."

"Best sophomore in the league," Luis says.

Pops dies laughing. And they go on talking like that for a while. Pretty soon, Luis's daddy, the lawyer from my hearing, sees them cutting up and comes over to join in. He says, "I tole my boy he oughta soak this up, gettin' to catch for a kid going to the majors. Can only help him."

"That's right," Pops says.

"Can only make him better. Can only show him what he's gotta do if he wants to end up playing ball professionally one day, too."

"That's right," Pops says again. They are talking about me like I am not here.

"Naw, I don't really want to go pro," Luis says. "I just want it to pay for my college. Have fun with it."

"It'll help with that, too," Pops says. "Craw, though, he's got bigger things on his mind than college. Don't you, Craw?"

I don't answer him. My guts are roiling like a spaghetti pot left on the stove.

"Don't you, Craw?" Pops says.

I just say, "Yep," so we can hopefully move on and talk about something other than Pops' plan for my entire life.

But they don't stop.

Cope Field

Pops goes on and on about how all the "good ones" get called up straight from high school. He tells them about my whole entire future like it's set in stone. Finally, when I am about ten nanoseconds away from pulling my own face off, Pops shrugs and says, "Y'all should get back to work."

Luis's daddy nods. Says, "Good luck," and heads back to the bleachers. And you'd think Pops would go, too. But no. He's gotta be part of this. In his head, he's got to be part of this. Most of the dads get run off the field, but Coach Rodriguez makes an exception since Pops pitched in the majors. Still. I wish Pops would show himself out. Because once he is on the field, all the focus is gone. And since he's on the field, some of the players stop warming up and start hanging around the bullpen, hoping he'll do what he always does. Share stories of the good ole days.

I throw Luis a pitch, but I can tell his heart isn't in it anymore. He looks at Pops when he soft tosses the ball back to me. "Who's the best batter you ever sat?" he asks.

Pops taps his chin. "Let me think."

I wing a fastball at Luis. It smacks his glove. He goes to his knees and soft tosses it back to me. I kick the ground and turn toward the field. The Poinsett Christian Saints, tidy in their navy-and-baby-blue uniforms, come pouring from a yellow school bus in the parking lot. I watch them walk up, their bat bags slung over their shoulders, cleats clattering like a thousand dice on the asphalt.

"I struck out McGwire and Sosa both," Pops says. "Middle of the home-run race, too."

"They homered off you each," I say.

"Okay, yeah, another at bat, they sure did. Later on in the series. I still sat 'em though. Name another person you know can say they sat McGwire and Sosa."

"That's insane," Luis says. "They was on 'roids, too, I heard."

"They was all on 'roids them days," Pops says.

"Were you on 'roids?" one kid asks.

Pops flashes his smile. The same one he used on all his posed baseball cards. "All natural, baby. Believe it."

Then he flexes his arms. Which are not buff, by the way. Just normal human arms. But it gets the desired reaction. Laughs from everybody. Luis even says, "Jeez, Crawford, you got to be the luckiest kid alive. My dad is a dumb *lawyer*."

Pops says, "Craw's got no idea how lucky he is."

I stare across the field, where Poinsett Christian is still getting their stuff loaded into the dugout. That's when I notice someone sitting in the stands near them, wearing some all-black Goth outfit that makes her look like a Spirit Halloween store personified showed up for a good old American afternoon of baseball.

Hannah.

And that's bad enough. But worse is who's sitting right next to her.

Big Time.

And he's talking up a storm, the way only Big Time can.

I see him point across the field at me. Hannah's eyes follow his finger. And she flashes a massive, black-lipped smile. I'm trying to say with my eyes, *What the actual hell are you doing here?* and either it's not getting across or else she don't care, because she cups her hands around her mouth and yells, "LET'S GO, CRAWDADDY!"

Big Time falls backward laughing. That is just the sort of dumb nonsense he's bound to love. My eyes cut between Luis and Pops.

Pops says, "Crawdaddy?"

EVER FALLEN IN LOVE (WITH SOMEONE YOU SHOULDN'T'VE)
BUZZCOCKS

Before I can conjure an answer, Coach Rodriguez yells, "Let's go, men!" trotting toward the dugout. "It's game time!" This gets some whoops and hollers from the other boys as they run toward their places in the field. I go ahead and join in. Even though being loud and hyped is not my usual MO.

Anything to get out of a conversation about Hannah and her stupid nickname for me.

We shut down Poinsett Christian in the first inning. Nine pitches, and I'm back in the dugout, leaning across the cinder blocks, spitting sunflower seeds and shooting the shit with Luis.

Pops stands by the fence, just outside the dugout. He likes to walk down there between innings so he can talk through the fencing at me. Tell me what I'm doing wrong. Let me know what he's seeing from a particular batter. Sometimes it's helpful. But right now, I just feel heavy in my chest. Like I'm on guard. Like can't I have one single conversation without him hovering over it?

"You know that girl?" Luis says, launching a chewed-up seed almost to the first baseline.

"Which one?" I spit my own seed. It lands on the chalk. The secret for distance spitting is you can't chew up the seed.

"The horror show on the end. Hannah Flores."

I try and hide my grimace. I was hoping to get outta here without having to acknowledge her presence at all. "Sorta. I mean, I seen her around some. How do you know her?"

"She used to go to my church."

I am surprised to hear she ever went to church. You'd think God would send lightning the moment she walked through the doors. Or else all the pictures of Jesus would start oozing blood.

"Why'd she call you Crawdaddy?" Luis says, spitting another seed. He clears mine by a few inches.

"Cause she's weird as hell, I don't know."

"She's a slut," Luis says.

Hearing that, my mouth kinda hangs open. I wasn't expecting him to be fond of the girl, but I wasn't expecting him to say that, either. "How do you know?"

"Because, Craw. Everybody knows. Plus, I heard she's ambisextrous if you follow me." He laughs at his own joke. But I am not sure what it's supposed to mean. And I am not sure why it offends me, either. Like I'm about to white knight for Hannah. Please.

"So who is she sleeping with then, Luis?" I shoot another seed. Short.

"Everyone."

"You?"

"Jesus. No."

"So who?"

"No sé, Craw."

"You said everybody. Everybody includes you."

"Por qué carajos me estás haciendo tantas preguntas?"

He knows I don't speak Spanish. This is his way of saying *I am done with this conversation*. But I am not done, damn it. I am starting to think a lot about the things folks say about people. How they cram you inside a box based on the box someone other than you built. I reframe the question. "How can you call her that if you don't know it's true?"

"Why does it matter, Craw? Who cares? It's just what people say."

"People say a lot of things, Luis. Don't make them true."

"Jesus." He pinches the bridge of his nose. "You are about to make me crazy. You like her or something? What is your deal?"

"No. God no."

"Then what?"

I stare across the field at her. She catches me. Grins a giant, black-lipped grin. Like some Batman villain come to life. I shake my head. "Forget I asked, Luis. How about that?"

"Fine, Craw. Fine."

But it's too late. This whole conversation has me frustrated. We got no outs, and there's time before I'm up to bat. So I step out of the dugout and take a walk. Clear my head.

But it ain't helping.

Cope Field

Not even a little bit.

No way around it. I walk around the dugout, behind the home-side bleachers and backstop, and hustle over to the fence near where Hannah sits alone. I check over my shoulder. Luis is staring right at me, this look on his face like, *What in the hell are you doing?* So far, Coach Rodriguez hasn't noticed. And, thank God, neither has Pops. But they will if I don't hurry. Because there are just three batters until I'm up. That could be as quick as three pitches from now...

I lean against the fence and clear my throat until Hannah looks up from her notebook, where she seems to be drawing a picture of a baseball player. I say, "Why are you here?" Straight up.

"Am I not allowed?"

"You are."

"Then why does it matter?"

"Because..." And I have to think for a minute. Why *does* it matter? A girl can come watch a baseball game if she wants to watch a baseball game. Can't she? "Because I never seen you here before."

"Oh, that's because I hate baseball."

"You hate baseball." I don't say it like a question. I look down at that drawing, still open on her lap. It almost looks like me.

"Hate all sports, actually."

"So you came here for what?"

"To support my community service buddy, of course."

"Don't say that out loud!"

"Say what?"

I lower my voice. "Community service."

"Crawford, why are you embarrassed? Community service is the coolest thing about you."

"Be quiet," I say. "What did Big Time say to you?" That little butthole says whatever thought comes to his brain. And to any person willing to listen. Who knows what he has said about me.

"He told me why you got community service."

Across the field, Big Time runs with some other boys out past the outfield fence. This is what they do instead of watching baseball. Instead of learning something. There's a long, twisty creek that runs alongside the field before disappearing into a culvert under the road. They're probably chasing mudbugs or little minnows over there. He's laughing his stupid red head off at something. At the plate, we are on to the next batter. Bases loaded. We are cooking. And I know I need to hurry back. Luis glares at me from the dugout, and he is getting a little frantic. Probably secondhand fear I am about to get my ass chewed.

Hannah adds, "Also a whole lot about outer space. Like, dude could not stop telling me all about it. He's a smart kid."

"He's stupid. What did he tell you about me?"

She leans back. Hitches one leg over her other knee. Wearing these torn-up black hose with spiderwebs stitched into them. "Don't worry about it, Crawdaddy."

She picks up her pencil and writes something in the blank space next to the baseball player. I squint to read it. It says, *Crawford Cope thinks baseball matters.*

This girl is messing with me. For fun. That's what this is.

I am happy to mess back.

"Hannah. Why are you here dressed like a wicked witch?"

"It's called an aesthetic. Why are you so interested in what I'm doing here?"

There's this old guy eating a chili cheese dog sitting behind her. He's got on sunglasses, but I am sure he is eavesdropping on our conversation. He takes a big bite, smears of chili on his cheeks, then dabs at his lips with a wadded-up napkin and nods at me. I look at him. Then at Hannah. Then back at him. "I'm not," I say.

The man with the chili dog just keeps stuffing that meat tube down his greasy throat. My God, I hate this guy all the sudden. Then I hear the crack of a bat. Yank my head around in time to see the ball go sailing into the air, the runners advancing. Luis bounces up and down in the dugout. Like, *Will you get your ass back over here?*

Coach Rodriguez's eyes land on me. At first, it's like he can't believe I'm not where I'm supposed to be. He shakes his head. Takes off his cap and runs a hand through his buzzed brown hair. "Vamos, Crawford! Vamos!"

Near the fence, Pops puts his hands on his hips and scowls.

Shit.

"Hannah, have fun," I say, heading back to the dugout.

"Don't count on it," she tells me.

Which is real funny. Why would you come to a baseball game if the aim is not to have a good time?

Cope Field

In the top of the third inning, we are up twenty-three runs. That is enough for a mercy ruling. Which is good because if it were a close game, Pops and Coach mighta got on my ass a little more. Instead, all I got was a stern "Do not do that again" from Coach Rodriguez and a "What in the sam hell is wrong with you" from Pops.

All I gotta do to end the game is sit the next three batters. Better than that, so far not a single person has got a hit off me. I've walked nobody. And yes, it's just three innings. But I still want to finish it with a perfect stat line.

There's this thing in baseball. A superstition.

You never say it out loud when a pitcher is close to a perfect game. You don't want to jinx it. You especially don't say it to the pitcher. Because then he'll get in his head. He'll think a little too much about perfection. Then he'll go ahead and mess it up.

I get through the first two batters.

And even though nobody has said it to me, I'm thinking about that perfect stat line anyway. Pops knows it, too. I can tell from the spooked expression on his face. The nervousness all over his body. He wants this as much as I do.

Luis throws me the ball. The batter, this barrel-chested kid with cannon arms, steps up to the plate. He crosses himself, roots his cleats into the dirt, and taps the plate with the end of the bat. Ninth in their lineup. Nowhere close to their best batter. Looks more like a football player. Should be easy. But I am feeling sick to my stomach anyway.

Hannah sits forward, her elbows on her knees. For someone who don't like baseball, she's pretty keyed in. I turn away from the batter, look up at the scoreboard. Then I stuff the ball into my glove and get in my stance, and it's like time slows down. A pitch routine may take less than thirty seconds. But my brain has all the time in the world to get in my way.

I have this core memory. Little league. Machine pitch. We were up 13–2 with the game almost over. I was on second base with nobody behind me. Pops was coaching, so he told me if the ball comes to my side, don't run. He said, pop fly—don't forget to tag up. But I was eight years old. And I was chomping at the bit to cross home plate. As soon as the ball was hit, I took off to third base. Problem: It was a pop fly. Right to centerfield. Kid made the grab. A miracle, really, at that age. Then he tossed it back to second. A double play. All because I did not tag up.

Luis calls for a four-seamer to start things off. I shake my head no. He shrugs, throws the sign for a curveball. I nod. Step into my throwing motion and send the ball sailing toward the catcher. It flies perfect, high and then low, inducing a brutal swing and miss from the big fella. Poor guy damn near spins himself all the way around. Luis snatches it just before it hits the ground.

Luis throws the ball back to me. I go through my whole routine. And my brain goes right back to that little league field. Pops tore his hat from his head, slammed it on the ground. He stomped it three times and started yelling. Slobber flying from his mouth like a rabid pit bull. And this is the part that turned what mighta been a bad but forgotten day at the ballpark into a core memory: I started to cry. Because I was small. And he was red-hot angry. Pops said right out loud to everybody, "Get this crybaby off the field."

Luis calls for a heater. I agree this time. Big Ole Boy will be hesitant to swing now. I'll mow him down. I sling the ball with precision accuracy. There's no radar gun to tell me, but I am betting we brushed 95. The ball smacks into Luis's glove. The batter blinks like he didn't even register it. Then he slams the bat into the plate in frustration.

Let it out, Big Boy.

One more strike, and we can go home.

Luis returns the ball. I go through my steps. And my head goes straight back to little league. I remember Pops wrenched my arm. Led me to the gate. Shoved me through and slammed it behind me. And all the parents just watched this. And nobody said anything. So it must have been fine, right?

I guess that's what Pops means when he says he's sorry for being so intense. But the other thing he says is true, too, I guess. He did it because he loves me. Because he expects the best out of me. Because he knows that I can do better than all the other kids. And if I had made *excuses* about how it's *just little league*, then in a few years, I'd be saying *it's just high school ball*, and that kinda attitude cannot be in the mind of a professional ball player.

Luis wants another heater. If I'm throwing 95 today, ain't nobody here hitting it. So why not? I'm feeling shaky and gross in my stomach. One pitch away from that perfect stat line. And all I want to do is go home and not think about it anymore. I nod once to Luis. Then I go through my pitching motion. Only, I step a little funny. And that funny step causes a chain reaction all the way up to my fingertips. The

Cope Field

ball pops out of my hand wrong, still angry with velocity, but . . . not accurate.

The ball smacks the kid in the shoulder. He turns away from me and howls in pain. And it's like, *Damn it.* Worst case in my mind was I'd give up a strike. I definitely didn't wanna hurt the kid. He bends at the waist, rubbing at his shoulder, damn near in tears.

A teammate yells out, "Rub some dirt on it."

And almost at once, this kid stands up straight, hands his bat to the batboy, and takes his free base, taking my perfect stat line with him.

I look straight up at the sky. Refuse to look at Pops. Close my eyes.

Then I mow the next batter down in three pitches.

Game over.

STILL WAITING
SUM 41

I can see Pops waiting by the truck. Just from how he is standing, I know what is on his mind. That stupid pitch. And maybe he's got more to say about me leaving the dugout. Could be he's linked the two incidents in his head. And maybe he would be right. If I had just cleared my head on the mound... if I had just rose to the occasion... been good at the right time... then Pops wouldn't have to say nothing to me. I am not so stupid to think I am the only pitcher in the world who has to battle their own brain on the hill. It's everyone. We all got our battles. So the question is—do you win 'em? Or do you lose 'em?

That is what Pops is trying to teach me.

But for right now, he can wait a minute.

After walking a line across the field telling the other team *good game*, and after getting high fives from all my teammates and hearing fifty people say, *So close, but at least we won!*, I find Big Time in the crowd. He's eating a little cup of frozen pickle juice. And of course, he saw that bad pitch, too. He learned from the best. He says, "Cracked under pressure."

He is joking. It is good-hearted. He wants me to laugh at it, to feel a little better about a bad situation.

I say, "What did you tell Hannah about me?"

"Nothin'."

"She said you told her why I got community service."

Big Time slurps that pickle juice. Green liquid at the corners of his mouth. He shrugs and says, "I told her you got angry manager issues."

"You told her what?"

"I told her you got the 'roid rage. Makes you hulk out."

"You little shit. That is not true."

He finishes off his pickle juice. "Don't curse at me."

"Then don't tell lies about me."

Cope Field

"It ain't a lie, Crawdaddy."

I do not want Hannah thinking I'm some incredible hulk, bending metal just because somebody ticked me off, so I hurry around the ballpark trying to find her and set the record straight.

Not on the bleachers.

Not at concessions.

Not wandering around between the fields.

Then I see her through several fences, walking across the parking lot. There is an older man with her. Tall, rangy, and slumped forward in the shoulders. His hair is long and greasy, and when he turns to the side, I can see his giant knob of a nose. I'd guess he was her father, except for his white skin. Pale as the moon next to hers. I hustle through the groups of people standing around chatting. A teammate calls out my name. Luis, maybe. But I don't stop. I hurry through the main gate and catch her climbing into this old beat-up Ford truck. She's halfway climbed in, looking down at me like, *What do you want?*

"I don't got 'roid rage."

She says, "Huh?"

"Big Time likes to joke around."

The man driving glares down at me. His right ear is cauliflowered, almost disc-like. Says to Hannah, "This your boyfriend?" He's got narrow, animal eyes. Like he might like to kill and eat me right there in the parking lot. There's a person hiding somewhere in those features, but it's wrapped up in something else. Something I've seen in Pops a hundred million times. It stops me cold.

"He's not," she says, looking out the window, away from both of us.

"Hannah ain't allowed a boyfriend," the man says, leaning across the truck toward me. "So get out of here. And don't bother her none."

Hannah looks like she might die. Even through her Goth makeup, and even though her face is turned away, I can see her cheeks turn red. Her fists clench so tight in her lap, her knuckles turn white. She did not want me to see this. To know about this. And I know that feeling all too well. Even though I am trying to keep it together, to figure it out, that is *exactly* how I feel at all times.

"I'm sorry," I say. And I mean it.

Hannah shuts the door. She won't look at me. The man revs the engine. Floors it leaving the parking lot, tires squelching on asphalt. I stand there feeling stupid. Like I barged into some world where I do not belong.

JOCK-O-RAMA
DEAD KENNEDYS

The whole ride back from the game, Pops drives in silence. He just sits there. Not speaking. And the act of not speaking becomes the act of me waiting for him to go off on that bad pitch. When we get home, it's underneath everything. He still hasn't spoken. So I can't let it go.

But maybe this one time, finally, in the history of all our baseball together, he is going to focus less on what went wrong during the game and more on what went right. We mowed through the other team like they were nothing. Plenty to celebrate there.

Still. I decide to keep quiet around him for the rest of the night.

Just in case.

He walks into the den while I am playing PlayStation. I'm half brain dead, my body sorta oozed out all over the sofa. I am damn near a liquid. Like I would not have been surprised if when I stood up a part of me stayed behind, stuck to the fibers of the couch.

Pops sits down in the recliner, brings up the footrest, then kicks off his boots, one smelly toe jutting from the end of his sock. He watches me play for a while, and I'm doing pretty good. Like *headshot, headshot, headshot*. He says, "This is nasty. Play a sports game."

I keep blasting. *Boom. Boom.* Blood and brain matter splattering. Just having the game of my life. Topping the leaderboards and all.

Pops picks up the remote and switches the channel to ESPN.

"Hey!" I yell, dropping the controller.

"You think that kinda game is good for you? Considering you are in community service for your anger problems?"

Anger problems.

I am tired of hearing this phrase.

He gestures to the television. "C'mon and watch the game with me. The Royals are playing."

"I was winning," I say.

"Winning what? At computer games? So what?"

"So, it's fun."

"But it don't matter. You want to win, go out to the batting cages and work on your swing. Maybe practice that pitch you goofed earlier. That's the kind of winning will carry you someplace. Don't nobody give a damn about your stupid video games."

"It's fun," I say again.

"Hell, Craw. Don't nobody care. Five years, you won't care, either. So why waste time? You got to pour your energy into something that matters. That's why I was so happy Brucie Boy hooked you up working on our field."

"Our field?"

"Yessir."

Brucie Boy. I remember he called the Judge that when we were in court. They'd known each other. Through baseball. High school chums, probably. And when the Judge gave me community service, he'd winked at Pops.

"You made this happen," I say.

"I pulled a few strings."

This wasn't punishment. This was orchestrated. Fake consequences. Someone else in the same shoes woulda had it worse. Might've even got locked up. Hell. Hannah was right. "What is going on with that stupid field?"

Pops' eyes go hard. "It's for the kids," he says.

"For them to do what?"

"To play baseball, Craw. What is wrong with you?"

"It's in Jerusalem. No kids live there."

"There's kids. All around the hills there. Folks will use that field, Craw. You watch. There was this group of folks trying to bring it back alive already. When I heard about it, I had to get involved. Gave enough money they'll put our name on it. Cope Field. Ain't that something?"

"It's something."

I don't know how to feel. I guess it is a good thing. But there is grossness underneath. Grossness I can't quite put a finger on. I stand up. Stay there for a minute. Thinking. Him watching me. Probably wondering what in the hell I am doing.

Then I just sigh and plop down on the couch. The Cards are playing the Royals. So, we watch the whole thing. And five innings in, baseball works its magic on me. I am just a boy watching a game with his daddy. Fetching him beer cans. Cutting jokes. Laughing at his. Big Time hears the commotion and joins in. I throw a frozen pizza in the oven, and it's like... this is us.

This is what it's all about.

These little moments, where the world outside don't matter.

There's goodness here. Underneath all the rough spots. There is goodness.

CIRCLES
DAG NASTY

Here is what I find out.

Cope Field used to be called Tomlinson Field. No one knows when it was built, but a newspaper article I found online says the last baseball game played there was in 1975. Nobody even knows much about the field's original namesake, Tomlinson. Somebody in the article speculated he was the man who owned the land before they put a little league baseball diamond on it. Said he sold it to Quiet County for $1. And baseball was played there on the regular... until one day it wasn't. It was this functioning facility. This place that brought joy and happiness to so many folks. Until one day, it didn't. Grass grew. Concrete crumbled. Paint peeled. And signage disappeared. Thinking about it has me raw. It reminds me of Pops. But I am not sure why.

SILENT TYPE
DISPATCH

Roger pulls up in his pickup truck and starts unloading paint cans. He's got clean rollers. Little paint tins. Rags. Screwdrivers and paint stirring sticks. One problem. Hannah is nowhere to be seen.

"Where's the girl?" Roger says, handing me a bucket.

I shrug. "What are we doing?"

"*I*," he says, heavy emphasis, "am supervising. *You* are painting the dugouts."

"What happens if she don't show up?"

"Then I got to tell the Judge. He'll decide what to do about it." Then his eyes move to something in the distance, across the highway. "Ah, there she is," he says.

Across the street, there is a small white farmhouse. Looks like it's been there since before Abraham Lincoln was president with not a single person alive since then who gave a care about it. And here comes Hannah, from around back. She stands there, thinking nobody can see her, clenching her fists at her hips. Just shaking. Pure fury. I can tell, even at this distance. Then her eyes dart up and lock with mine. She looks scared, only for a second. Then she smiles, puts a little hop in her step, and hustles over.

She says, "What's up, fellas?" Like everything is normal, and we saw nothing. And I am not one to question this kind of thing, so I just hand her a roller and tell her we're gonna paint the dugouts.

"Look," Roger says. "Long strokes. Don't leave no streaks. We painting them white on the small sides. Blue on the big sides. Blue trim up by the roof."

Royals colors.

As if Pops would have picked anything else.

I just want to slap some paint on these things and get out of here. So I carry all the stuff over to the visitor dugout and start cracking off the lids with a screwdriver. Hannah walks past me and into the dugout, and I'm figuring it's another day of me working and her drawing in her notebook in the shade.

Fine.

I dump a giant blob of white paint into one of the rolling tins and squish the roller through it. Zip that up the cinder blocks. And repeat. Three. Four. Five times. Brain drifting through time and space all the while. Here but not here. Wondering if this whole place is gonna be done up like some miniature redneck version of Kauffman Stadium, where the Royals play. That's Pops for you. Reliving his glory days. Making sure not one person in this whole community forgets where he went before he came back here. As if they ever could. There is a shrine to the man in the high school. His jersey retired and everything.

"Hey." Hannah kneels beside me.

"Figured you was staying indoors."

"I'm bored. Could use a little company."

I laugh a little. But she starts painting. For a while, we don't talk. I'm a little surprised. This is the perfect chance for her to overshare some insane detail about her life nobody wants to hear.

"You played good the other day," she says.

"Thanks."

More silence.

Then: "Why did you run to the truck?"

I'm checked out again. Not listening. Here but not here. "Huh?"

"After the game. How come you ran to our truck like that?" She takes three more passes with the paint roller.

"Because I wanted you to know whatever Big Time told you about me wasn't true."

"Yeah, but why did you care?"

She's got white freckles of paint on her cheeks and nose. A clump of white in her hair. She tucks it behind her ear, which I just now notice is stretched at the bottom with a little gauge. A silver hoop hangs up near the top. "I don't like people thinking things about me that aren't true."

"So tell me the real reason you're here then."

"It's complicated."

"I have time."

I keep my mouth closed. Keep on painting. We are making good progress, covering up the old, dirty brown paint. Making something old into something new. Beautiful, in a way. Painting that dugout starts to feel good. Hannah works with her tongue poked out, her eyes scrunched up. The longer we go, the more little flecks of paint speckle her skin. And for the first time, I think I am seeing her. I mean really seeing her. You can look at a person a million times and see nothing but what everyone told you to see. Hell. You can look in the mirror and see the same thing.

Things are not the way people say they are.

Not all the time.

Hannah rubs her cheek with the back of her palm, leaving a smear. She catches me looking. "What?"

"Nothing."

She puts her paint roller back in the tin. "You were smiling."

"No, I wasn't."

"That might have been the first time I've seen you smile."

That can't be true. I smile, same as everybody. I block off the last few cinder blocks with a few swipes of the roller. From the corner of my eye, I can see Hannah is still looking at me. And that gets heat rising from the pit of my stomach, all through my cheeks. Can even feel it in my ears.

She picks up the roller, pushes it through the paint. "It's a nice smile," she says, her voice soft. Almost a whisper.

Funny how a kind sentence can put hurt in your guts. No idea why. Kind words should feel good. But on me they feel like puking up a razorblade.

I don't know what to say.

So, I say nothing. A whole hour of awkward silence as we finish up the white sides of the dugout. Hannah says, "You don't talk much."

I don't say a thing to that. Why would I talk much?

"You don't like me, do you?" she asks, a little later. And I can't let that one stand.

"I don't know you."

"You could get to know me. We're stuck here anyway."

"You talk enough for the both of us." And I can see this hurts her feelings. I let out a deep breath. "Sorry. I just never have talked a lot. Don't have a lot to say, I guess."

"I don't believe it. Everybody has a lot to say."

"Do they?" I chew on that a minute. Seems like nonsense to me. Some folks got books in them. My brain is like the old West, out where the outlaws live. Hot sun. Shimmering horizon. A tumbleweed blowing through. Maybe a vulture picking sinew off a dead animal or something. "Don't seem that way to me."

"So you're the strong silent type," Hannah says.

I like that. I give her that smile she likes so much and tell her, "That's me."

EVERYTHING IS ALRIGHT
MOTION CITY SOUNDTRACK

When we are finished, Roger gives us bottles of water. We sit on the tailgate of his truck, slurping them down. The whole time we've been painting, Roger has been running the backhoe on the backside of the property, pulling up shrubs and trees, moving them into a huge pile in the center of the field. Looks like a lot more fun than whitewashing a dugout, that's for sure. But he is covered in sweat when he walks up. His shirt, completely soaked. And I don't mean just the pits, either.

Hannah's cheeks are red. Little stray hairs clinging to her face.

"It's a hot one," Roger says, as if we don't already know.

Sitting beside Hannah, I realize again how short she is. She can sit on the tailgate and kick her feet. Like a kid. Which she does. We sit there, not talking, looking around at each other and the field. We've only been out here twice, and already our work is noticeable. Before you'd have driven by and thought, *Oh look, a piece of garbage field with no reason for being here.* Now, you'd drive by and think, *Oh look, a bunch of rednecks painted those useless buildings for no reason.*

Definitely does not look like a baseball diamond at this point. No way, shape, or form.

Cope Field.

Good Lord.

"Are we done for today?" I ask.

Hannah says, "I got time. I can do more."

Roger spits on the ground. "Reckon I'll turn ya loose." He gets the paperwork from the truck and has us sign our names to prove to the Judge we showed up. Hannah signs hers with big loopy letters and draws the O like a little skull. I write mine like a normal human being.

I get in my truck and crank the engine. Wait for it to stop blowing hot air. In the mirror, I can see Hannah walking across the street.

Back toward the old white house up on the hill, where she came out earlier today looking like she wanna have a fight with somebody. You can walk all kinds of ways. Normal. Cocky. Or with your shoulders slumped down with zero confidence. Right now, Hannah is walking like somebody who don't wanna go where they are going.

Up at the house, I can see a shape in the window. A hand pulling back the blinds.

I open my door. Holler out, "Hannah."

Her head snaps around.

"You wanna sit in here with me? Get cool for a minute?"

Her eyes crawl back up to the house, then back to me. She nods one time, then hurries over. She struggles to climb up the lift kit, so I reach across and give her a hand. Then she plops down beside me in the seat.

She doesn't say anything.

Not one single word.

"Hannah?"

"Sorry."

"What?"

"My heart is racing."

Up at the house, the window curtains close. A second later, the front door opens. Out comes a man. Shirtless. Tattooed from his belly to his neck. Skin pale as something that mighta crawled up from beneath the earth, spiderwebbed with blue veins. Long, greasy hair. And that old, flattened cauliflower ear. He has a bottle of Jack dangling from one hand. A lit cigarette in the other. He brings the cigarette to his lips, staring at us with Clint Eastwood eyes, breathing smoke and fire like some kinda demon.

"Your father?" I ask.

"Step."

"What's his problem?"

She shakes her head. Like, *Who fuckin' knows*. And that speaks to me. Because I've been there. "You want me to drive you around a while?" I ask.

"Please."

"Will it make it worse?"

"Not if he passes out before we get back."

I put the truck in drive. "Then I'll keep you out a long time."

I don't know where to take this girl. And it is not lost on me that we live in a small Arkansas town. Every person we drive past is likely as not gonna call up Jim Bob or Curly Sue down the street and let them know Hannah Flores is sitting shotgun in my truck. The last thing I need is to hear from Luis or anyone else on the team about being seen with someone like Hannah.

"You swim?" I ask her, thinking maybe she'd like to get in our pool. That's a place nobody gonna see her but me, Big Time, and Pops.

She says, "I don't have a suit."

"You can swim in your clothes. It don't matter."

"No."

"You want to go somewhere and walk? There's some deer trails up behind my house. Pops puts out feed, and if you sit up on the ridge, you can sometimes see them come down and eat."

"Maybe another time," she says. She looks so defeated sitting over there. Her head against the window. Her eyes vacant. It's a look I know pretty good. She's leaving her body and mind behind. Pressing pause on the moment. Because the moment sucks a big fat one.

I start naming everything I can think of to cheer her up.

"We could drive up to the Buffalo. Get our feet wet? How about coffee? We can drive all the way into town. Like one of those fancy Starbucks-type places where they put all the cream and sugar and shit in there? Or we could go see a movie. I got time."

No.

No.

And no.

"What about food? You hungry? I'll pay for it."

She perks up at that. The vacant look leaves her eyes some. "What?"

"Food. It's about lunchtime."

"I'm starving."

"Then what do you want?"

We go back and forth on this for like half an hour. The problem: She's hungry, but she don't want me to pay, but she don't got money, either. Okay, fine. So we will eat cheap, she says. But nothing cheap sounds good. So, I suggest BBQ. Because Goddamn can I eat some BBQ. But she says that's too much.

"You shouldn't spend that kind of money on me."

And I'm like, *Hannah. I do not care. Let's eat.*

Finally, the choice is made for us, because I'm just about out of gas.

Cope Field

And I got no clue where we are because I've just been driving north on the highway, not paying attention. So when I pass this little gas station–diner combo, I figure might as well because who knows how long it'll be before we see civilization again if we keep going.

I buy some gas first. Then I open her door to help her down the steps. Because this lift is stupid. I admit it. It's something Pops did after he broke some stuff in my room after I yelled at him. My fault again. Who am I to raise my voice at the man who gave me everything? The man who was there for me all those times Momma should have been but wasn't? I should not have pushed him. But he felt guilty anyway. Those are the times the wallet opens. Sometimes I get to pick out something I want. Other times he guesses what he thinks I might like. This is one of those guesses that fell flat. Might as well put a big pair of wrinkly truck nuts on the back.

Hannah hops down the last step. And for a second there, I'm just holding her hand.

She doesn't pull her hand away. And for some reason, neither do I. She looks up at the diner and says, "Thanks, Crawford. You really don't know how much this means to me."

STORY OF A LONELY GUY
BLINK-182

By the way, she eats like a coyote. Frantic. Like something bigger might yank her plate away at any second. That sounds mean. But it is the truth. She orders a kid's meal and eats the whole thing before I can even finish half my chicken tenders. So I ask her if she's still hungry, and her eyes go wide like, *Aw damn.*

"I can get you something else," I say.

First she says, "No." Then she says, "Are you sure?"

"I'm sure. Get any food you want."

So this time, she gets a grown human–sized burger. By the time it gets on the table, I'm done with my meal, so I sit there sipping my soda and watching her eat. About halfway through the second plate, she slows down some. Leans back in the seat and says, "Sorry."

"For what?"

"For eating like a pig."

"More like a starved dog."

She laughs a little. But not much. "I haven't ate anything since school yesterday."

"Why not?"

"I've got no food at home." She doesn't get embarrassed about it. She just adds, "Actually, there is food. What I've got is a stepparent who bogarts all the Twinkies."

That does not make sense to me. She must be able to tell by my face, so she shares this long story about her stepfather. Says his name is Sam Ledbetter, but he goes by Shotgun. Or Shotgun Sam. She just calls him Asshole. Or The Asshole. These are all answers to questions I do not actually ask her. But she tells them anyway. She tells me her momma married him when she was little. But it really started getting bad around the time she began going through puberty, because Hannah says she was a late bloomer, and he would comment on her body any chance he got. Tell her she was filling out. Or that she was "finally getting tits."

"And he'd say or do so much worse," Hannah says.

I do not want to know what could be worse.

"He had all this money but no job. I did not think about it back then. But now, you know, it's pretty obvious. Asshole would disappear in the shed around back for hours at a time. Come out smelling like cat piss. Or fingernail polish remover. Or some other smell not typically associated with storage sheds. Since he had money, Mom let him run with this hardcore inclination he was now FATHER™ and pants-wearer and general ruiner of what little bit of a home life we had.

"Then, about a year ago, he started saying I was getting fat. Started calling me Roly-poly. Said no man is ever gonna look at me. Said I must be 'sneaking food,' which, by the way, I was not. So he started locking everything in the house. The fridge is locked. The freezer is locked. All the cabinets are locked.

"I have caught him sitting down eating an entire frozen pizza by himself. Not one slice left for me. He's not even ashamed about it. He'll just smile at me. His mouth all full of cheese."

Me thinking she eats like a starved coyote now feels a little mean. Saying it right out loud like I did feels even worse. Pops has never locked our cabinets saying me or Big Time is too fat. Sort of the opposite, really. Big Time's got some meat on his bones. A thick little kid, for sure. And all anyone ever says is, "He's gonna be a good football player one day."

But.

If Pops did lock up the cabinets. Believe me, I would have them off their hinges the first time Big Time told me he was hungry.

Actually, I'm getting heated sitting here listening to her. I don't really know this girl, but I want to break down the door to her house. She eats the rest of her burger while I sit there and fantasize about some made-up fistfight I'd have making sure she got enough to eat. Shotgun would come into the kitchen like, *What the hell?* And I'd be like, *What the hell indeed.* Boom. Baseball bat right through the cabinet. *Your skull is next, buddy.* I'm completely lost in this daydream.

"Crawford," Hannah says. Her plate is empty.

I pay for everything. And she says thanks. And while I am waiting for the clerk to count back my change, I am thinking I just had a full conversation with this girl. I talked when I was supposed to talk.

I listened when I was supposed to listen. And it was easy. I am always on my guard. Always scared I might say something that goes wrong the moment it leaves the tip of my tongue. But not with her. It's like I can relax a little. So when Hannah asks if we can swap phone numbers, I don't have to think hard to say yes.

The clerk hands me back some quarters and a few ones. I tell Hannah, "Don't thank me. I did nothing for this money. Pops just gives it to me."

"You're lucky," she says.

And she's right. Of course she is right. I have everything I could ever want. But something still puts turmoil in my stomach. I can't explain it. And if I can't explain it, then I can't fix it, either. How can two opposites be correct at the same time? How can I fit those things together inside my brain?

I can't.

That's God's truth.

I cannot. And the space between them makes static. Dissonance. Can thoughts hurt like touching fire? I am here to tell you they can.

But maybe that is only my anger issues talking again.

We roll down the windows on the way back. And we don't talk. Just listen to the sound of trees whizzing past. Wind in our hair. Hannah points at the center console and says, "Bluetooth?"

I hand her my phone and tell her to go nuts.

"What kinda music you like?" she asks.

"Country." She makes a face like she might puke. So I add, "Rap."

Which draws even more disgust.

"Fine, what do *you* like?" I ask.

"Punk."

I roll up the windows because I can't hear her over the sounds of the road. "Did you say punk?"

"Yeah."

"Isn't that like... old people music?"

"People still make punk music, Crawford. But yeah, it's got some history behind it."

She hits a button on my phone and cranks up the volume. The sound of drums fills the cab, and Hannah starts nodding her head in time with the music. It's almost cool. Then the guitar starts. All these fast, erratic riffs. Even that is tolerable. But then the singing. My God, the singing. Some guy yells over and over about how much he hates Walmart.

I am not kidding you.

Walmart.

This goes on for two minutes then ends as abruptly as it started. Hannah smiles. "What'd you think?"

"That was full-on circus music."

She laughs. "You're not listening to it right."

"Not listening right? What's right?"

"Punk is an ideology. One sec. I'll make you a playlist. Homework, if you will."

"I'm good, thanks."

But she lets the music rage on, looking down at my screen, adding songs to a Spotify playlist. Every once and a while, she stops and thinks for a minute, chewing on her lip. Then she'll have some eureka moment, add a few songs, and go back to thinking. When she hands me the phone back, she's named the playlist *Crawdaddy's Musical Education*, with a little blue mudbug as the icon.

FACE DOWN
RED JUMPSUIT APPARATUS

I do not have to wait long at all to meet Mr. Shotgun Samuel. He's standing on the front porch when we roll in. Sun low in the sky. The wind finally deciding to turn cool. Little mamba of lightning bugs floating like crazy in the baseball field across from her house. Could be a postcard for the South, if not for the acidic smell wafting through the trees, the gangly half-human meth skeleton lurking on the porch.

Hannah says, "Damn," when she notices him there. She'd been hoping he'd pass out. But there's nothing to do about it, so I drive up to the house and let her out.

Shotgun brings a cigarette to his lips. Clint Eastwood eyes still intact. Says, "Where the hell you been?"

"I had a school project," Hannah says, keeping her distance.

"Like hell you did."

Feels like I should leave. Like I am watching someone take a dump through the space in a bathroom stall door. But I put the truck in park instead.

His eyes cut toward me. Then he flicks the cigarette on the hood of my truck, ashes going everywhere. "What you doing with him?"

"A school project, I said."

"Tell him to get the hell out of here."

She rolls her eyes. "I'll see you around, Crawford."

But I see where this is going. There's no way I am leaving her here alone with Shotgun Sam. I'm like, *Hell no*. I am having flashbacks to Pops when he is getting into one of his moods. So I open the door and step out of the truck, leaving it idling.

At first, I am Mr. Polite. "Name is Crawford Cope. I've been working on that field across the way with your daughter."

I see him mouth my name to himself. "Cope. Cope. Cope." Like he thinks he might know this name. But he's probably too strung out.

Those neurons aren't exactly firing. He shakes his head and says, "This your boyfriend?"

Hannah says, "No." Then, to me: "Please get out of here."

"We have rules in this house," he says. His hand drifts to something hidden behind a slat on the porch. "Rules about when to be home. When you can leave. How we clothe ourselves. Rules about boys. You know why we have rules like that?" His hand finds whatever he is looking for. I am about ready to dive for cover, but he pulls out a bottle of Jack, puts it to his lips, and just glug, glug, glugs the stuff down his throat.

"Alright," Hannah says. "Why don't we just go inside." She walks toward him, tries to turn him toward the front door. But he jerks away from her, speaking directly to me.

"'Cause the little whore can't keep her hands to herself. Just like her momma. One thing I ain't doing. Raising no gotdamn grandbaby from some slut what ain't even my blood relative."

I am thinking about nothing but driving my thumbs through this dude's eyeballs. Then something clicks. He figures it out.

"Cope," he says. "You're the baseball kid." He laughs. "Jesus Christ. You're Hunter Cope's kid. You done grown up. I barely recognize you." He laughs again. "But now that I see it, I can't *not* see it. You're him made over."

Shotgun staggers to one side, still holding that bottle by the neck. He has the word LOYALTY tattooed in a half-circle around his belly button. Lightning bolts all up and down his torso. A giant eagle with a sword in its talons over his chest. He comes down the steps and nearly falls, long, greasy hair swaying side to side. He is a good three inches taller than me. Scary as hell. But woozy on his feet because *drunk*.

Hannah says, "I won't do it again. Let's just go inside and get you to bed. You've had too much." Then, to me: "Crawford, please leave."

Not happening.

"I don't know what you are talking about," I tell him. "I don't know you."

"I'm sure you don't remember." He is so close I can smell his acrid breath. Like he puked and swallowed it.

Hannah grabs his wrist. Tries to pull him back toward the house. He jerks his hand away, staggers to one side. His hand moves right past my face.

You hear stories about time slowing down.

About people in car wrecks noticing crazy small details. Having all the time in the world to soak in the bullshit.

You hear about time slowing down for a batter in a baseball game. How they can see the stitching on the ball. Something that by all accounts ought to be impossible.

This was one of those moments for me.

I didn't ask to be here for this. Yet here I am. Am I meant to see this? Am I meant to do something about it?

In that fraction of a second, I can see him throwing that backhand. Can see the trajectory—where that hand will land if he keeps it going. Hannah is too focused on pulling at him to avoid it.

So I do the only thing I can.

I tackle The Asshole to the ground.

THNKS FR TH MMRS
FALL OUT BOY

At least I try to.

I drive my shoulder into him. Wrap up like a linebacker. Drive him backward a few paces, but he shifts his feet, and we stay upright. Shotgun reacts like a complete maniac. And I don't mean he gets angry. The dude starts laughing. Howling. Like he has lost his mind. And it is so out of the woods, I am more or less shook. He starts saying, "Ole boy wanna fight?"

Hannah screams, "Crawford!"

I drive my feet harder. Getting low. Wrapping my arms around his legs. Whole time I can hear Hannah yelling and cursing. And she isn't yelling at Shotgun. She's yelling at me. Begging me to stop.

But.

Too late now.

Shotgun teeters, then topples. But on the way down, he somehow turns me backward. Instead of me landing on top of him, I end up between his legs, my arms pinned down under his knees. And I got no clue how, but the play button on that playlist Hannah made for me gets hit in my pocket and the truck starts blaring this insane punk music. Shotgun looks at me. Wild insanity in his eyes. Says, "What now, big man?"

I buck around underneath him. Trying to get free. But this skinny bastard is like a machine of wires and bolts. I can't turn him. I can't free myself. If he wanted to, he could stick a knife right through my forehead. "Get off me," I tell him.

Hannah's playlist rampages from my truck, all drums and electric guitars. The lead singer barks something, but I can't understand him.

"You opened this can of worms," Shotgun says.

True enough. But I go ahead and tell him to get the hell off me again. He thumps his palm in the middle of my chest. "You gonna be calm?"

I look up at Hannah. Her face is grave. Her eyes wide, saying, *Please stop this.*

The singer from the playlist screams about burning it all down. And it's like... *Right there with you, man.*

"I am calm," I say, looking back at Shotgun. His face is nearly hidden in a curtain of greasy hair. For a second, I am not sure what is going to happen next. Then he swings his leg off me like he's dismounting a horse. He stands up. Offers me a hand, which I don't take. He shrugs and staggers off. Finds his bottle of Jack, which landed in the yard without breaking but fell sideways and burbled all its whiskey into the grass. He looks at the empty bottle and says, "Look what you done."

"This was a mistake," Hannah says.

Burn it all down.

He shakes his head. Sadly. Like he might cry. He says something I can't understand as he walks back toward the porch. We watch him go up the steps and disappear inside the house.

Then Hannah hurries over to me. I pull myself to my feet. I'm expecting some kind of *thank you* because I have been a real Goddamn hero today, buying her food and saving her from her idiot stepdaddy.

She slaps me right across the face.

I am double shook. "What in the hell?"

Burn it, burn it down.

"What is wrong with you?" she says.

"He was gonna hit you."

"What are you talking about?" she screams.

What in the hell? I got no words for this girl. Was I supposed to just stand by and watch him hit her? "I saw it, Hannah. I saw him fixing to hit you."

She stands so still. Her fists clenched at her sides. She looks like a spring about to come uncoiled. A lot like the way she looked this morning when she came around the side of her house, thinking no one could see her. For a long moment, we just stare at each other, neither sure what to say or do next, music blaring. Finally, she walks over to the truck, reaches inside, and kills the engine. All at once the music stops, the silence deafening after all that screaming, and she turns to face me.

"Listen very carefully," she says slowly. "Shotgun might be an asshole. He might ruin my life on the daily. He might bogart all the food and call me names. He might be a dealer. But he has never once put his hands on me. If you'd have just *left* like I asked you to, he'd be inside asleep on the couch right now. I know how to deal with him. You don't take him on. You redirect him somewhere else."

"I did the right thing."

"Jesus, Craw. Why do guys think they gotta punch their way through everything? You made everything objectively *worse*."

All my words have dried up inside me. I walk to the truck. Look at her one more time. I say, "Well, I'm sorry then."

Then I drive home.

Halfway there, I crank up the music. Country music warbling—not the damn punk nonsense. Me with the windows down. Lost in my thoughts. Thoughts that go in every direction imaginable. Trees flying by the window. A big yellow moon creeping up through them. I start to feel sick over what happened. Start to see it with a bit of distance. I am not sure what was right and what was wrong. I really did think he was gonna hit her. Because I have seen that kinda thing happen before.

It is dark before I roll up in our driveway.

Pops is on the front porch, plucking at a guitar. He stands up when I get out. I walk straight toward him but stop halfway. Fold my arms across my body. There's this pregnant feeling in the air. Like I oughta speak. I oughta tell him what happened to me. What I done. But it's falling heavy on my shoulders now. I got anger inside. It's like those YouTube videos said. Something triggered me. And I snapped. Maybe I wanted to fight him. Maybe the whole thing already lived in my head, and it was me who brought it to the surface.

Pops pulls me into a hug.

I go tense, but he doesn't let go. He squeezes me tight.

He whispers, "Are you okay?"

I don't say nothing. He just keeps squeezing.

That night, Hannah texts me. She says: *ur an idiot*

ME: I am an idiot.
ME: But I am sorry.
HANNAH: everyone is sorry

I don't know what she means by this. So I lie there staring at my phone, heart racing, hoping she'll elaborate. A few seconds later, I see she is typing another message.

HANNAH: i keep thinking

But then she doesn't say anything else. It's like, *What in the hell?* Why say half a sentence and then stop? So I go ahead and nudge her.

ME: What have you been thinking?

I get a miles-long text.

HANNAH: go back over my whole life thinking about stuff that has happened to me. ppl get so mean. so shitty. say all kinds of fake things about me. got so much worse after momma got arrested. i been punched. at school some girl just punched me in the stomach when i walked past her in the hall. said skank keep your distance. like what the hell? i don't even know this girls name. that is not the first time that kinda thing has happened. wont be the last im guessing. thing is all this time not one person ever stood up for me. mom never once stood up to shotgun.

I have no idea what to say. So I just reply: I'm sorry.

I almost fall asleep waiting for her response. My phone vibrates in my hand.

HANNAH: even tho u are stupid and wrong, u stood up for me
HANNAH: in your stupid jock way
HANNAH: so i guess that counts for something
HANNAH: thank u ♥

part two | the strong silent type

crawdaddy

ABOUT A GIRL
THE ACADEMY IS...

Coach Rodriguez teaches my history class. A lot of times, he keeps it easy. But today, after a half hour of everyone being loud and not listening to him, he claps two erasers together and yells, "You don't wanna listen? How about an essay assignment?"

And we're all shook.

You push someone until you can't push them no further, I guess.

"I want you all to interview someone you live with," he says. "And I want five hundred words about their life tomorrow."

Someone asks, "What does this have to do with World History?"

Coach Rodriguez says, "Do you live in the world?"

"Yes."

"Then it's World History."

Everyone quiets down after that, and we take turns reading out loud from the book about some ancient guy named Hannibal. What I am gathering about this guy is he was a man born with his whole future picked out for him by his father. He was born to hate Rome. Born to fight Rome. But even after being born for something, he still failed at it in the end.

Thinking about that has me feeling some kind of way. Like baseball is my Rome. Hell. That don't make sense. But it's still wiggling around in my skull for some reason.

A few kids try and make another case against the homework assignment before the bell, but I already know Coach Rodriguez is not one to go back on his word.

"Craw," he says, before I can leave his classroom.

"Yeah, Coach?"

"Do yours on your old man. Would be real interesting, I bet."

Of course.

Everybody wants to hear the same ten stories about Pops over and over again. But then Coach Rodriguez says something I am not expecting.

"Ask him about what it was like growing up here. Ask him how he ended up in the majors from a little place like this. That's the part nobody ever talks about."

I walk out of class, thinking about that statement.

It's funny—and not haha funny.

Because that's the part Pops almost never talks about, either.

ME: You ever heard of Hannibal?
HANNAH: like silence of the lambs?
ME: What?

This is during lunch. I'm looking all over the cafeteria for her because I feel like the world's biggest jerk for not knowing her name before community service. Like how do you go to a school as small as ours and not know every person in your class by name? You go to a place like this, or live in a small town like ours, and everyone says, *Everybody knows everybody.* But it isn't true. Even in the smallest of places, there are those who fall through the cracks.

Hannah's not in the lunchroom. I take one look at all the baseball players sitting together, and my brain says, *Nope, not today.* So I walk down the hall, carrying my sack lunch in one hand.

I peek in classrooms, thinking maybe she had to work extra during lunch on a project or whatever. But nope. No clue. I take out my phone again.

ME: Where are you?
HANNAH: in my secret cave

Ah. Okay. The very place a troll would eat if trolls were real. Makes sense.

ME: I'm serious.
HANNAH: unused classroom in the back of the music lab

The music lab. Maybe the only classroom on campus I've never been inside. It's at the end of a long hallway, across from the gymnasium. You gotta walk past about twelve athletic trophy cases to get there, which is where they keep Pops' retired jersey, plus the state championship trophy he won. Plus a picture of him when he was my age. A real weird thing. It's like some alternate universe picture of me. Me but not me.

I hate it.

I slip inside the room. There's a girl at the piano playing sad-sounding music. She doesn't look up at me, so I don't bother her. But then she says, "Are you supposed to be here?"

So I say back, "Are you?"

She stops playing and gives me go-fuck-yourself eyes. "Yes. I am. But you're not. So leave."

I just start throwing open all the doors, looking for this so-called unused classroom, being as loud and obnoxious as I possibly can. I open one door, and two teachers look up from their lunches like I just caught them making out.

"Sorry," I say, shutting the door.

Three rooms later, I find Hannah sitting alone in an empty classroom, scratching an anarchy symbol into one of the desks with the sharp end of a protractor.

"Crawford," she says without looking up.

"Can I eat with you?"

"Aren't you afraid somebody might see you?"

I step inside and shut the door. "We're in your secret cave. So no."

"Pull up a seat, Crawdaddy."

She's got on this denim jacket. Threadbare. Looking like someone with no clue how to make jackets took a crack at it back in the 1970s. There's a patch on the sleeve that reminds me of the Ghostbusters logo. Except instead of crossing out a ghost, it's crossing out a swastika. No Nazis. A good life philosophy, I figure. There's also a bunch of band names I don't recognize like Dead Kennedys and Ramones, plus a piece that looks like it was torn from an old T-shirt that shows some big-eyed anime girl wearing a sailor costume. I tug the sleeve of the jacket gently. "What are you wearing?"

"It's my battle jacket."

Okay.

No further questions. Except one, I guess. There's a rainbow pride flag in the lapel, which makes me think of what Luis said about her that day on the fence. He called her ambisextrous. Which I think means he was calling her gay. But I am not sure. I touch my own chest where the pin is on hers. "Are you?"

"Am I what?"

I tap my chest again. Raise my eyebrows. "You know."

"Lesbian? Are you asking if I'm a lesbian?"

"Yeah."

"Why does it matter?"

"It doesn't."

"Then why did you ask?"

"Because you have that pin."

"Maybe I'm just not a shitty person."

"Okay. Fair enough."

"Sit down, Craw. You're hovering over me, and it's weird as hell."

I slide down the wall and start going through my lunch. Pops don't pack lunches, but he keeps plenty of snacks in the cabinet. So I make whatever I feel like. Which today is six packs of fruit gummies, some tortilla chips, a banana, a can of Coke, some Oreos, and a pizza Lunchables, which was meant for Big Time's lunch, but I snuck it because *hell yeah pizza.*

"Okay, but Hannah, are you?" I say. Because I cannot leave well enough alone.

"Why do you want to know, Crawford?"

"Someone told me you are."

"Well, they aren't far off. How about that?"

Not far off. What's that mean? And she raises a good question. Why do I want to know? Probably the same reason I keep on thinking about her all day even though I tell myself I shouldn't. Some little ape bouncing around in my skull wants to know: Do I have a chance in hell with this girl?

I start eating, and already I can see Hannah giving me side-eye. "What?"

"Nothing."

Her lunch is exactly that. Nothing.

Right then, I remember about the locks on her pantry doors. "You got a lunch?"

"No."

"Why not a school lunch?"

"Because every time I go get a free lunch, LeAnne or one of her dumbass friends gives me shit about it. I'm not that hungry. And I don't want to deal with her."

I toss her a couple packages of fruit chews, which she eats without talking. When she finishes the packs, I ask if she wants one of the mini pizzas. She does. So I give her that, too. And the banana. By the end, only thing I end up eating for lunch is one pizza, one pack of fruit chews, and the Coke, which she says is "nasty" and "bad for you."

But she also says, "Thank you."

"Why you hiding out in here?" I ask her.

She puts the protractor down on the desk. "I don't know. I hate it here. But I'm stuck here. So I look for ways to make it as tolerable as possible. And that means not eating in the cafeteria next to people who think it's fun to fuck with me."

"So where you gonna go after?"

"After?"

"After school."

"Home, I guess?"

"I mean after you graduate. If you hate it so much, I figured you had your escape all planned out."

She chews the inside of her lip for a second. "Yeah."

"Yeah?"

"Yeah, I had a plan. But it won't work. So I gave up on it."

I don't have anything to say to that. I stay quiet. Eat the rest of my lunch crumbs.

"Did you know Anna Carol Wood?" Hannah asks. She finishes the last bite of her lunch, picks up the protractor, and goes back to scratching that anarchy symbol in the wood. The name sounds familiar, but I have to admit I don't know her.

Hannah says, "She was my only friend. A year older than us. Graduated last year. Really big into theater and band and choir."

She says it as if it should jog my memory. It doesn't.

"We had this plan about getting out of here," Hannah continues. "Get scholarships, go to the same school, and be roommates. Get out of this place and never look back. It was all working out, too. She had immaculate grades. Top of the class. Had to give a speech at graduation and everything. She had a full-ride scholarship. And I was right behind her, hitting the books and doing all the extra credit assignments, making sure my grades were up to snuff, too."

She stops. Scratches the wood some more.

"So what happened?" I ask.

"So, her momma got sick with cancer. And next thing I know, Anna Carol is saying she needs to go work at the chicken plant so she can take care of her."

"Damn."

"A couple months later, she texts me that she's pregnant and getting married and they have a trailer a county over and I should come visit. I didn't even know she was seeing anyone. And just like that. Life over. It's like . . . nobody leaves this place, Crawford. You can plan and plan and work and work, and it will always find a way to pull you back in. Look at your dad. He got pulled back here, too."

"Damn," I say again.

"So I gave up," Hannah says. "What's the point? Squeaked by last semester by the skin of my teeth. Which really goes to show you how low the academic standards here really are. Anyway, what's the point of working yourself to death if it gets you nowhere in the end?"

A part of me wants to tell her some nonsense to make her feel better. *You can get outta here, Hannah. Believe it!*

But I know it's just that.

Nonsense.

You really can get trapped here. I have lived here long enough to see it.

Hannah finishes the anarchy symbol. She blows the wood dust off the desk. "Why were you asking about Hannibal earlier?" she asks.

"No reason. Why did you come to my baseball game?"

"Also no reason."

We are a pair with no reasons between us.

At baseball practice, I ask Luis if he ever heard about Hannibal before, and he says the same thing as Hannah. "That movie scared the hell out of me."

I just shake my head and tell him, "Never mind, you work on catching. I'll work on pitching."

Luis and I are developing this psychic connection. He will call for a pitch. And it's like, *My guy, I was thinking the exact same thing.* I don't think I would ever say this out loud, but he has this easy way about him. It's like he breathes out calm. And you breathe it in, and that makes you calm, too. Real good trait for a catcher to have. Real good trait for anybody to have, really. I wonder how many VR meditation YouTube videos I'd have to experience to get there myself.

"Hey, Craw," Luis says after a minute or two. "How come you ate lunch with Hannah today?"

I nearly drop the ball. "How do you know about that?"

"People talk, Craw."

"People make shit up."

"Craw, come on, man. If you can't talk to your catcher, who can you talk to?"

I sigh. It's not a good argument. There's plenty I won't ever tell him about. But I can tell he is not leaving this alone until I give him some kind of answer that satisfies his curiosity.

"I been havin' to do community service with her on Saturdays," I tell him, throwing him a heater but not all that hard. It pops into his glove. He drops to one knee and returns it. "I just went in there to ask her a question about it."

"I heard you was in community service."

"You heard? People are talking about it? What are they saying?" I ask, really just glad he's moving on from the whole Hannah question.

"Nothing."

"Not one thing?"

"No. Who cares?"

"What do they think I did?"

"Well, I guess they do talk about that."

"What do they say?"

We aren't practicing at all by this point. Just soft tossing the ball back and forth. He lifts up his catcher's mask and tells me there are a lot of theories.

"Some are saying it was some kinda scuffle with your papá," he says. And that gets my heart rocketing around in my rib cage because it is too damn close to the truth. But he shakes his head, breathes out that calm, and says, "Nobody believes it. You got the best daddy possible. Plus, we all know you don't have a mean bone in your whole body. Except when you're on the hill. On the bump, you're... un asesino."

"I'm a *what*?"

He smiles. "A killer."

I laugh a little. But I'm not done asking my questions. "So what do they think?"

"Like maybe you got busted with weed or something."

I laugh again. "Naw, not that."

"I know. People are dumb."

Coach Rodriguez hollers at us to get back to work. So we start throwing again. After a while, Luis says, "Craw, what did happen?"

I can't hardly look at him. There is a part of me that wants to say it. To release it out of my belly and let it float up into the stratosphere and never come back. But all up and down, my throat tightens. I can't say a damn word. I throw to him as hard as I can, hoping he don't bring it up again. Hoping the effort needed to catch my heater is enough to distract him.

He takes his hand out of his glove after a catch. Shakes it at his side. "Damn, man. You don't gotta kill me with it."

After practice, I head back up to the school because I left my whole-ass backpack in sixth period Algebra. How do you wander out of class without grabbing your backpack? Beats me. But I did it. And it's not the first time, either. I get so . . . *lost* inside my own head sometimes. Here but not here.

It's a short drive across campus, and I park right by the front doors and hustle inside, praying to the divine whatever that the door to the classroom is still unlocked.

It's nearly five in the evening, so I'm surprised the commons is bustling with activity. There's a bunch of cheerleaders on the ground with giant rolls of paper, ribbons, and other craft materials making prom decorations. They got red, white, and blue paint containers all around them. Paper stars. Little American flags. One of the girls, LeAnne Wilson, smiles at me when I hurry past. Says, "Hey, Craaawford." Dragging my name out like that.

I nod and say, "Sup."

Hannah sits on the stage across the room, her drawing notebook open across her lap. She doesn't look up from whatever she is working on, which is a good thing. Because I don't got time for conversations with her.

It is weird, though. Hannah still being here. What for?

She glances up when I walk past. I nod and say, "Hey, Hannah."

She smiles. "Hey."

But I keep moving toward the hallway.

School is a weird place to be after hours. It has the same feel as a hospital. Or a graveyard. Feels bizarre. Almost mystical. Maybe it's because half the lights in the hallway are out. And that is for real spooky.

The door to the classroom is still open, but all the lights are off. I find my backpack sitting on the floor in the back. I scoop it up, throw it over one shoulder, and head back out. I already had baseball practice, but Pops will want me and Big Time in the dungeon for at least an hour tonight. If we're lucky, he'll let me take Big Time out there alone and we can just goof off, maybe play some catch if we feel like it.

Halfway back to the commons, I can hear people yelling.

I hurry up. Curious, but not expecting much.

When I round the corner, Hannah is standing in the middle of a circle of girls, blue paint running through her hair, down the side of her face, pooling on the floor around her Chuck Taylors. Her fists clench at her hips, and even from behind, I can tell she's about to lose her shit.

"It was an accident," LeAnne says.

"You did it on purpose."

"I swear..."

But some girls behind Hannah giggle, holding containers of red and white paint. And I'm taking this in slow. They move toward her. The first girl dumps white paint over Hannah's head. Hannah jerks upright, like she's been zapped with electricity. She turns toward her attackers just in time for the second girl to upend her can of red paint. "Oh, man," the girl says flatly. "Another accident."

I oughta break this up.

But what am I gonna do? Beat these girls up?

I don't have time anyway. Hannah pulls her fist back and decks this girl right in the face. She spins backward, her mouth hanging open, Hannah's blue knuckle prints on her cheek. The girls start screaming and scattering like there's a snake in the cafeteria. But Hannah goes to work. She grabs the red-paint girl by the hair and pulls her to the ground, swings a leg over her body, and gives her four hooks like left, right, left, right.

And I'm over here like: 😱😱

Then, cool as a hardened criminal, Hannah rises and turns toward LeAnne.

"Don't!" LeAnne says, holding up her hands. "My dad's a cop."

Hannah grabs her by the front of her shirt. Pulls her close. "Don't *ever* touch me," she says. "Ever."

The two girls she beat up pull themselves together. "I'm fuckin' bleeding," one of them says.

"Thought you liked gettin' touched by girls," the other says. "You slut."

Hannah's eyes shift around the room. They land on me.

And she seems to shrink. Like she's ashamed I saw her like this. But she's got no reason to be ashamed. She's a certified badass. I feel like I should do something. Say something. But I remember what happened last time I threw myself in the middle of her life.

Hannah lets go of LeAnne's shirt. She's surrounded, but it seems like the fight is out of everyone. One of the bleeding girls says, "It's not worth it, LeAnne."

LeAnne shrugs. Makes pretend like she is in control of the situation. Says, "Fine," and they head to the lady's room to clean the blood and paint off their faces. When they are gone, Hannah looks at me.

"Let's get out of here," I say.

She nods.

We walk down to the gymnasium, where the basketball team is practicing. I hold on to her elbow. I don't know why. My hand just landed there. Hannah leaves patriotic footprints everywhere she goes. We slip into one of the unisex bathrooms meant for the coaches, and I shut and lock the door. Hannah leans against the sink, leaving little smears of paint.

I look her up and down. "Why are you still at school?"

"Shotgun comes when he feels like it. If he don't, then I walk."

I start yanking paper towels out of the dispenser. I get them wet in the sink. Hannah stands completely still. Her eyes stare straight at the floor. And I'm not sure, but I think I see teardrops streak the paint on her face.

"You okay?"

She tries to wipe her eyes. Smears paint instead. She laughs bitterly. "So damn stupid."

"Yeah. They are."

"No. I'm stupid."

"How the hell are you the stupid one?"

"Because. I proved them right. Everything they say about me. It's all true. I come from people who are no good. So I'm no good, either. Craw, I made fun of you for punching your way through your problems, and look what I did."

"You *are* a good person. Better than me by a hundred miles."

"Shut up."

I step a little closer to her, still holding the dripping paper towels. I reach up and clean a little paint away from her cheek. She doesn't resist. So I take her head in one hand and wipe away the mess with the other. I go through my entire stack of paper towels in no time, and she's barely any cleaner. But we stand there for a long minute, my hand on her cheek. Her eyes turned upward at me.

She is trembling.

"You know what she said when she walked up to me? Before she dumped the paint?"

"What?"

"Said she heard you and I were spending time together."

I wipe away some more paint. My heart is racing. I have no clue how LeAnne woulda found out something like that, but it tells me folks are talking. All this time, I was worried people would think less of me if I spent too much time with Hannah, but not one person has treated me different for it. No. It's Hannah whose life has been made worse. Just by being friends with me.

"I'm sorry," I say. And I mean it. I wish I could explain to her how much I mean it. "Do you want me to stay away from you outside community service?"

She smiles weakly. For a second, I think she is going to wrap her arms around me. Hug me. And I find that I am wishing she would. Instead, she pulls back. Puts a little distance between us. "No. It's fine. They'd pick a different reason if it wasn't you. I like talking to you, Crawford. That's all I need from you. I don't need you to win baseball games. I don't need you to fight people for me. I just need you to listen to me when I talk. And I need you to reciprocate."

"Reciprocate? How?"

She reaches up and touches my cheek. Then she gives it a small playful smack. "Drop the strong silent nonsense and talk to me."

"I do talk."

"I mean *really* talk to me."

I don't know what to say to that. I don't even know what she means. So I just tell her fine. I'll try. One more thing for me to work on, I guess. Maybe there are VR meditation videos about that, too.

"I'll drive you home," I say. "You don't need to be walking in the dark."

"I'll get paint in your truck."

I step back, huck all the wadded-up paper towels in the trash, and open the door. "There's been way worse stuff in my truck, believe me."

She screws up her face. "Wait, what's been in your truck?"

I'M JUST A KID
SIMPLE PLAN

I finally get home after dropping Hannah off. She made me listen to that stupid playlist the whole damn way. And I will admit, some of them songs are catchy. But most of them are pure noise.

Pops sits on the porch, picking the guitar. Don't even look up at me when I walk past. Not until I say, "Where's little man?"

He stops playing for one second. "Where you think?" he says, then goes right back to the strings, playing some old country song with that chugging train type of rhythm.

Where you think? means in the pool.

I tell Pops, "I got to interview you for some schoolwork later. Don't let me forget." Then I walk all the way around the house and through the side gate.

Here's Big Time in a nutshell.

He's floating in the middle of the pool, his butt halfway through one of those Froot Loop–shaped floaties. He's got all these smaller floaties in the water near him, with snacks on them. There's a bag of Doritos on one floaty. Another has a little cooler filled up with sodas. On another floaty, he's got a paper plate loaded up with pizza rolls. All of these floaties he has looped together with a bit of rope so they won't drift away from each other. Dude is kicked back. His hands laced behind his head. Sun bouncing off those reflective wraparound pro-rassler shades. He kicks a little foot in the water until he spins to face me. "Sup?"

"What up, Big Time?"

"Oh, nothing. Doing my thing."

"I see that." I kick off my Jordans and sit on the edge of the pool. Dip my toes in there. Big Time floats over and asks if I want some pizza rolls. They're a bit soggy, so I say no thank you.

"Your loss," he says, popping a few in his mouth.

Cope Field

"You work baseball today?"

He looks at me over the top of his glasses and says, "What do you think?" in a tone that means, *You know Pops. Obviously we did a million baseball drills today.*

"Where did you get those dumb glasses?"

"These glasses are rad. I found 'em in Pops' closet. They're his from when he was in the league."

Going through Pops' things is a risky gamble. He might yank a knot in your tail. Or he might not care at all. You never can tell with him. I guess the glasses suit Big Time with no objections from Pops since he's still wearing them. I let out a long breath.

"You know what I been thinking about?" Big Time says.

"What?"

"Stephenson 2-18."

"What in the world is Stephenson 2-18?"

"It's a red super giant. Or maybe an extreme red hypergiant. We ain't too sure."

"What?"

"It is the largest known star, Craw. You could fit thirteen quadrillion Earths into it."

"I don't want to talk about space, Sutton."

He sits up in his little floaty. I can see my own face reflected in his rassler glasses. Little man's getting passionate. "You can't even comprehend thirteen quadrillion Earths!"

"No, I guess I can't. And I don't want to."

Big Time settles back down. I sit there quiet. Not looking to talk. But I'll say this about Big Time. He is an observer. Like an old person stuck inside a little chubster's body.

He paddles a little closer to me. "Long day? Why don't you crack open a cold one and tell me about it."

He throws me a Coke, which I don't catch because I was not expecting it. It plops into the pool and sinks to the bottom. Big Time says he'll swim down and get it later, no worries. Then he throws me another can. This time a Sprite. I pop the tab and take a swig.

"What's on your mind?" Big Time asks.

"Nothing."

"Something is. I can tell about these kinda things."

"Well, I don't want to talk about it."

"Confession is good for the soul."

I blink. Like, *What did you just say to me?* I swear to God, sometimes this kid opens his mouth and some old grandpappy ancestor starts talking through him.

"Look, Craw, we was made to talk with each other."

"We?"

"We're brothers. Brothers talk."

For a second, I thought he meant "we" as in *all people*. Brothers, I can get behind. Everybody in the whole stupid world? No thank you. "Okay, fine. I'm thinking about a girl I know."

"That one from the baseball game."

"That's her. Which, by the way, I hate you told her I got anger problems."

"You do be having them though," he says ponderously.

"That is not true."

"That Judge says you have angry manager problems. And so does Pops. Pops said once you get going, you don't know how to stop yourself. Don't worry, Craw. I am the same way about ice cream sandwiches. Once I have one, I can't stop myself no matter what. Craw, sometimes I'll eat three or four of them suckers."

"Alright. Fine." No point arguing.

"That girl emo or what?"

"I don't know what she is."

"Well, what you think about her so much for?"

"I don't know."

"Is it a bad thing to think about someone?"

"Sometimes. Like in school when I ought to be learning. Or sometimes at baseball practice."

Big Time snaps off his glasses with one hand and squints at me. "What?"

I got no idea what his deal is. So I just glare at him like, *What's the problem?*

"You mean to tell me this girl is on your mind so much you can't *practice* right?"

"I said sometimes. Not all the time."

He leans back in his floaty. The back of his mullet just barely touches the water. "I think you like this girl."

"False."

"Not false. Gross. But not false."

"Gross?"

"All girls is gross, Craw. Read a book."
"You might feel different about that one day."
"Bet you I don't."
"I'll take that bet. Besides, that ain't what I'm saying. I'm saying I don't know how I feel, and it's driving me straight up crazy."

Big Time doesn't answer me right away. We sit there for a long time. Me sipping that Sprite. Him just floating. Glasses on. Pink swim trunks with little blue dolphins on them. Mullet adrift. Pizza roll crumbs on his stomach. Finally, he says, "I think you do know. It's just too gross to admit."

Pops ain't a cook. But he has this one meal he can do, and it's full-on comfort food. He don't break it out often. But when he does, it's a good day.

I smell him cooking that evening. I'm floating through cow fields on my VR headset, listening to this old boy tell me how to wrangle my anger problems, and my stomach starts growling. And it's like okay. We gonna eat good tonight.

I walk down the hallway and to the kitchen bar. He's got all these veggies simmering in bacon grease with garlic and salt. Plus some ground beef browning in another pan. Just looking at all the ingredients—beef stock, tomato paste, beans, a whole slew of different seasonings—I know what he's got cooking.

"Chili?" I ask.
"Yessir."

Hell yes.

Pops makes a mean pot of chili. His secret comes at the end. Once everything cooks together, he adds a whole bar of dark chocolate plus some brown sugar to the mix. He says it elevates all the flavors. I don't know about that. All I know is it is my favorite meal.

I sit down at the counter while he cooks, feeling pretty happy about my favorite meal. But Pops has baseball on his mind, of course.

"Don't get too comfortable. We getting some reps in later," he says.
"I figured we would."
"I ain't at all satisfied with how you been pitching this year."

I don't know what to say to that. I know I goofed up some. But I have done a lotta good on the hill, too. Why can't we ever talk about that?

There's a scrap paper on the counter with cartoon spacemen drawn all over it. Big Time's doing. But it reminds me of my homework assignment, and I figure now is as good a time as any. I pick up a pen. "I got to interview you for homework before we do any of that."

"What do you wanna know? About baseball?"

"Kinda."

"What you mean kinda?"

"Everybody can Google you and learn about your baseball career. I want to write the stuff don't nobody know about."

He shakes some hot sauce over the chili. "Okay, ask away. Some stuff don't need to be told though. Our business is our business."

"Just basic stuff, Pops. Like what was it like growing up here?"

Pops says, "I might have had the best childhood there ever was. Splashing in the creeks. Running all over the mountains. Acting stupid back before cell phones made stupid permanent."

"And practicing baseball, right?"

"Sure. Your papaw coached the high school team, so I had extra coaching, just like you."

By the time I knew Papaw, he was *older'n hale*, as he woulda said. He still loved watching baseball, but he didn't do much more than sit in his recliner and watch games and old Westerns on his satellite television. He was a good guy. Always called me Rutabaga, like as a nickname. But I never did make much sense out of it. "What was he like as a coach? I only remember him as a papaw, which I figure he gone soft by then."

Pops smiles. He shakes some orange powder into the pot and gives it a stir. "Soft as cotton. He was a mean old cuss, to tell you the truth. Always on my ass for one thing or another. Sometimes it seemed like I never was good enough for him."

"But you went pro."

"Yeah, I did. And let me tell you, it was *because* he was hard on me I done that. I know you think I'm a hard ass. But I am nothing compared. And I thought the same of him back then. But looking back at it, I know everything he done was just to make me better than I woulda been on my own." He tastes the chili. Thinks for a second. "You know where I'd been without him?"

"Where?"

"Acting a fool with foolish people. I never woulda got out of Quiet County. Come taste this."

I stop writing and stand beside him. He drops that bar of dark chocolate in, and I watch it ooze into liquid. Then he gives it a twirl until it disappears into the beans and meat and sauce. He dips a spoon in, then holds it out for me.

It tastes perfect.

Savory. Sweet. Heat around the edges.

Takes me straight back to being small.

He gets bowls from the cabinet and puts them on the counter. Then, before he hollers for Big Time, he says to me, "I know we got our problems sometimes, but you know I love you, right? That I only want to see you succeed? That I never mean to hurt you?"

He speaks soft. With sincerity.

But his eyes remind me of that night in the baseball dungeon. Him on the ground. Blood leaking from his head. The baseball bat in my hands.

"I know, Pops," I say.

This man pushes hard. But I think I can see he is pushing me in the right direction. Just like his old man did for him. Maybe they are right. It's me with the problem. It's me who don't listen. Me who escalates. That thought settles in my stomach. Sours everything. Pops fixes me a bowl of chili with sour cream and cheese on top, just the way I like it. But I don't hardly eat it.

BABY, I'M AN ANARCHIST
AGAINST ME!

Roger hands me and Hannah leather gloves. Walks us to the back of the truck. There's these metal tubes back there. Painted black, but all chipped up, showing the oxidized metal underneath. I got no idea what I'm looking at. But Hannah grabs one and asks, "Are we post setting?"

Roger says, "Spray painted some big orange dots out there. Need a post in each dot. I already laid the posts out. They need to go about three feet deep."

I pick up the other tube and stare at it like, *What in the hell am I supposed to do with this?*

Roger says, "I'd wear them gloves." Which automatically means I will not. There's a lady present. And even though it's Hannah, some small part of my stupid little monkey brain wants her to think I am tough as a silverback.

"You looked at that T-post driver like it was a live snake," Hannah says as we walk across the field.

"I got no idea how to use one."

"It's not hard. I'll show you."

We walk to the first orange blob of paint in the grass. Hannah shimmies her hands into a pair of leather work gloves, then sticks the post upright and slides that metal pipe over the top. A little lift and tap, lift and tap, and I can see the post inching its way into the ground. It's slow going, though. And not even six inches in, Hannah is already wiping sweat with the back of her hand, huffing and puffing and saying every cuss word you can think of.

"Let me take over," I say.

"Be my guest." She hands me the post driver, then she takes out her phone, cracks the volume all the way up, and lies back in the grass. That punk rock playlist of hers, of course. I didn't ask to listen to music, but I can't deny all these angry sounds got me feeling some kinda way. Like I might could drive this post straight to hell.

I go to town on that bad boy. Because again—idiot monkey brain says, *Impress girl good.* Ten or fifteen strokes in, I stop and look at my palm. The skin is broken open, weeping clear liquid. In other places, pockets of fluid bubble like someone injected juice into my hand. They have machines for this, I am sure of it.

"That's why you wear the gloves," Hannah says, thumping a pair in the center of my chest. She must've tucked extra in her back pocket before we left Roger's truck. I guess she knew my ape brain would come to its senses before long. But I'm not ready to call it quits just yet.

"I'm fine," I say. And I go back to work. Just shredding my palms worse. Hating myself for it the entire time. Like, who programmed me to be this stupid? Someone did. I definitely did not arrive here on my own accord.

"Crawford," she says.

But I keep going. Hammering the post until it's almost two feet in. Takes for-fucking-ever, and I still have an entire foot to go.

Hannah slugs me on the arm. "Will you stop being stupid?"

Baby, I was born stupid.

I look at my hand. Bleeding.

And my first reaction to the blood is: Good.

Because there's another part inside my skull that's got nothing to do with impressing Hannah. Some part I can't all the way untangle. It's like . . . fixing this place should cost blood. This place with my name on it. With Pops' name on it. It should take something from me. Blood. Sweat. Pain. You can't fix anything without giving something of yourself. Of that much I am completely sure.

We only get two posts in the ground all day. At the end, Roger comes over and says, "This was not my best idea."

And I'm like, *What was not your best idea?*

This goofy moron says, "I'll see if I can't get aholt of a gas-powered post driver this week. Take care of the rest easy."

And it's like, *Are you kidding me?* Why not do that to begin with? I stand there gritting my teeth. And Hannah, thank God, just as mad as I am, goes and says it right out loud.

"Why make us waste a whole day?" She puts her fists on her hips.

And I think back to the day she beat up LeAnne and those other girls. Hannah is someone who can scrap.

Roger just says, "Look, y'all are out here to work. So it wasn't a waste of time as long as you worked. Y'all ain't here to finish this field. You're here to put in so many hours until your community service is served. So don't worry about it. The field will get finished up with or without you."

Well.

That's all I can handle for today.

In the truck, my hands start to burn for real. I sit there looking at them. Like, *What in hell have I done to myself?* There's a tap on my window. And there's Hannah, with her hands behind her back, her toes turned inward at each other. I roll down the window. She looks down, turning her foot in the dirt like a little kid about to ask for candy.

"What?" I say.

"You wanna go driving again?"

It is about noon. And I am starving. "Hop in."

Hannah's face turns bright. Happy. Like the kind of happy you wish you could put in a bottle. Keep it around your neck. Take little sips off it when things get bad.

Warms me up inside. The idea of it. That she would be happy just to be around me. I'm starting to realize I feel that same way, even if I don't show it on my face as much.

I look in my rearview mirror, and there's old Shotgun Sam, standing on the front porch, cigarette dangling between two fingers, eyeballs watching my tires kick up gravel and dust. Last I heard, he didn't like me running around with Hannah too much. I'm not looking for more chaos in my life. So I ask her what's her plan to deal with him this time?

She says, "I can deal with him. Don't worry about it."

But of course I do.

I worry about it the entire time we are driving.

crushcrushcrush
PARAMORE

"Just don't take me back," Hannah says. We are at that diner, stuffing burgers in our faces.

"Ever?"

She leans back and smiles. "Wouldn't that be nice?"

I got a mouthful of food, so I chew on the thought and the food at the same time. Imagine, if you will, Crawford Cope, blowing across the continental USA in the pickup truck his pops bought him, spending his pops' money, whole time telling everyone he's never going back to live in Quiet County. No baseball. No more fights with Pops. No nothing.

But running away solves nothing. It fixes *nothing*.

All it'd do is drive a wedge even further through the middle of our family.

After we eat, I haul ass down the highway. Take some back roads I know, to where a bend in the Illinois Bayou is perfect for swimming or just sitting on the bank, watching clouds bounce back reflections in the water. The river is a good distance from where you have to park, but enough rednecks have walked to it over the years that it's not too hard to get down there. We reach the water's edge. Listen to the sound of it swirling. Little tadpoles scatter to the depths. It looks beautiful. Honestly, like God's face turned upward. But Hannah scoffs and says she won't swim in any kind of creek or lake because she read a news article online that said they are full up on brain-eating amoebas.

I kick off my Jordans and walk a ways out into the river. Until the bottom of my shorts start getting wet. "Look, someone hung a rope swing from that tree. Nobody's hanging a rope swing over water famous for brain-eating amoebas."

Hannah stands at the edge of the water. Her toes almost touching.

"You don't always know they are there. They surprise you. They get up your nose and eat your brain."

This seems made-up. But she is serious. She takes out her busted-up phone to show me, but there's no signal.

"Just dip your feet in," I say.

But she won't. So I walk back toward her and sit down on a big rock. I pull my Jordans close, tuck my phone inside one shoe, my socks in the other. Then I stretch my toes in the water. And even though we got a nice clean swimming pool back home, I swear to God this is better. The water has some current. This teal color out deep. It's almost unbelievable. The river is low, baked down by the sun, so the far bank is a tangled mess of tree roots and rocks. *A snake's playground*, Memaw woulda said. God, I can almost hear her voice. *Y'uns get away from there fore you get your ass a cottonmouth.*

That woman was more afraid of snakes than any person I have ever known. I swear probably two-thirds her whole life was spent worrying about snakes. You could show her a drawing of a snake you made in school, and she would tell you to keep that thing away from her eyesight.

Hannah takes off her shoes. She sits beside me and dips her toes in the water. We don't talk for a long time. But the woods do some talking for us. Water bubbling. Trees breathing. Birds speaking. And behind that, the Arkansas Anthem: locusts buzzing.

"What about if it really was you and me," Hannah says after a long time.

"What?"

She looks straight ahead across the water. "What would you do differently?"

"I don't know what you mean."

"If it was just you and me in the whole world, what would you do differently?"

I chew on that for a while, not all the way sure what she is asking me. "I guess I'd do everything the same."

"Would you?"

"I just said that I would."

"What about if we left and never came back? Like we were talking about earlier? Just left forever. But together."

"I got baseball practice."

"If you went on the lam, you'd have to give up baseball."

But baseball is as intertwined with my being as my own skin. To imagine never playing baseball again is to imagine pulling out my own guts. No thank you. I'll keep my guts in the belly sack where they belong. There are times I hate baseball. But there are times I hate my own body, too. I am trying to think of how to explain this to her. I say, "Do you love anything?"

She says, "Punk music."

"You love it so much you can't imagine being separate from it?"

She shrugs. "Sure."

"That's me and baseball."

"Does baseball make you happy?"

Trick question. I don't answer.

Hannah says, "Okay, fine. Then tell me why you play."

Another loaded question. A hundred million different reasons. I just say, "The life lessons, I guess."

"And what are those?"

"If you hit the ball only three times every ten times you step up to the plate, you're called a good hitter. That is seven times striking out. So, baseball to me is all about failure. You fail and fail and fail. Until you don't. You can strike out all game and still hit the game-winning grand slam. You can hit every at bat and still lose the game. Being good isn't enough. You gotta be good at the right time. That's what's the most important. Do good at the right time."

It strikes me this might be the realest thing I've said in my entire life. It is too close to the epicenter of my soul. Too much friction there. So I add, "Jesus, Hannah, can't we just sit here and be quiet."

"I want to know about baseball."

"And I want to sit here and be quiet."

She lets it go for a while. We listen to the birds. Then she says, "You made it sound beautiful."

"What?"

"Baseball. I always think about it being full of idiot jocks. But you actually made it sound beautiful. Like a poem."

"Oh."

"You aren't like you seem."

"Nobody is."

"I know I said you were a strong silent type, but I don't think that is true. I think you got a lot going on in there. You just don't let anybody know about it."

I keep my mouth shut. She puts her hand on the rock next to her. And I am suddenly intensely aware her little pinky finger is about a centimeter away from mine. There is a little black ant going this way and that around the rock. It stops at her finger, then hops on. And I'm thinking here's this whole other thing happening at the same time me and Hannah are sitting here. At any given second, all around us, there are a thousand different animals and insects doing all kinds of hidden things. There are tummies getting fed. Little sacred lives moving about. Momma critters caring for their young in secret. In a weird way, it means we are surrounded by love at all times.

"What are you thinking about, Crawford?"

I realize I've been staring at her, checked out.

I look back across the water. I tell her, "Not one thing," and I leave it at that.

WHAT HAPPENED TO YOU?
THE OFFSPRING

Since she won't swim in the brain-amoeba water, and she don't want to go home yet, I start pitching out new ideas. Among them: Let's go swim at my place where there's no kinda parasite bugs to crawl up your nose and kill you. Which, by the way, I Googled as soon as I had signal, and it was *not* science fiction.

"I don't have a suit," Hannah says, trying that same old excuse as before.

So I pull into the Wally World and tell her, *We are getting you a suit because I am not burning through a whole tank of gas anytime you gotta hide from Shotgun Sam. Which, evidently, is gonna be every Saturday from now on.*

She says, *Okay, okay, I get it.*

But here's weirdness: buying a swimsuit with a girl you are barely friends with.

We walk to the ladies' section, and there are all these mannequins with huge breasts and tiny waists standing around showing off the hottest bikinis of the year or whatever. Hannah says she hates swimming suits. And she hates the part of the department store that sells them. And I don't blame her. Imagine going to the boys' section and seeing mannequins with giant, impossible-sized wiener bulges.

I want to say to Hannah, *This is all nonsense up here.*

But I get it.

"You go wait in electronics. I'll find something," she says.

So, I go stand there. Watch some baseball on the televisions. She comes back with a suit wadded up in her hands. At least I think so. Turns out to be a men's T-shirt with anime characters on the front, plus a pair of basketball shorts. Also men's variety, where the leg goes all the way down to the knee.

"This isn't a suit," I say.

"I told you I hate them."

"Yeah, but you might as well swim in your clothes."

"I figure I can leave this at your house. That way I always got something to change into."

I don't really care that much. So I don't argue. I pay for the stuff, plus some snacks.

You can tell a thing or two about somebody based on what kinda snacks they like. She picked out Funyuns, which are S-Tier, meaning she has immaculate taste in junk food. When we get back in the truck and start driving down the road, I start to get a picture of the rest of our afternoon lined up in my head. And by God if I am not feeling pretty happy about it.

I am realizing it's not so bad having somebody around who likes to talk. Who likes to pry words out of me. Lets me stop living in my head so much. I can just focus on what she is saying. And focus on what I am going to say back to her. And it's... I don't know. I kinda *like* it. The only other time I am even close to present like that is on the mound or in the batter's box.

We are going to go swim.

Pops might see I have a girl over and decide to grill up some burgers or steaks.

We will splash around.

She might touch my leg.

But when we pull in to my house, there is an old Ford truck in my front drive I do not recognize.

Hannah's like, "Shit, shit, shit." Sinking lower and lower into the passenger's seat.

Then I remember the truck from the parking lot at the baseball field. When Hannah came to my game in her Halloween costume.

"What's Shotgun doing here?" I ask.

Hannah shakes her head. "I don't want to know."

"Follow me," I say, throwing the car in park.

Hannah shakes her head again. "Can't we just leave?"

"I just want to peek through the back fence. See what's going on. We won't let them know we are here."

She thinks for a second. Then says okay, and we sneak out of the truck like Navy SEALs, running low along the side of the house so nobody can see us through the front windows. We come to the privacy fence around back, and we peek through the slats.

Shotgun stands on our back deck. Weird as hell. And there's Pops with him. They are talking in low tones. Then Shotgun laughs and claps Pops on the shoulder. At the same time, Pops goes into his pocket and comes out with a wad of cash. Shotgun palms the money and takes out a baggie full of little white pills.

I grab on to the fence to keep from falling over.

Little pieces of information start to fall into place in my brain. Shotgun is a *dealer*. Shotgun already knew Pops when I met him. I'd thought it was because of baseball. But it wasn't. Shotgun had been *Pops'* dealer when Pops got hooked on pain killers after his surgeries.

But he beat it.

Pops told me he beat addiction.

That it was hard. But he did it for me. He did it for Big Time.

Because he loves us so much.

My hands are shaking at my sides. I feel that fuse burning inside me.

Beyond them, which I did not see at first, there's Big Time in that snack craft of his own making, not paying attention to anything.

A drug deal. Right in front of the kid.

My stomach turns upside down. I am beyond words. Pure fury. I have worked so hard to keep this family together, thinking the whole time Pops was doing the same.

I throw open the gate and make a beeline toward them.

Shotgun smiles real big to see me, his eyes darting back and forth between me and Pops.

Pops looks like a kid who got busted stealing from the cookie jar. He still has the damn pills in his hands, not even bothering to hide them in his pocket. Real stupid. Puts my whole damn brain on the fritz. I am an unthinking automaton. Completely separate from my own mind.

There's this buzzing metal feeling in the air between us all.

Like a storm fixin' to happen.

And that storm is me.

I yank the baggie out of Pops' hand. He makes a grab at it, but I am too fast. I step between them, turning sideways, and with one quick movement, I grab the stack of bills from Shotgun's hand. Then I haul ass away from them. They are both left there, slack-jawed. Like, *Hey*.

Then all at once, they come to life behind me. Hollering and scraping. Shotgun is like, "My money!" And Pops is like, "Craw. Please! I *need* those!"

"Like a hole in the Goddamn head!" I yell back at them. There's a propane grill on the far side of the pool. I hustle toward it. By now, Big Time is sitting up straight in his snack contraption. He's added a daisy chain of drinking straws so he don't even gotta lift his head to sip soda. He lowers his shades like, *What in the hell is happening?* My heart breaks seeing the confusion and fear on his face. Here is a kid who wanted nothing but to swim. And here he is, seeing me lose my shit again. Not understanding the reason. Just thinking, *Here goes Craw again with his angry manager problems.*

There are no words for it. No actions to fix it.

I am screaming wordlessly. Hearing my voice rise as if it is not my own.

I don't *have* anger problems. In this moment, I *am* anger personified.

I throw open the grill and crank on the flame. Pops is closing in on me, so I turn the entire grill sideways to put it in between us. Screaming and cursing at him the whole time. There is no restraint now. No holding it back. It's crashing out of me like a ruptured dam. I hold up the cash like, *I'll do it. I swear to God, I'll do it. One step, and I'm hucking this in the fire.*

Pops yells, "Don't!"

But I do. Because I was never planning to do anything else. Money first. That stack of bills goes up in yellow flames. Then I throw the baggie on top, throw my head back howling. I'm half mad by now. Completely bonkers. I start yelling the first thing that comes to my head. "We having us a mother fuckin' barbecue!"

Pops throws his hands on either side of his head. "That was a thousand bucks, you idiot!"

Shotgun appears beside me. He musta gone the other way around the pool. His hand closes on my wrist. I slam the barbecue pit closed with my free hand. Spin and punch him across the face. But he doesn't break away from me. He steadies himself. Then he turns me. Shoves me backward against the grill. Shoves me halfway over the grill. My feet coming off the ground. The whole thing topples over, and I go rolling backward across the deck.

Big Time bursts into tears. Starts paddling his little craft toward the ladder. I think he is running for his life. But no. He's saying, "I'll kill you! Leave my brother alone! I'll kill you!"

Shotgun lands on top of me. He's slobbering and spitting. Pinning me down to the ground. Me fighting and failing like hell to upend him, to get back in control of the situation.

Cope Field

I'm like, *Pops better do something*. He's not gonna sit there and watch his own son get beat on by Samuel Ledbetter.

Right?

I can count my own heartbeat. Twenty-three since he first got on top of me. I grab at the front of his shirt. Throw stupid, ineffectual punches. I keep expecting him to strike me. Or to choke me. But he doesn't. He looks me square in the eyes and says, "You better calm down, boy."

Then Pops' huge boot crashes into the side of Shotgun's head.

He goes tumbling sideways. Tries to stand, staggers, then falls into the pool. Pops stands between us. A Goddamn pistol in his hand. I roll over and puke in the grass. A long moment passes with Shotgun under the water. Silence. Like a normal backyard barbecue. Big Time squats beside me. Puts his tiny hand on my cheek.

Then Pops is screaming. Shotgun is screaming. Pops saying, "Put your hand on my kid again, and you're a dead man."

A statement meant to invoke fear. But Shotgun's got a wire twisted somewhere in his brain. He thinks it's funny. He throws his head back. Then his hands up. He pulls himself out of the pool and stands dripping on the concrete. "I'm leaving."

I watch him walk toward the gate where I left Hannah.

She must have seen the whole thing.

And now, he is gonna find her. And in the heat of this stupid moment, who knows what he'll do about it. Shotgun fumbles with the latch. Cursing under his breath. He checks over his shoulder. Pops still has that gun trained on him. And we are in this almost comical moment, watching Shotgun fail to wrangle the gate.

"You lift the thing," Pops says. "The latch. Lift it up."

Shotgun pops it open. He says, "Fuck you all," before opening it the rest of the way. I am expecting to see Hannah. Terror on her face. I'm expecting to be forced to live through the moment Shotgun realizes she is with me. Wondering what will happen next. There is still a gun in play, after all.

But Hannah isn't there.

The girl has absconded.

When things calm down, Pops sets the grill back up. Then he sits down on the deck. His head falls into his hands. He does something I am not expecting. He cries. And the thing about it that bothers me the most is how much I do not care. I'm like, *You should cry*. But the longer we sit there, the more I listen to him sob, the worse it feels.

He cries so hard. Big Time sits beside him. And he starts crying, too. Pops looks up at me, tears streaming down his face. I cannot remember the last time I saw this man cry, and something about that breaks my heart in half. I remember him telling me to dry it up so many times over the years. Reminding me that boys don't cry. And he always was my example for that. Nothing ever shook him.

But now?

He is broken. And that breaks me, too.

He says, "They put me on painkillers after my Tommy Johns. I reckon I needed them for pain management back then. But . . . I don't know, Craw, I got hooked. Started using 'em too much. Taking more and more. Pushing myself to the limit."

I sit down on the deck beside him. He has told me this story more than once. But I hear him out again.

"Can't you see it weren't my fault? I didn't ask to have no Tommy Johns. And when I was in the league, it was easy to keep getting the script, and it got worse and worse and worse. Your momma about left me over it."

"Momma did leave us," I say.

He laughs ruefully. "That's right. She did."

For a long time, he just cries. Little wet spots hitting the concrete.

"After I got cut for good and it was clear nobody was going to sign me, the doctors started telling me they couldn't prescribe no more on account of the pills being habit forming. They even labeled me as an addict in their system, which meant I couldn't get my medicine at all. But my arm still hurts, Crawford. It still hurts and won't nobody do a thing to help me with it." He pauses, cries for a while, then takes a breath to collect himself. "We moved back here. I met Samuel Ledbetter. Played ball with him in high school. But our lives could not have gone more different directions. Samuel helped me out for a while. He was my dealer."

Big Time says, "What's a dealer?"

This makes Pops cry harder. Big Time puts an arm around him. His head on his shoulder. Big Time says, "It's okay. I was scared, too. I even said I was gonna kill him. Right out loud. Can you believe that?"

I feel so tiny sitting here.

Cope Field

Like a little boy.

No power whatsoever.

"You told me you got clean. Told me you done that for me and Sutton," I say. "Said you done it because you love us. Because you want to keep us together. And you said the drugs was tearing us apart." The statement yanks tears out of me on the way. I fight against them. Wipe at them with the back of my arm. "Why go back to them now?"

Pops looks right at me. "I hurt all over, Craw," he says. "I messed up. Got weak. But I promise you. Never again. After seeing that man attack you... after seein' what I brought in this home..." He shakes his head, tears streaking down his grizzled cheeks. "No more. I promise you both. No more."

Wish I was back at the creek. Now that Hannah has something to swim in, we could go there. Risk the brain-eating amoebas. Or maybe sit by the water. I never should have thought to bring her to my house.

Hannah wasn't outside that gate when Shotgun left.

Did he find her around the side of the house? Force her to ride back with him? Or did she run into the woods? Was she out there right now?

I text her: *You okay?*

A few seconds later, the screen lets me know she read it. Or someone did.

But she don't answer.

I am so scared she saw me flip out like that. Now she will see the truth. I am too broken to be around. I am not safe. She is better off staying far away from me. And now she knows it.

Where does that leave me?

I want to call her and spill my guts. But another part of me is like, *Really, Craw? Are you losing your mind?*

Maybe I am.

Maybe that's the cost of growing up with someone like Pops.

You lose your mind.

I fall asleep with the VR headset on. Drifting high above snowcapped mountains. The sound of wind in my ear. A gentle voice telling me, *"Let go of your anger. Let go of your hurt. Focus on the love that's around you.*

Focus on healing. Focus on calm. Focus on loving yourself. Focus on only the things that really matter."

On repeat.

Over and over and over again.

Until my alarm wakes me with a start in the morning.

LITTLE THINGS
GOOD CHARLOTTE

Hannah is giving me a pure and proper ghosting. Which I guess I deserve. I text her again this morning, and I don't even get a *hello how are you* back. I'm like, *Fine, okay, I get it.* But then she is not at school today. Or the day after. And I am thinking I should go by her house. But also, I am thinking I will only make it worse if I do.

Like this is my fault.

I can tell it is my fault.

Now Hannah knows the truth. Me tackling Shotgun wasn't a onetime thing. It's a cycle. Something triggers me. I go off. And she don't need to be around that. I cannot blame her one bit. What am I going to do? Roll up to her house and say, *I am sorry I am full-on crazy, but I promise I'll never be full-on crazy at you.*

That's what they all say.

By the end, she will be like, *Listen, being friends with you was all the way a mistake. So please stop texting me.*

At the same time, it's like, *Hannah, just talk to me.*

Please.

I need somebody to talk to me.

Friday.

Still no Hannah.

I'm feeling a bit like a walking bruise.

And what for? Who even is Hannah Flores to me? A friend I had for a moment in time. A friend folks told me to stay away from. I want to look at myself in the mirror, say, *What is wrong with you? Why are you feeling this way? You barely know this girl.*

But I am in the bullpen at Little Creek, over in Abner County, warming up my arm because we are down 3–1 and Coach Rodriguez thinks I can turn things around. And I know we are a county over, and Hannah doesn't exactly got wheels, but for some reason, I keep looking over by the visitor's-side dugout, hoping she'll be sitting there in her Gothy makeup.

But she's not.

Of course she's not.

I hurl a bunch of pitches at Luis, all of them popping off my fingers wrong. Flying wild. Or with not enough heat. Whole time, Luis is like, "What's with you, Craw?"

And I'm like, "Don't worry about it, don't worry about it."

"Well, I am worried. Because this is a conference game, and we need to win it. And basically, you are our only hope at this point in time."

"If it was so important, Rodriguez oughta have started me on the hill."

"Well, that was a little strategy," Coach says, appearing at the net. My cheeks go bright red knowing he heard me talking critical about him. But he plays it cool. Because nothing shakes Coach Rodriguez. "Mighta backfired a little. But Little Creek ain't bad at the plate. Reckoned it was better to save you for later than to burn you out early."

"I can pitch a complete game."

"Maybe you can. Maybe you can't. Depending on all kinds of different things. We all got our limits, Craw. High school boys *especially* have their limits. Besides, we got three innings left. An eternity. More than enough time to turn things around, once you pin them down at the plate."

I think back over all my bad warm-up pitches. All of a sudden, there's not a lot of confidence inside me. My mind is somewhere else. And it needs to be here.

Coach Rodriguez gestures for us to follow. "It's time," he says. "Vamos."

Here's the rundown. There are six innings in a high school baseball game. We are in the top of the fourth, trailing 3–1. Little Creek has been eating all afternoon, collecting seven hits across four innings. But! Thankfully, not moving many of them across the plate.

Enter Crawford Cope.

Every kid on that field thinking, *Aw hell, this is Hunter Cope's kid.* And let me tell you, that kinda moxie goes a long way in baseball. Like, you step up to the plate already thinking in your head that the pitcher you are going against is the best around, that he learned from an actual MLB pitcher who sat Sammy Sosa and Mark McGwire both, then maybe you decide somewhere deep down that there is not a chance in this world some scrub like you is gonna get a hit against him.

Or, if the batter is cocky... the exact opposite.

This kid thinks he can pitch?

I'm about to show him I can hit.

I'm about to get a hit off a future pro baseball player.

I'm about to embarrass this kid.

And sometimes that is just as bad as thinking you won't get a hit at all.

It's like: Keep it chill. That's your best bet.

It starts to spit rain from the sky. There are low gray clouds hanging over everything. Wind near cold enough to set your teeth on edge. My brain goes all over the place. Luis calls for a heater to start, tapping his inside thigh with four fingers. He wants to shock 'em with my speed. And I do not disagree.

There is a quiet place I go when I am about to pitch. A silent meadow in my head. Tune out the noise. Tune out the distraction. Focus. Only this time, there's Hannah in that meadow. There is Hannah every time I close my eyes.

Damn it.

Where is she?

Is she okay?

I wish she would just let me explain myself.

First pitch flies wild. Thudding against the backstop. Luis throws off his catcher's helmet and scrambles for it. But it's the top of the inning. No runners advance. No nothing. Still, I catch Pops' glare. He's hanging on the backstop fence. Looking at me like, *What in the hell is wrong with you?*

That does not make it better. Or easier.

Worse, the ball is wet from rolling on the ground. I try and dry it on my jersey, leaving little smears of mud. But it's one of those things Pops is always saying you gotta rise above.

Next pitch flies funny, too. A little low. Luis has to drop to his knees to block it. By now, I am starting to cuss out loud. Coach Rodriguez throws out his hands. Pops roves along the chain-link fence like a starving lion at the zoo. I try and tune him out. Tune out Coach

Rodriguez. Tune out everything. Find my meadow. Can almost feel the cool breeze. The grass. I stand on the hill alone. Choosing a pitch behind my back. Luis calls for another heater. Let's get this right before we move on to something else. I look down. Look up. Touch my hat. Wipe the sweat from my brow. Step forward. Come down hard. Feel my hand drag through the air behind me. Windmilling. Commanding the ball to fly right.

It's a good pitch.

Not a great one.

The batter steps. Torques his body. I hear the bat make contact. Yank my head around to watch it go.

And go.

And go.

And go...

Until it lands safely on the other side of the fence.

BLEED AMERICAN
JIMMY EAT WORLD

After the game, all the other players file onto the bus. But Pops walks up to Coach Rodriguez and says, "I'm taking my boy. That good?"

"That's good," Coach says.

And so I'll be stuck in the car with this man for the full hour it takes to drive back home. It's full-on raining now. And I'm soaked through to my underwear. When I get in the car, Big Time sits in the back with two bottles of Prime, dry as a bleached bone in the desert. He tells me one Prime is for me, but Pops says I didn't earn it. Which is the stupidest thing in the entire world. Earning a bottle of sports drink. Come on.

"I don't want it," I say.

Pops stands outside, talking a little bit to Coach Rodriguez before they go their separate ways. Pops has a little umbrella, but Coach is just standing there getting soaked. Because you can't get wetter than wet, I guess. They're talking about me most likely. I gave up three hits by the end. Only the one run. And since we never got our bats going, we took the L.

Big Time cracks open both bottles and drinks from one, says *Ahhh*, and follows that with a drink from the other. He goes back and forth between them. We are talking ten minutes of this. Slurp. *Ahhh*. Sluuuuuurp. *Ahhhhh*. I am about to lose my mind. And it's like, *Pops, will you hurry up and get in this car and murder me?* Because I can take no more of this nonsense. After about the fiftieth slurp, *Ahhh*, I yank around in the seat and lay into him. "What in the hell are you doing, you little idiot?"

He says, "Hydration stations."

Like what does that even mean? "Stop slurping like a big old pig. You are driving me crazy."

And I shoulda guessed this would happen. Big Time brings a bottle to his mouth. Dips his little chubby lips in. Stares right at me. Sluuuuurp. And what follows is the most deliberate *Ahhh* that has ever been uttered in the history of mankind.

"I am going to kill you," I say. "I swear to God."

The driver's door opens. Pops shakes off his umbrella and gets in. And even Big Time has the good sense to hush up his stupidity. He caps both bottles of Prime, stuffs them in the cupholders, and fires up Minecraft on his tablet, the blue glow underlighting his face and mullet. Not a peep. Might as well not even be here.

Pops starts the engine. He puts a hand on the back of my headrest while he backs up the truck. For a long time, he does not say a word. Only, not saying a word is saying everything. There's that weight between us. No, weight is not right. It is more like electricity. Buzzing. Like it buzzed between us by the pool the other day. Like it did in my elbows when I brought that bat down on his head. I'm realizing Pops feels it, too. And he wants it there. Because he wants me to feel *exactly* how disappointed he is.

I want him to yell at me and get it over with.

But he doesn't.

We drive the whole way home in complete silence. But in our driveway, when I go to get out of the truck, he snatches me by the wrist. Pulls me across the console so we are face-to-face. His eyes are somehow wild and vacant at the same time. His body tense. I can smell his sweat. His body odor. His foul breath. Acrid like an empty beer bottle. But hidden somewhere behind spearmint.

That look in his eyes jars something in my memories.

Him and Momma fighting.

Him there. But not there.

I try and pull away from him. But his grip is like a vise.

He spits the next words at me. Like he is aiming to kill me with them. "Do not *ever* embarrass me again."

One hundred pitches. Me. Pops. Big Time. That giant indoor monstrosity behind our house. Pouring rain outside sounds like a buncha snare drums going bonkers on the corrugated roof.

Big Time finishes off both Primes before moving on to a family-sized bag of Doritos, sitting cross-legged in the turf. Little orange crumbs and dust clinging to his fingers.

All I want is to go to my bedroom. Turn on the PlayStation. Point a cartoon gun at cartoon players. And pull the trigger. Shut up my brain. Not think about baseball. Not think about Pops. Not think about community service. Not think about...

But there is no getting out of this. So, I do my due diligence. Go through every pitch he asks for. Try to keep my form correct. My first step. My release. My timing. Endure his yelling and screaming each time I make a mistake, growing more and more irate the longer it goes. Before we stepped on this practice field, I'd thrown at least fifty pitches at the game. Now he is asking for a hundred more. My arm is dead. Dull ache in my tricep and down the backside of my upper arm. I get no zip on the ball.

"Weak," Pops says. "That is what is wrong with you. Zero mental fortitude."

But it is not a matter of toughness. It is a matter of can and cannot. I sling another, pain firing electric all the way to the tips of my fingers, leaving them numb. The ball flies straight through the strike zone and smacks the backstop.

I double over, holding my arm.

"Craw, you have got to learn to dig deep. Anybody can do good when it's easy. You got to do good when it's hard. That's the difference between just alright and greatness. Greatness does the right thing—the hard thing—even when it seems impossible. You hear me?"

"Coach shoulda started me. Not my fault he let them get up on us."

Pops' eyes narrow. He's never been one for excuses. "Coach trusted you. And you let him down. That's on you, Craw. That's on you."

Pops is right. But at the same time, my arm is straight up on fire right now. I need to stop before I do some real damage. The daily maximum pitch count in a high school game is 110. That's a rule for a lot of reasons. Because a kid might can throw more than that. But not long-term. And if you leave it to folks like my pops, folks with that drive to win so deep it eats them from the inside, they will pitch that kid's arm into oblivion unless some rule out there stops them.

"You done with me yet?" I say.

The wrong thing to say. The wrong tone. The wrong everything. "You giving up already? You going soft on me? You know who didn't give up? You know who ain't never once given up in his whole life?"

I stare at him. Not saying anything. Big Time pops a chip in his mouth. Bites down. The crunch louder than seems possible, even over the sound of the rain.

"Me," Pops says. Thumping his chest. "Me! You think I made it all the way to the majors by giving up? No. No, I did not. My old man would not have that. Believe me. He pushed me, Craw. Like I am pushing you. Maybe you hate me right now. But know that this is love right here. This is what love looks like. Makes me so *embarrassed* watching you play like that. You're mine. And you oughta know better. But you don't. I reckon that is my fault. I reckon I take that personally. But it ends today, Craw. Ends right now."

He is ranting now. Full-on ranting.

Big Time crunches another handful of chips. That *buzz, buzz* electricity moves all over the place. Weight and pain between me and Pops. Made double anytime I look at Big Time because I know—I *know*—every single thing happening to me will happen to him, too. He crunches those chips, and I see Pops' eyes snap toward him. Pops' brow furrows, and he rushes across the room.

"Look," he barks. "Look at what you are doing."

Big Time's eyes go wide. He looks down and around. "What am I doing?" he says, through a mouthful of chips.

"Look around you," Pops says, offering no kind of explanation.

This is Pops' way. Wanting you to know you messed up. But also wanting you to guess how. Not easy when you are a kid. But I have played that game long enough to get good at it. He is mad because Big Time is getting crumbs all over the artificial turf. It's not like you can easily bring a vacuum out here to clean it up.

Big Time has no clue.

And everything in me is begging him to figure it out before things snowball into something worse. Snowball into something like *last time*.

Big Time takes an exaggerated look around, still not understanding. Pops yanks the boy to his feet, hand under the kid's armpit. So hard, Big Time's pro-rassler sunglasses topple off the top of his head. He steps backward without realizing, crunching them. Pops' visor glasses. The ones he wore throughout his baseball career.

Pops looks down at the broken glasses, still holding Big Time by the arm, a slow crawl of realization moving over his face. And I am wincing already. Knowing whatever is coming will be big. I am half ready to run. Half ready to grab a bat and bust this man over the head again.

"Those were irreplaceable," Pops says.

Big Time sputters an "I'm sorry!"

But it don't matter. There aren't enough *I'm sorry*s in the world for Pops.

He shakes Big Time by the arm. Then forces him to his knees, his face inches away from the Dorito crumbs. "You see the crumbs now, you little pig? You see the damage you do? Just by being here? Breaking my glasses? Ruining our turf? 'Cause you don't think. You don't think of others. Don't think of nothing but your fat little stomach."

"Pops," Big Time says. "You're hurting me—" His voice breaks in half. And tears start rolling down his cheeks, breaking free off the tip of his nose and falling into the fake grass. "Please, Pops, you're hurting my arm."

I can't take no more.

What am I supposed to do?

All this talk about me having anger problems. And it's this. Underneath everything. It's this all the time.

All this talk about doing good at the right time. It's all I've ever done!

But if you do good even when it's hard, they'll stick you in community service.

Tell you you're lucky.

Tell you if you hadn't come outta the ball sack of Hunter Cope, famous MLB player and local legend, you'd have been shuffled off to juvie with all the other riffraff.

You are *lucky*, Crawford Cope.

You are *so* lucky.

Pops wrenches Big Time's arm around his back. Forces him face-first to the ground. Starts telling him how fat he is. Fat as a piggy. Squeal like a pig, you gone eat like one. Says to him, "Why don't you eat them crumbs up off the ground right now?"

Big Time gives up begging. He is full-on screaming. His eyes rise from the floor and find mine like *Help me*, which sets a feeling in my guts like a downed electrical wire. Like a snake striking. Like me, with a baseball rolling between my fingers, on a good day, on a day things fly right, staring down a wide-eyed batter who's never seen a pitch over 70 miles per hour.

Do the hard thing. It's the only fragment coalescing inside my skull.

My muscles tense. My fingers tighten on the baseball in my hand.

Big Time cries out in pain, tries with all his strength to wrench away from Pops.

I look down. Look up. Touch my hat. Wipe the sweat from my brow. Step forward. Come down hard. Feel my hand drag through the air behind me. Windmilling. Commanding the ball to fly right.

All in a fraction of a second.

I watch the ball fly from the tips of my fingers as if on a rope. Pops rises. Unaware. But my arm. The pain. All my mechanics were off. Pops turns toward me as the ball curves past his face and thuds off the metal wall behind him.

He turns Big Time loose. Stands upright. The sound of rain on the roof is so loud in my ears. He says, "You fucked up now."

I shake my head no.

That was a choice.

That was the *right* choice.

"You... fucked... up," he says again.

He takes a step toward me. His eyes so empty. I am flashed back through time. Back to when Momma was with us. Back to her begging him to stop. Back then, sometimes I wondered, *Stop what?* But there are other memories. Ones where I knew exactly what was happening. Ones I try not to think about too much. Her bruised up. Her punching at his chest. And him not stopping. Never stopping. Sometimes me getting between them.

And even then...

He would not stop.

Pops likes to blame the pills.

But is it really the pills?

No. I'm starting to think it's just him.

He walks straight toward me.

His expression never changing.

I run out of the building and into the driving rain.

ONLY ONE
YELLOWCARD

I cannot get over how nice it feels outside, driving my truck full tilt through the back roads of the Ozarks. Windows down. My foot on the gas pedal, all the way to the floor. Little flecks of rain hitting my face. Tires barking and squalling around the wild curves. I lean my head out the window and holler at the moon like some kind of maniac. Because maybe I am half crazy. And maybe I oughta act like it a little more often. Nothing but trees around anyway. And 'cause it's just me and my insanity, I crank on that angry punk rock playlist of Hannah's.

Out near Jerusalem. Brain on autopilot. I whip into Cope Field. Soon-to-be Cope Field. The playlist raging that same angry song as when I tussled with Shotgun. This field is nothing right now but a mowed lawn, two crappy buildings, and a bunch of fence posts, which I almost smile to see that Roger has finished up without us. Probably using some heavy piece of equipment that gets it done lickety-split because Lord knows his fat ass is not ruining his hands or his back T-post driving.

That's for us delinquents.

Us bad kids.

Us monsters who huck baseballs at our fathers. Who beat them over the head with a baseball bat.

I drive through the yard, rolling to a stop near the visitor's dugout. Hear the lead singer scream at me to burn it all down.

I hesitate there a minute, then floor it and bounce my way out to the center of the baseball field. I yank the wheel to the side, throwing my truck into a spin, slinging mud everywhere, digging deep rivets in the grass. I'm half hoping to lift the truck up on two wheels, sending it rolling end over end, me inside.

Burn it, burn it down.

My headlights canvass the field. The dugout. The distant tree line.

Hannah's house. Crank the wheel around and around. The engine roaring through the drumming sound of rain. Field. Dugout. Trees. House. Over and over. Headlights cutting through the dark until, on my third or fourth pass, they cross over someone standing in the road.

I hit the brakes. Absurdly expecting a police officer. Or Shotgun. Out here to bring further hell upon my life.

But it's Hannah. Standing there, rain-slick and beautiful. Confusion in her eyes. And that look snaps me back into the *what in the hell am I doing* reality of the moment. I have ruined this field. Destroyed it. Rivets so deep it will take months to repair them.

Hannah hurries across the field, and I kill the music. She crosses through my headlights, climbs up the lift kit, and stares in the window. I roll it down.

"Having fun?" she asks.

I can't look at her. We haven't spoken all week, and here I am tearing holes in the field across the street from her house. Acting out my anger in front of her again. "You better get away," I say.

"Get away? Crawford, what are you doing out here?"

"I don't want you to see me like this, Hannah. You should leave."

"Why are you saying this?"

I look down at my hands, still white-knuckled on the steering wheel. The whole interior of my truck is muddy and wet. And the rain comes a little harder now, hammering the glass. Drizzling through my open window. Hannah climbs inside, even though I asked her to leave. No surprise. She always does exactly the opposite of what I want her to do.

"Are you okay?" she asks.

"You want me to stop being the strong silent type?"

"I want you to do whatever is going to help you." Then, when I don't answer her: "Crawford, why are you acting like this?"

I was born into this. No choice given. God pointed his finger, said, "Crawford Cope. Rich but poor at the same time."

Poof.

Here I come. Not even knowing God said that about me. Bumbling along thinking about how lucky I am to have a famous daddy. Asking for whatever toy I want and getting it. Everyone telling me, *Wow, that's your dad. You're so lucky. That's so amazing.* Then, as the years go on, everyone saying the apple sure don't fall far from the tree. Saying that to me. And me watching him hit Momma. Him hitting me. And now, him going after Big Time.

I want my apple as far away from that tree as possible.

I am broken because of it. The last thing I want is Hannah Flores getting sucked into my mess. Pulled into orbit with Hunter Cope. With me. With all this ugliness. She's gotta go. And she's gotta get her ass out of Quiet County. She deserves better than this place.

She deserves better than me.

"Crawford, please tell me what's wrong." Her voice coming from the dark. I can barely see her face, except for a little pale blue sliver along her cheek and jawline. Light drifting down from the sky.

"You need to get out of this truck right now."

"No."

"Right now, Hannah." I am tensing up. Almost ready to raise my voice. To sound like Pops. And I can tell she can sense it. That electric feeling comes back. The one I felt the day I tackled Shotgun. And when I hit Pops with the baseball bat. It's like everything in me wants to get away from that feeling. Or else harness it. Turn it loose on whoever is causing it. And right now, that person is Hannah.

This is the problem.

Me.

My anger issues.

She don't budge.

"I'm fucked up," I tell her. I wait for her to react. But she just looks at me like, *And?*

She's not getting it. So I put a little more edge in my voice.

"You need to get out of this truck and get as far away from me as you possibly can. 'Cause you know why I got community service? I beat my old man with a baseball bat. Busted him open good. You seen me attack your stepdad. You seen me freak out beside the pool. And tonight, before I headed over here, I threw a baseball as hard as I could at Pops, hoping to kill him with it."

She's silent.

Good.

"So, yes, you oughta get out of this truck. Because I am a piece of shit with anger management problems and no clue how to ever fix them, just like Sutton told you."

I wait for her to agree. To tell me, *Wow, you are garbage, Crawford. I shoulda seen it sooner.* But she doesn't. Her hand touches my back. She scoots a little closer to me. The rain sounds like swelling music.

She says, "Crawford."

That's it.

Just my name.

Just someone saying my name with zero expectation behind it.

Our eyes meet. She says, "What's happened?"

I open my mouth. No sound comes. I press my fists into my eyes and lean forward on the steering wheel.

"Crawford, you can talk to me. I promise."

I shake my head no.

When she nudges me, I look up at her. She is blurry through my bleary eyes. She puts her hand on my cheek. Speaks slowly. Deliberately. "I'm here. I'm listening."

I'm here.

I'm listening.

Those words split me in half. We learned about the Manhattan Project in World History. How they split the atom to make the nuclear bomb. You split something small like an atom, you can blow up a whole city. You split something even smaller, say an emotionally stunted boy from the Ozarks with a father like Pops... what happens then? Does he explode, too?

Her thumb brushes beneath my eyes. Her touch is electric. But a different kind. Not like the kind that buzzed between me and Pops or between me and Shotgun. A good kind of electric.

"He hits you, doesn't he?" Hannah says.

I burst into tears. It just comes outta me. From nowhere. I press my hands into my eyes as hard as I can, trying to suck the tears back in, trying to get it together. But I can't stop.

"He doesn't," I choke out. I don't know why.

I cry for a long time. I punch the steering wheel.

Hannah says nothing.

She just witnesses my breaking.

"Listen," she says eventually. "If you want to talk some more, I am here. If you don't, that is okay. But I think you really should tell somebody what's going on. Somebody who can help you. I would like that person to be me. But I understand if it's not. The main thing, Crawford, is that you don't have to be alone."

She leans her head against my shoulder. Smells like flowers and fruit mixed together.

Her touch sends warmth through my entire body. I start to cry a little bit again. I lean my head against hers.

"Strong silent type, remember," I say. I mean it to be funny. But it lands hard. Like a thrown rock.

I kill the engine. Hours pass. Rain falls. And Hannah fills the quiet with stories about her life. About living alone with Shotgun. She says he's every bit as bad as I imagine him to be. But at least he never hits her.

She says Shotgun treated her bad when her momma was around. But now that she's gone, it's even worse. Turns out a lot of the stuff people said about Hannah and her momma is not true. But a lot of it is. Truth and lies mixed up together.

"Momma would be trying to quit drugs," she says. "Going through withdrawals. I'd play on the floor with my tea set, nursing her back to health with fake tea. Momma loves this story. How sweet and attentive I was. Wiping sweat off her face while she dealt with the shakes. She'd tell me, 'Don't ever do drugs, baby girl.' At four, I thought drugs were like ibuprofen or something. I remember scolding The Asshole for downing a handful of Tylenol when he drank too much. It's funny—I never got on them for the alcohol because seeing them drunk was normal dot com for me."

She tells me when she got older, her momma told her right up front she used to turn tricks for methamphetamine. Said she had to let her know, because that's how she got pregnant and that's where Hannah came from to begin with. That's why Hannah doesn't have a daddy.

And it's like, *Damn.*

This stuff happens. Right under our noses. Right across the classroom. And what do we do? We identify this person. And we make extra hell in their lives by excluding them. Calling them garbage. Calling them sluts. Or whatever other foul thing we think can tear them down even further than they already are. At least I had the lie of Hunter Cope to fall back on. Because make no mistake, that lie protects me almost as much as it harms me.

"But that's *not* who you are," I tell her.

"Please. It's exactly who you thought I was when we met."

I look away from her, out the window. She's right. "I'm sorry," I tell her. And I mean it deep down. "I was really, really, really wrong."

She says, "I was wrong about you, too."

We both go quiet. The rain is like gentle music. Like something I might could sleep to. Her head's in the crook of my arm. Her shampoo or perfume or whatever smelling like flowers. The feeling of her breathing near me. Her not talking. Me not talking. My brain saying, *Craw, you oughta kiss this girl.*

But I decide no. No kissing. Because I do not want her to think she has been out here spilling her guts and all I am doing is thinking about putting my mouth on her.

Around midnight, the rain slacks. By now, Pops is probably starting to get near frantic wondering where I am. Probably thinking he ought to call the police. Probably stopping himself for fear I might tell them what he done.

"It's stopped raining," Hannah says.

"Yeah."

"I should go."

She scoots away from me. Opens the door and steps out. Without thinking, I get out, walk through the mud and water, and meet her on her side of the truck. She is already walking back toward her house. Not even realizing I'm out here.

"Hannah," I say.

She turns. Walks back to me. Doesn't say a word. Her eyes lift toward mine. There's expectation there. My brain is rolling circles inside my skull, screaming, *Kiss her, you literal moron.*

Instead, I say, "Thanks."

"For what?"

I shrug. Gesture around. "Everything."

Her eyes never leave mine. I'm held in that stare. Afraid to look at her. Afraid to look away.

"Crawford," she says.

"Hmm."

"We been out here for four hours."

I scratch the back of my head. "Yeah."

She smiles. Confident. Cool. Like, *Yeah, this boy's a little stupid, but he's cute, so I'll walk him there.*

She says, "Aren't you gonna kiss me?"

I have kissed three people in my life. Only one counts, because two of those kisses were with cousins when I was little. Gross, I know. But we didn't know better. We just sat around in a circle on Memaw's front deck, taking turns kissing each other. Like little chickens. Peck. Peck. When Memaw found out, she went completely bonkers. She told Pops she "about had a conniption fit." Which, if you've never seen one of those, skip it.

I move in slow. Eyes half open. Her features soft in the moonlight. She puts her hand in the center of my chest.

Our lips touch.

One second. Two seconds.

Then I relax. Ease into it. Her arms go around my neck, fingers tracing through the hair on the back of my head. An electric feeling, like the tingle in your elbows when you make bad contact at the plate. Except this buzz goes all through me.

She pulls away. Smiles. Then comes back for more.

They make whole movies about this kinda thing.

And I can see why.

We separate, but our arms stay around each other. Her chest pressed against mine. My hands on her hips. She goes back down on flat feet. Still looking up at me. And she says it all. Says it with one word. Something I mighta taken the entire damn dictionary to say.

"Wow."

BAD TIME
ALKALINE TRIO

As I'm driving back through the trees on those old, familiar take-me-home roads, it feels like being pulled up from the bottom of a lake, fishhook barbed through my lips, some unseen thing yanking me toward hell.

I might coulda stayed in that kiss forever.

But no.

That fishhook yanks me. That Goddamn fishhook.

I'm thinking about what happened in the Baseball Dungeon before I destroyed Cope Field. Pops wrenching Big Time's arm around his back. Telling him to eat, little piggy. Eat them crumbs. I threw a baseball at him. Then what? I went out to my truck, and I left.

I *left*.

And I stayed gone for more than four hours. Four hours of Big Time alone with a pissed-off Pops.

What was I thinking?

I press my foot harder on the pedal, the engine roaring like some beast come up from hell. One good thing about Pops' *I'm sorry* giving: This truck has the guts of a monster. Together, we roar through the backwoods. Headlights casting long shadows through the trees. Glittering in the eyes of a coyote caught crossing the road.

By the time I pull up to our house, there's real panic in my stomach. I leave the truck running, door hanging open. Hurry up the steps and unlock the door. Whole time, I'm listening. For what? I do not know.

I throw open the front door. Step into the foyer. Still listening. Straight ahead, I can see into the living room. The soft undulating blue glow of a television, the big seventy-two-inch one Pops had his eyes on at the store a while back. He must've gone and bought the thing. Maybe by way of apology to myself and Big Time?

I hear the sound of a baseball game. Some old game from ten years ago. The Royals. Of course. And there's Pops on the hill. Checking for the sign. Tugging down on the brim of his hat. Leaning forward. Nodding. Selecting a pitch. Rising up.

"Crawford," Pops says.

He's sitting facing away in the recliner. Melted into it, more like. Some spooky sound in his voice. Like he is not a man, but a wraith. A pretender. He asks me where I've been without looking away from himself on the television.

"Where's Big Time?" I say.

"I asked where you been."

"Where is Sutton?"

Pops lowers the leg rest of the recliner. He rises like a vampire from its coffin, then snaps around to face me. "This is *my* house. I ask the questions, and you answer them."

He wavers on his feet. Like a gust of wind might knock him down.

And I realize.

He's stoned.

Even though I burned those pills the other day, he must have found a way to get more.

I hurry down the hallway. He lumbers after me, thudding against the wall, nearly falling. I reach Big Time's room. Try the knob. But it's locked. I reach back to hammer with my fist. About to holler his name. But Pops' hands fall on me. He slams me against the wall, claps a hand over my mouth, and gets in my face. Veins bulging up in his neck. Truth is, I don't fight against him. I'd rather let him pour that anger out on me. Beat me to a bloody pulp. Do whatever it is he needs to do. So long as he keeps all of it off Big Time.

He drags me back down the hallway, one fist wadded up in the front of my shirt, the other yanking my hair. We tumble back into the living room, that big television showing close-ups of his face, blue and flickering in the dark.

"Where did you go?" he screams.

I bury my words.

He bellows. Wordless. Spit hitting my face.

And I realize something. This man don't care where I went. Not really.

He's more worried about *who* I talked to. He's worried I went to the sheriff or the police or got ahold of the school guidance counselor. He's afraid I spilled my guts. Broke that promise I made him outside the courtroom to *keep my mouth shut*. Hell. That same promise I made him on the edge of my bed when Momma disappeared.

"I went driving," I say. "To blow off steam. Don't worry. I didn't talk to nobody."

His grip on the front of my shirt slackens. He pats the center of my chest with an open palm. "Oh. Oh, okay. Alright. That's good. It's good to blow off steam. Believe me."

"I just drove like a maniac. Then I came home. That's all. Is Sutton okay?"

"He's in his room." Pops oozes back into the recliner. Wrestles a blanket out from underneath himself and covers up. On the television, he's just struck out his sixth batter of the game. The announcer says, *"Hunter Cope just might be the Royals' best chance at a World Series this year."*

I start back down the hallway. But Pops calls out to me, "Hang on a minute, Craw."

I freeze in the hallway. Half curious. Half terrified. That's a line he likes to keep me on.

"After you left, Big Time was foolin' around with that pitching machine out there. Got it off-kilter. Where it wasn't aimed right."

"Okay."

"I didn't know about it. But it was off, right? Not pointing down through the strike zone. I couldn't tell, is the thing. So I went about it business as usual."

"Shit," I say.

"He took a sixty-miler to face. Swol' him up real good."

"Shit."

"He'll be fine, Craw."

I start back down the hall again. Pops calls out, "I know what you think of me."

I don't say nothing.

NOT TODAY
MXPX

I use a screwdriver to unlock Big Time's door. Stand over him in the dark. He is snoozing good. His mullet splayed out on the pillow around his head. A little line of drool from the corner of his mouth. But he is lying with his face obscured by some pillows. I can't tell how bad the damage is.

I nudge him. He smacks his lips.

I nudge him again. He looks at me with one eye. Then he sits up. The pillow falls away.

The left side of his face is swollen purple. Shining. There is a break in the skin across the bridge of his nose. Some crusted blood circling his left nostril. His eye is sealed completely shut.

"Jesus," I say, sitting on the edge of the bed. "What happened?"

Big Time blinks at me. Then he says, verbatim, exactly what Pops said before I came back here. Every line. Like this whole thing is some stage play, and this is the role he must play. The script he has memorized.

"Did Pops hit you?"

Big Time blinks. Then he says it all again. "After you was gone, I was playing with that pitching machine out there, even though Pops told me to never touch it without permission. I guess I got it messed up, got it where it wasn't aimed right. Because I got hit right after. Pops didn't know about it."

"Did Pops hit you?"

"With a baseball, yeah. But it weren't his fault. Ain't you listening?"

"Did he *hit* you?"

Big Time plops backward onto his pillows. He rolls so he is not facing me. He says, "I'm sleepy, Craw. Leave me alone."

"No, tell me the truth. No matter what he says for you to do, you tell me the truth."

"I'm sleepy, Craw."

"Sutton. Tell me."

He looks at me over his shoulder. And even with one swollen eye, I can tell he is getting annoyed. Not that I care. This kid will annoy me on purpose for no reason at all. But this right here, what we are talking about right now, it's important. It's worth a few *bad* feelings. Everything I done up until now has been to keep Big Time safe. All the meditation videos. All the working on my anger. All of it to fix a problem that wasn't of my own making. All of it to make Big Time's life a little better than mine.

And look how I failed.

"I done told you he hit me, but it was an accident," Sutton says. "And I also done said *I am sleepy*, and I don't want to talk to you no more."

"I'll leave you alone if you promise to tell me the truth."

Sutton sits up in bed, snatches a book he'd fallen asleep reading, and hucks it at me. The heavy space encyclopedia lands with a thud and a flutter of pages on the floor beside my feet. "I told you the truth!" he yells. "Jesus Christ on a biscuit. Will you get the hell out of here?"

I don't know what else to do, so I go back outside to turn off my truck, which I damn-near forgot I'd left running. Then I come back inside and go to bed. Lie awake thinking I read someplace if you get hit in the head, you probably got a concussion 'cause your brain rattles around in there like a bean in a can. Thinking I read you shouldn't sleep for like twenty-four hours after that. Like maybe you could die, even. And I'm starting to get more and more irate. Because at the very damn least, Big Time needs to be seen by a doctor. I almost pull him out of bed and drive him there myself, but I stop in the hallway and think hard on it.

If I take him, what happens then? Will they take him away from Pops? And if they take him away from Pops, will they take him away from me, too?

I can't let that happen.

I do a little more Google Doctoring, and it says you gotta wake 'em up every few hours to make sure they're okay. Ask them questions and stuff. Simple things, like *Who are you?* and *Who am I?* and *Where are we?*

So, I stay up all night, popping into Big Time's room every couple of hours to shake him awake. Him getting more and more annoyed with me. Not understanding. Thinking I'm just messing with him to be mean.

"Why won't you leave me alone?" he bellows, hiding under his pillow.

"I need to make sure you don't got brain damage."

He throws the blankets back and sits straight up. "Brain damage? Craw, you have gone absolutely batshit insane."

It is 3:30 a.m.

Out in the living room, Pops is asleep in the recliner. A different baseball game on the television. Not one of his, thank God. I stand over him a little bit. Being a creeper. Thinking about smothering him under a pillow for a little while. Wondering how long you gotta hold a pillow there to make someone dead. And can I pin this man down that long?

Truth is, I *am* a little batshit insane by now, pacing all over the house. Knots inside my stomach. I try and play a video game. Take my mind off things. Blast through some fools.

But no. My brain is a hundred million miles away, and I am just wasting time. I take out my phone and text Hannah: *You up?* Knowing the answer is, *No, Craw, no person with any kind of sanity is still up at this ungodly hour.*

But a few seconds later, my phone buzzes.

HANNAH: wide awake
ME: Can I call you?
HANNAH: of course

She picks up the phone on the first ring. Says, "Why are *you* up?"

And I don't even know.

But I do know my heart won't stop racing. And my brain is on a little gerbil wheel inside my skull, stuck on maximum speed. The gerbil is dead, by the way, just spinning loops inside my head for infinity. I don't say any of this. I open my mouth. The words won't come. It's all buried deep. Under granite. And I got no way to dig it out. So I just say, "Why are *you* up?"

She shuffles around on her end of the phone. "I'm always up. Call me anytime, and I'm up."

I sit on the edge of my bed. Still fully dressed. Then I topple over. Flop on my pillow. "Will you sit here on the phone with me?"

"Crawford, is everything okay?"

"Everything is fine."

"No, it isn't. What happened when you got home?"

"Will you just stay on the phone with me?" I put the phone on speaker, then place it on the pillow next to my head.

"Do you wanna FaceTime?"

"Sure."

She hangs up. Calls back. Now her face is on my screen, lit up by a pale blue glow. She's got the blankets pulled up over her shoulder. Like a little hood around her head. "Have you thought about tomorrow?" she asks me.

"What's tomorrow?"

"Saturday."

At first, I'm like, *Who cares?* Saturday. Community service. Some little cute part of me wants to say, *At least I'll get to see you.* But then it hits me. I tore the hell out of that field. And they'll find out around the same time we show up to work. "They won't know it was me."

"No. But... you can't keep a lie off your face."

"What's that even mean?"

"It means when you're lying, everyone can tell."

"False."

"True. Know how I know?"

"How?"

"You said nothing was wrong earlier. Now I can see your face. And you're lying. You don't have a good poker face. Something is wrong. You just don't want to say."

My cheeks burn. I can't even look at her. I roll away from the screen and look up at the ceiling. Just trying to hide my so-called lying eyes from her.

After a while, she says, "Crawford, you got to talk to somebody. Maybe not me. But somebody. You got to tell them what's happening to you."

I pick up the phone. Stuff the pillow under my head. "You know," I tell her, "I am pretty sleepy after all."

"Crawford."

"And we gonna have a lot to do tomorrow."

"Crawford, come on. Why is it so hard for you to talk to me?"

That question cuts.

I am surprised how hard it cuts.

I say, "I think I'm gonna roll over and try and sleep."

"Alright, Crawford."

I hang up the phone. I roll over. But I do not go to sleep.

TEENAGERS
MY CHEMICAL ROMANCE

SATURDAY.

Used to be a good day. Used to be a *wake up, eat cereal, and watch YouTube* day.

Now it's community service day.

I'm not sure what time it is. Sure feels like I only just shut my eyes when Pops comes into my room. He's got on his soft face. Uses his soft voice. "Hey, Craw. You sleep alright?"

And I know what's coming before it even gets out of his mouth.

"I was thinking about taking you and Big Time out to breakfast," he says. "Then I'll drop you off for community service. Take a look at our field."

I sit up straight.

"Then, I was thinking after you was done working, we'd drive down to Little Rock. I got money burning a hole in my pocket. And I wanna treat you boys to somethin' good."

Oh Jesus.

I throw the covers back and scoot to the edge of the bed. Check my phone. It is 6:15 a.m. The thought of Pops being among the first people to see the damage I wrought on Cope Field has my heart hammering in my chest. And he'll know it was me, too. Right away. No question.

"If it's all the same, I'd rather drive myself," I say.

"Well, how about you drive us all then? We can all do a little work on the field together. It'll be good family time."

"I think I'd rather just drive myself. Alone."

Pops makes a sour face. But it's playful. Not mad. Because he is in *I'm sorry* mode, which means all the stuff he'd take as personal disrespect is now allowed to be a funny back-and-forth between folks who love one another deep down.

"Well, I ain't of a mind to make you do something you don't want to do. Not today. How about you just meet us for breakfast? Then we'll head out to Little Rock soon as you get home."

I tell him, *Fine, okay, that's good.* Just anything to get him out of my room and not asking about seeing the damn field all of a sudden.

By the time I'm out the door, Pops is in his truck, Big Time riding shotgun, his head looking worse in the daylight than it did last night. Pops rolls down the window. Music blaring. Aviator glasses on. He leans out and hollers, "You go muddin' last night?"

And I'm like, *Oh damn.* Stop dead in my tracks. He's talking about the remnants of Cope Field still clinging to the sides of my vehicle. I laugh a little. Play cool. Tell him I drove it in circles round Briar Creek. "'Cause the water's low."

He nods. "Done that in my day." Then he slaps the car door through the window. Grins huge, and says, "I'm starved. Meet you over at Dewayne's!"

Lord, he's feeling good.

And that's got me feeling bad for sure.

I hop in my own truck and drive into town. Pull in to Dewayne's as Big Time is climbing out of the truck. He stands there. Head swollen up. Hands on his hips. Managing to carry that shiner with some amount of eight-year-old swagger.

"You okay?" I ask him, once I'm outside.

"Doing good, broham. How are you?"

"Didn't get much sleep."

"Pops gave me extra melatonin. I slept like a baby up in heaven on a cotton cloud."

"Do you remember me talking to you last night?"

He looks side to side. Pops comes around the front of the truck, pats his stomach with both hands, and says, "Let's eat."

And that's the end of our conversation. No way Big Time is getting real with me if Pops is standing in earshot.

We go in. Order. Shovel eggs and toast and waffles into our mouths. The waitress asks about Big Time's bruised-up face, but Pops don't even have to answer.

Big Time says, "Battle scar. I took a baseball to the face."

The woman laughs. "No doubt he's your son," she says to Pops.

Pops says, "No doubt at all."

Big Time repeats the same story again anytime someone asks. He's eager to say it. And I have this sinking feeling in my stomach. Because

Cope Field

I know why. Hunter Cope is a legend here. A hero. So if he says something happened, folks will believe it. And who are we to speak up against the man who put this entire town on the map?

Makes me feel a little like crying.

But I hold it together.

A little later, Pops wanders around the diner talking to folks. Signs some autographs, even though I got no idea how anybody in this stupid town don't already have his autograph by now. He sits with some old-timers for a while, and they belly laugh. Big Time tries to explain his newest space rabbit hole to me. But my brain is like a puddle of grease water. No good.

It's getting close to community service time. I tell Pops I'm heading out. He's belly deep in good-ole-days stories, the whole table inclined toward him, fascinated by the glamorous and apparently hilarious life of a Major League Baseball player. But he stops mid-sentence. Tells the table, "This is my boy, Craw."

"Aw, we know Craw," they say.

"Well, you gonna know him better in a few years."

"Bet scouts get hard thinking about this kid," one of them says. It's a big fella, wearing a yellowing oxygen tube on his face and pulling a green tank behind him on wheels. This sentence he uttered, which might be the grossest thing any person has ever said about me to my face, is the height of comedy to the entire table. Those old-timers stomp their feet laughing. Their faces turning red. One guy, I swear to God, snarfs coffee.

"In a manner of speaking, yeah," Pops says, chuckling a little. "We had a call from the Royals last week. They're sending someone to watch him play next game. Isn't that exciting? Thousand bucks he gets called up right outta high school."

I stand there. Stunned. We play in five days. To tell the truth, I'd rather have not known. Jesus Christ, I feel like garbage. "When did... when did that happen?"

"They called up last week. I told you about it."

He did not. But there is no sense arguing.

One of the old-timers says, "I'll take that bet. They don't call up high schoolers much no more. They'd rather send them to D-1. Get 'em coached up."

"Then what? He'll play a farm team somewhere. Maybe peter out," another says.

141

Pops starts arguing. "No, no. Trust me. He's got the best private coach alive. He's going to the big show."

And I'm like, *Peace*. Because I don't got time for that. I hurry out to the truck. Waving two fingers at Big Time as I go out the door, a little bell chiming overhead. And I'm in the truck lickety-split, backing out of the parking lot and roaring toward my doom at Cope Field.

DIRTY LITTLE SECRET
THE ALL-AMERICAN REJECTS

Roger stands in the middle of the field, looking like somebody shot his dog in front of him. Shaking his head. Staring down at the mess. I stand nearby, my arms crossed, trying my hardest not to throw up.

Thing is, I destroyed this place to hurt Pops. But I can see it hurt Roger, too. And that feels real scummy inside. Didn't Pops say there was already an effort to fix up this field before he got involved? This whole project is probably Roger's baby.

"You okay?" Hannah asks, breaking the silence.

"Who would do something like this?" Roger asks. His eyes dart between us. But there is zero accusing in them.

Hannah says, "A lot of bad folks in this world."

I just rock back on my heels and try to look calm.

"You know I live right over there," Hannah says. "And I heard some noise last night. After that storm rolled out. I peeked out my window, and there was this old white Jeep doing circles in the middle of the field."

Roger nods, listening. "Old?"

"Like '80s style. Maybe '70s. I don't know my Jeeps that well. Anyway, I ran out on the porch because I was thinking, *My God, who would want to destroy some baseball field in the middle of nowhere?* After all that work we did, too. I mean, geez. So I hollered after them, and I think they heard me. Or saw me. Or something. Because they hit the highway right away after that, back toward town."

Roger glances up the hill to where my truck is parked. Still coated in mud. He says, "I don't even know where to start to fix this."

Then he don't say anything else. He walks back to his own truck and gets on the phone. It's like, *Start with what?* Start with the field? Start with that gonzo lie Hannah just issued?

I stand there looking around at my mess. In the daytime, it's worse than I thought. The field had been nice and soaked. There are dozens of deep, circular grooves zigzagged all across the infield. The outfield isn't much better. And guess what? I knocked down the posts me and Hannah put up last Saturday, plus the ones Roger put up later on.

That mistake cost me some fresh scuffs and dents on my rear bumper, which Pops has not as of yet noticed, thank God. I didn't even feel it when it happened. Which is par for the course. Not feeling things, I mean. Like, my body was doing stuff, yes. But I was one hundred percent checked out. Separate from my own self. Like a ghost. Or a combat veteran. Or both at the same time. Checked out right until the moment Hannah Flores climbed into my truck.

"What do we do?" I ask her.

"Just play dumb," she says. "It'll be fine."

"No, I mean, how do we fix this?"

"You *want* to fix this?"

"It's weird, Hannah."

"What do you mean?"

"I mean how I feel about fixing it is weird."

"I can do weird. Tell me."

We walk to the dugout to get out of the heat. She sits on the bench, and I hang on the fence, trying to find the words. "You know how they gonna name this field after my Pops?"

"Yeah."

"Well."

She tilts her head a little. Like a confused puppy.

I sigh. I know what I want to say. What I want to say is: *Before, fixing this field felt like fixing everything. Fixing my life. Fixing my father. Weird thing, I guess, is that's the same reason I came out here and destroyed it. But now I just feel like the only person I really hurt was Roger. Pops is just gonna throw money at it.* But I cannot force the words past my lips.

Roger walks over carrying a pitchfork. We stare at him like he's Jason Voorhees or something coming over to jab that thing through our brains. He sticks it in the ground and says, "This is all I can think of."

"Huh?" Hannah says.

"To fix this." Then he plucks it out of the ground, walks to one of the tire ruts, and levers the spikes down through the grass. I don't understand what he's doing at first. But then I see he's sorta lifting up the part that I squashed down so that it's more or less level with the undamaged parts of the field. He does it a few more times until one of the rivets looks even. Then he passes the pitchfork to me. "I'm gonna head into town. Gonna pick up another pitchfork. Maybe some dirt. I don't know. Ask someone up there if they got any ideas how to fix this. Reckon I better call your daddy, too. Let him know what's happened. Hannah, you think you could tell that story about the Jeep you saw to the police."

Hannah shrugs. "Nah."

"What? Why not?"

"A cab."

Roger and I make the same face. Which is like, *The hell does that mean?*

Roger shakes his head. Gives up. "Alright. We'll talk more later. You two take turns with that fork till I get back."

When he's gone, and we've watched his truck disappear around the bend, I turn to Hannah. "A cab?"

She shrugs. "All Cops Are Bastards."

Two hours of jabbing that damn pitchfork in the ground. Two hours of lifting up sod. Trying to make it even. And really, looking back at our work, it still looks terrible. Like you can tell someone drove all over this stupid field. I don't think anything can fix the mess I've created except maybe more dirt. Professional landscapers. Time. Money.

Hannah talks through the first hour. Telling me this story about The Asshole. She's like, *Do you know why folks call him Shotgun?* And I'm like, *No. No, I do not.*

"Well"—and she's taking her turn with the pitchfork while I stand there dripping sweat all over the place—"he doesn't run with a great group. Let's just say that. They're all losers. Stuck up their own white asses. The story goes, and this just the way he tells it, they used to control most of the meth market over in Abner County. This was back when he was like twenty or something. Long before I came around. There was this fella who took a whole boatload of their stuff saying he wanted to sell for them, but instead he just smoked all of it. Then, when it came time to pay up, he was like five grand in the hole. So one of the guys—some high-up guy—tells The Asshole to go over there and rough him up."

"This is all very *Breaking Bad*."

"You can say that 'cause you don't live it." She jabs the pitchfork in the ground and wipes sweat off her forehead with the back of her arm. "Jeez, it's hot."

It occurs to me Roger left with the water cooler. We're out here where we might bake straight to death with no water. "So what happened with Shotgun?"

"Oh, yeah. Well, he goes out there, right? Has a shotgun with him. And he kicks down this guy's door. The guy hits his knees right away. Starts begging and crying and saying, 'Don't kill me, don't kill me, don't kill me.' And Shotgun was never planning to kill this guy, right? Just wanted to scare him because a dead guy can't pay, right?"

"Right," I say, like I'm in on this somehow. Like I have one single clue what in the hell she is talking about.

"So he says to this guy, 'You know how in cartoons they can plug up a shotgun with their finger?' And this guy is white as a ghost saying, 'Uh-huh' and 'Yes, sir.' So The Asshole's like, 'You ever wanna try that? See if it can work?'"

"Jesus."

"So they did. I mean, Shotgun did. He was like, 'Plug up the gun with your finger. See if you can save yourself.' And this guy doesn't have a choice, right? Shotgun says he does it. Stuffs his finger right in the barrel of the gun. And Shotgun pulls the trigger. Takes this guy's whole hand off. And while he's down there bleeding, Shotgun just laughs and says, 'Hell, I guess that don't work.' Folks started calling him Shotgun after that."

This is some kinda Paul Bunyan nonsense. As in, I'm not buying it. I roll my eyes. Tell her, "Yeah, right." Still, at the same time, all I can think about is the day at the barbecue pit. How I burned up all his money. All of Pops' pills.

How Pops pulled a gun on him.

If this nonsense is true, Shotgun don't seem like the kind of person who forgives and forgets. Seems like the kind who gets motivated by that sort of thing. Like, *You done this to me. So I'm gonna do this to you.* Schoolyard bullying but turned up to eleven. The kind where somebody is liable to end up dead. And I got this sinking feeling in my stomach that somebody might end up being me.

"No. It's true," Hannah says. "Wait, let me rephrase that. Shotgun *says* it's true. Could be he's full of it. I would not be surprised. It's like one of those fish stories where the fish is bigger every time you tell it. Except, you know, for meth heads."

We work for another hour, waiting for Roger. Half dying because there's no water. Eventually, we give up and walk to my truck. I lower the tailgate and sit down. Hannah's so short she's gotta scramble to get up there. Gentleman thing to do woulda been to help her up. But, you know. It's funny to watch her work at it.

We sit there, sweating. Her talking. Me nodding. Listening. Looking down the highway for Roger. Before long, we are so close our shoulders are touching. I put my hand on hers. She looks up at me. Smiles. Then laces her fingers into mine.

"You know," she says. But then she doesn't say anything else. Her words have dried up. Like mine always do.

"What?" I ask her.

"Nothing."

"Something."

"It's just . . . I never thought I'd like being around a baseball boy so much."

"There's a lot more to me than baseball."

She smiles. Looks away. Her cheeks a little red. From the sun? From the work? From talking to me? I am not sure which. Maybe all those things combined. She says, "That's exactly what I been trying to say to you."

Across the street, the screen door to her house flies open, banging against the wall with a rattle of glass. She lets go of my hand and scoots an inch away from me. Shotgun steps out on the porch, a bowl in one hand, something small and black in the other. He stands there for a second, looking across the road and into Cope Field. He's got this look on his face. This squinty-eyed look. Like he's trying to figure something out. Then I realize: He don't see us. And he's looking for Hannah. His head sweeps back and forth until he finally turns toward my truck. He nods. "Working hard?" he hollers across at us.

"We're waiting on Roger," I say.

"Who the hell is Roger?"

"The guy in charge of this field."

He shakes his head. Laughs. He's always laughing at everything, seems like. Then he puts the bowl and the black object down on the front porch. He walks around the side of the house and returns thirty seconds later with coils of orange extension cord, which he hucks down in the grass.

We watch him like, *What the hell is this?*

He sits down and picks up the black object. He plugs it into the extension cord. It comes to life. Buzzing, like a little lawn mower. An electric razor. He's working without paying us any attention. But we're transfixed, and I don't know why. He swipes it upward and back through his long grungy hair. Matted, greasy locks fall around his shoulders. Drift in the wind like wisps of poplar seed.

One pass. Two. Each swipe revealing his skin-slick skull underneath.

As we watch, we hear an engine rumbling through the trees behind us. I turn in time to see Pops' truck come around the bend. He's driving fast. A little crazy. And I can tell just from the way his car moves he knows about the field. And he's already figuring it was me.

SUCH GREAT HEIGHTS
THE POSTAL SERVICE

Pops stands at the side of the road overlooking Cope Field. Big Time stands nearby, still looking like he just got out of a boxing match with Mike Tyson. I can hardly stand the sight of him, it makes me so sick. And Hannah's eyes go back and forth between him and me like, *What the hell?*

Big Time says, "I got hit with a baseball," to head off the imminent question.

Pops spits tobacco juice on the ground. Shakes his head. "Well," he says.

I'm between him and Shotgun, who has walked down to the end of his driveway. Swaggered down, more like. Throwing his shoulders from side to side, like he thinks he's some tough guy.

I'd be lying if I said I am not afraid of him, especially after what Hannah shared. As he walks past us toward Pops, I can see he has a tattoo on the back of his head.

The grinning mouth of a skull. The looping coils of a snake, its fangs bared. The entire thing inked as red as blood.

"Hannah," I say, my voice timid in my own ears. Like I am afraid if I open my mouth too much, I might throw up. Or start sobbing. Or both at the same time.

This is the same tattoo I saw under the dim blue glow of Christmas lights.

Except I must have something twisted in my memories.

That tattoo was jet-black. This one is red.

Tattoos can't change colors. Can they?

Pops don't see him. He's too busy looking at how I massacred his namesake. "You done this, didn't you, Craw?" he says. His voice low. Grumbly. Like there's gravel in his throat.

Hannah shakes her head behind his back. But I can't lie to him. He already knows. Lying will make it worse. Before I can speak, though, Shotgun calls out, "Well, lookie who we got here. Mr. Big and Tough."

Pops turns. His eyes narrow. "What are you doing here?"

"I live here, Mr. Pro Baseball. Tell me, you bring that peashooter of yours with you today?"

Big Time says, "I remember you from the pool. You better get outta here."

Shotgun bends at the waist. Hands on his knees, so he is eye level with Sutton. He says, "Quite the shiner you got there, little man. You get in a fight?"

"I got hit with a baseball."

Shotgun's face is grim. Serious. "You sure that's from a baseball?"

Pops stands very still. Like some gunslinger in an old Western movie. He says, "Craw, get in the truck."

I say, "Hannah."

It just comes out of my mouth. I think it's because I don't want to leave her here. Out in the road. With a worked-up Shotgun to keep her company.

Pops seems to read my mind. He says, "Her, too."

"You can't take my daughter. I'll call the law out here."

"The last thing you want is the law out here."

Shotgun laughs. Because of course he does.

"Hannah," I say again, looking at her. Whole world buzzing. Vibrating. Shaking me out of my skull. Like when I struck Pops with that baseball bat, and when I threw that baseball at him. My soul, leaving my body. Watching the world from above. Going on a little bon voyage of its own. Because here, this moment, this everything. It hurts too much and too deep to stay.

Another truck comes around the bend.

Roger.

He rolls up. Hanging halfway out the window. Grinning huge. Too dumb to sense the tension. Says, "What's up, fellas?" He climbs out of the truck. Grabs a pitchfork from the back and hands it to me. Then to Pops, he says, "Guess you got my message."

"I got it."

Roger shrugs. Rolls his eyes. "Vandals."

Shotgun makes his way back up to the porch. Didn't like his odds, I guess. From his pocket, he takes a straight-edge razor and stands there, scraping it across his head. No water. No nothing. Just cue-balling his dome down until that tattoo shines bright red in the early afternoon sun.

That sick feeling kicks up again in my stomach.

That *is* the tattoo I saw back then. But I am absolutely *sure* it was black.

Pops watches him for a few seconds. Then turns his attention to Roger. "What's the damage? Give me numbers."

Roger says, "No damn clue. Come on. Let's have a look."

They wander down to the field, leaving me, Big Time, and Hannah up on the road.

"Come on," I tell her, making my way down the hill. She hesitates a second but follows. I step inside the dugout and sit on one of the benches. Mainly because I don't want to be in Shotgun's line of sight anymore. She sits beside me, so I take her hand again. Rub a thumb in circles on the back of it.

"Are you okay?" I ask.

"Not really. Are you okay?"

"Not really."

She puts her head on my shoulder, and we sit there breathing. Not speaking. I want to ask her about that tattoo. Ask her if it ever was a different color. But that sounds so stupid. I sit there trying to piece together what I know about tattooing. It's not much. Mainly things absorbed from television. Are there books of tattoo designs you can pick from? Is it possible for two people to have the same design? Seems likely. About a million people throughout history probably got some variation of snakes and skulls inked onto their skin.

But on their scalp? Less likely.

It seems the kind of thing Hannah might know about.

I want to ask her.

And I want to tell her why.

I want her to know about Momma. About how she disappeared. About the man I saw standing under the Christmas lights.

But another part says, *No.*

Says, *Be quiet.*

Shut up. Don't tell nobody. Don't say one single word about it.

This is my burden. Not hers.

Hannah has enough to worry about all on her own.

"You don't deserve all this," I say.

She raises an eyebrow. "What?"

"All this bullshit. I'm sorry I got you pulled into it. I keep trying to help, but I just keep making it worse."

Hannah rolls her eyes. "Crawford. Shut up."

But I won't. I got this worry in the back of my head that after today, I might not see her again. Pops will take away my wheels. Take away my phone. Or worse. "You know how you said I oughta tell somebody what I'm dealing with?"

"Yes."

"Well, maybe you should, too."

"What are you talking about?"

"I'm talking about not giving up. Keeping on even though stuff is hard. I know my old man is an asshole, but he's right about one thing. You gotta do good even when it's hard."

"Don't be ridiculous, Crawford."

"I'm not."

She sighs. "Nobody cares about some poor punker stuck forever in the Ozarks."

"That's not true."

"Yes, it is, Crawford. Nobody cares."

"I care."

She shakes her head slowly. Opens her mouth. Closes it. She folds her arms across her chest.

That might have been the most honest two words to ever come out of my mouth. We stay there in silence for a while longer. Then I tell her something that's been itching my brain for a long while. "Remember that day in your secret cave, how you said you were trapped here like Anna Carol?"

"Yes."

"Well, I don't believe it. I don't believe one person or thing on this planet could trap Hannah Flores. Not even dumb old Quiet County."

"Crawford..."

"I'm serious. This whole place is beneath you. You should be out in Seattle or someplace cool with people who are going places. Maybe New York City. I can see you as like an author or a poet or someone else big and important. Someone who changes people's minds."

"Stop." A tear streaks down her cheek.

"Hannah." I turn to face her. I can hear Pops and Roger talking outside. And I got fear in my stomach over what might be coming my way. But in this moment, I don't care. It's funny: I am so twisted up and anxious over what I done to this field, over what Pops might do to me once we are alone, but thinking about Hannah off somewhere, being happy, being powerful...

It puts a smile on my face.

Like ducking under an awning during a thunderstorm. It's raging out there. But for right now...

I'm in here.

"You deserve better than this place. You sure as hell deserve better than me. You deserve someone who will talk your ear off. Let you in their heart to live there. You just gotta let yourself go get it."

From beyond the dugout, Pops calls my name.

I kiss her cheek. Her eyes crinkle up at the edges.

I taste salt.

Then I stand up and head outside, where Pops is waiting with his hands on his hips, a scowl on his face.

We don't know exactly how much damage I did, but Roger guesses several thousand dollars. Pops groans and puts both hands over his eyes.

He wants me to ride with him to town, where he's meeting a landscaper to talk prices. I try to get out of it, but he snaps his fingers at me. Says, "In the truck." Arguing will only make it worse.

"What about my truck?" I ask, still hoping for some kinda way out of riding with him.

"Leave it. We'll get it later."

So, I climb in.

Pops floors it, and we peel out, white smoke billowing behind us. I sink down in the passenger seat. We fly down the highway, and Pops is tense. Like a loaded animal trap, right on the edge of snapping closed on some poor critter's neck.

And it's me.

I'm the critter.

Only I'm on edge, too. It's like, him being on the edge of breaking automatically puts me on the edge of breaking. I wring my hands. Look out the window. Try and take deep breaths, count backward from ten like those stupid VR videos suggested.

But nothing works.

Big Time sits behind me, his feet on the back of my seat. Every second or two, I can feel them. *Thud. Thud.* Or one long press into my back. I want to say something. But saying something might set Pops off. So I sit there. Getting twisted up. Boiling.

I start looking up tattoos, trying to keep my mind occupied, typing in the search engine: *Can two people have the same tattoo?*

Big Time kicks the back of my seat three more times before I can get enough signal to populate results. But pretty soon, I have the answer. Yes. Most tattoo parlors got those books filled with pick-n-choose tattoo designs. They call it *flash*. Which I guess means it is possible for Shotgun and that man who ran off with Momma to have gotten the same tattoo.

I am not sure what to think of that.

Some part of me maybe wanted it to be Shotgun.

Because then I could ask him: Where did my momma go? And how did you help her get there? And Pops said you two ran off together, so where is she?

Big Time kicks my seat again. This time, he whispers, "Boom, boom, baby."

And I can take no more.

I whip around and yell, "Kick my seat one more time. I dare you."

Big Time looks like Shrek, his head is so bad swollen. But getting beat up by Pops—or hit with a baseball or *whatever*—hasn't yet driven the life out of him. He grins. And sure as hell, he kicks the back of my seat with both legs as hard as he can.

I am about to come over the seat and get him in a choke hold, but Pops yanks the back of my shirt, forcing me into my seat.

"Do not," he says. One finger in my face. "Do not touch that boy."

What a thing to say to me.

"Look what you done to him!" I say. It comes out before I can stop it. "Look how swollen he is!"

Pops slams on the brakes. "Look what I done? Look what *I* done?"

He throws the truck into park. Gets out and marches to my side of the vehicle. I slam the locks on. He stares at me through the glass. Then hits the automatic unlock button on his keys. I slam the locks on again. For a while, we do that back and forth. Locked. Unlocked. Locked. Unlocked. Me finding it a little funny. A little scary. Pops finding it all the way infuriating. Finally, he gets smart, has his hand on the door handle at the same time he hits the unlock button. He pops the door open before I can stop him.

Cope Field

I hear myself yell. Scream almost. I sound like a child in my own ears. Like a baby crying.

He pulls me from the truck and into the road.

I WRITE SINS NOT TRAGEDIES
PANIC! AT THE DISCO

HANNAH: are u alright?
HANNAH: sorry about everything that happened yesterday. i wish i could help
HANNAH: hey, i'm worried about u
HANNAH: crawford…talk to me
Read 9:39 P.M.

SWEETNESS
JIMMY EAT WORLD

Little tapping.
    Tap. Tap. Tap.

My eyes flutter open.

I'm not sure where I am at first. But there's my Nolan Ryan poster, with his bloodied face. My pillows. My blanket. And lookie. My little toes stickin' out from the end.

I don't move right away. Maybe I dreamed that noise.

My head feels like a jellyfish afloat in a sea of puke. I sit up, but everything in me says, *Don't move so fast, you idiot. Lie back down. Go to sleep.*

Tap.

Taptaptaptaptap.

It's coming from the window.

Okay, I decide, *it's real.*

I force my feet on the floor and peek through the blinds, not sure what I might find. Could be a woodpecker, for all I know. Or a serial killer with a butcher knife. Which, okay. Bad news. But at least I wouldn't have to see Pops in the morning.

Hannah peers at me through cupped hands.

I'm shocked for a second. Then I open the window and help her in. "What are you doin' here?"

She looks around my room. "You didn't answer my texts. I was worried."

"How'd you get here?" I lean out the window, looking across the lawn and out to the highway. Half scared she stole Shotgun's old Ford, and the next thing that's gonna happen is him appearing at my window with his namesake in hand. Tellin' me, *You know how in cartoons they sometimes can stop bullets by pluggin' the gun with their finger?*

"I walked," she says.

"That is a long-ass walk."

"Yeah." Her eyes dart to mine. She steps toward me. One hand falling on my chest. Then moving up my body. When she nears my face, I flinch.

She whispers, "Sorry. *Sorry.* Crawford, you look awful."

"Thanks."

"What happened?"

I sit down on the bed. Plop back, pull a pillow over my face, and don't say anything. She lies down beside me. Then she puts her head on my shoulder. One arm across my chest.

We lie like that for a long time.

Maybe I fall asleep.

I'm not sure.

Her hand rubs circles in the center of my chest. I feel the warmth of her touch, of her breath. And I'm thinking—this touch is put on me out of kindness rather than anger. It is sad to say, that is not an experience I am used to. So under my pillow, without her seeing... I let out some tears.

"Why is my life like this?" I ask her.

"I don't know. But you don't deserve it."

I take the pillow away from my face. Look at her in the dark. The moonlight through my window is soft on her skin. Caught in her eyes like little swimming pools of light. "Neither do you," I say.

She looks away. "Stop saying that."

I sit up. Turn her chin toward me. Look her straight in her eyes. "You're a beautiful person, Hannah. And you deserve the best there is. You deserve to get outta this place. You really do. I hate what you said the other day about giving up. About Anna Carol, and getting trapped here. Don't get trapped here, Hannah. You're too good for it."

Her cheeks turn red.

So I lean forward and kiss them. Once on the right. Once on the left. Her eyes crinkle up in a smile against my lips. "I mean it," I say. "Once you get outta Jerusalem, take nothing but the best from every person you meet."

"I'll take you with me."

"Where would we go?"

"Where do you wanna go?"

I squeeze her a little tighter. Think about that question. Where would I go if it was up to me—and only me? I am not sure I have ever asked myself that question before. "I wanna go to the top of a mountain. Where I can see the whole world below me. Throw up double birds and yell *fuck you* to the whole thing."

She laughs. "How very punk rock of you."

We touch foreheads, talk in whispers. "You rubbed off on me, I guess."

"Crawford, tell me what happened."

I kiss her forehead. Buying time, really. Hoping it will change the subject. I do not want to answer her. But I know Hannah well enough by now to know she ain't gonna let it go. Sure enough, when I break away, her eyes are locked on mine, waiting for an answer. I look away from her. Close my eyes, draw in a deep breath, and force the words out. "Pops got after me. He knew it was me that wrecked his field."

"He hit you, didn't he?"

I open my mouth. Close it. I still can't say it. Goddamn it, why can't I say it?

I clench my teeth. Think of Big Time. Maybe this all started because of my anger issues, but there is one thing I am sure about. Big Time did nothing wrong. And look what happened to him.

I nod my head one time. It's such a small movement. But huge in its own way. And it hits me: This is the first time I have ever told a soul. Ever implicated Hunter Cope in anything more than expecting my best. It's the lie Pops carefully constructed all my life. A lie I am complicit to.

"Jesus," Hannah whispers.

"Hannah."

"What?"

"I thought I was gonna die."

There is a long pause. I listen to her breathing. She starts to say something. Then stops.

"What?" I ask.

"You have to tell somebody."

"I just told you."

"I mean, you have to tell the police."

"Tell them what?"

"What you are going through. Someone can help you."

"I can't do that."

"I'm serious, Crawford. People will listen to you. And they'll want to help you."

My words dry up. Hannah don't understand. She don't understand Big Time doesn't want folks to know, either, that if the wrong people found out, they might break up our family. She don't understand that for as big as Pops is to the community, he's even bigger to Big Time.

I kiss her soft on the lips. And this time she does let it change the subject. She presses into me. Her hands moving behind my head. Fingers dancing through my hair. My whole body goes electric. But in that good way. Without even thinking about it, we end up face-to-face. Her on top. Her touch hurts where I am bruised. But my brain says, *Shh. That don't matter. Not right now.*

I slide my hands up her body. Over her hips. Her ribs. Under her shirt. I stop before I get anywhere significant.

"Is this okay?" I ask.

She shakes her head no. So I don't do anything else.

She says, "Are you mad?"

"No, Hannah. Of course not."

She puts her arms around me. Presses her chest against my chest. And I hold her. And she holds me. Breathing in rhythm.

I am glad she is with me. Near me. That of all the people in this world, it was *her* who came to my window the night after Pops pulled me into the road and beat me until I thought I might die.

"I got a stupid idea," she says.

"What?"

"There's this dance next month."

"Prom. Does *Hannah Flores* want to go to prom?" I am teasing. But my heart sorta does a somersault. Like I actually would go to prom with Hannah. Walking on the dance floor. Me dressed up fancy. Her wearing her battle jacket. Everyone stopping to look at us. Like, *Crawford Cope and... Hannah... together? Really...?*

And it's not like I care by now what they think.

But they'll make sure we hear them.

They'll make sure they say what they're gonna say loud enough they can spoil the night for us.

Spoil it for her.

Hannah clears that up real quick. "No, stupid. There's a punk show in Little Rock that night. And like three bands I like are playing. Small venue. And I've never actually gotten to go to a live show before, because there's barely a scene here at all, so... I was gonna see if you... wanna blow off the dance. Unless you already have a date?"

"Nope, no date."
"Good."
"That's good?"
"I think so."
"Alright, Hannah," I tell her. "I'll go to a punk show with you."
Hannah makes a squeaky noise. Wraps her arms around me and squeezes me tight. Then she kisses me all over my face. Which kinda hurts. But I kinda don't mind.

I'M NOT OKAY (I PROMISE)
MY CHEMICAL ROMANCE

Pops won't let me go to school for several days as my face heals. So I sit in my room, drifting over mountains and oceans in my VR headset. I am barely even listening to the voice at this point. And nothing about this fake space feels good to me. I take off the headset and pop in my earbuds, fire up that punk rock playlist Hannah made for me. Angry, screaming voices fill my skull. And I sit there thinking maybe I get it. Punk rock is about screaming *fuck you* at a world that has fucked you.

After a few days, he tells me to get back to class.

"You got a game tonight," he says. "You can't miss school and play in the game. So you better go."

"Okay."

"And Craw, that scout is coming, remember? So it's real important you show up." He leans against my doorframe. And my insides are white hot, begging the universe for him to go away. I wish *I* could just leave. But I can't leave Big Time behind. Look what happened last time I left him here alone.

"I'll show up," I say, hoping that'll be enough to get him to go away.

He hesitates. Rubs the lower half of his face with one hand. "Crawford, if anyone asks you—"

"I'll tell 'em I wrecked my four-wheeler."

"That's good. I only want what is best for you."

"I know that."

"Good. We all make mistakes. But we forgive each other. And we keep going."

I clench my fists under my blankets where he can't see.

Pops rubs his head, right where I hit him with that baseball bat. He says, "You oughta know exactly what I mean."

There is a long, uncomfortable pause. Finally, I choke out, "I know."

Cope Field

Pops nods slow. Steps away from the door. "Good," he says. "I'll see you at your game."

Principal calls me out of art class. Whole time, the teacher was going on and on about chiaroscuro shading or some nonsense. My brain was in a fog. Principal says, "You okay, Crawford?" when he sees me. And I barely register the question. Some autopilot part of my brain mumbles, "Four-wheeler accident."

He eyes me good. Then says, "Well, follow me."

He walks beside me, his keys jingling on a carabiner hooked through one of his belt loops. Big belly barely held back by his button-up shirt.

He has me sit outside his office.

My head pounds. I put my palms into my eyes and wait.

For the last couple days, I got this problem. It's like, I'll be sitting there. Not thinking about anything. Then all of a sudden, I am crying. Full-on bawling. Happened at dinner last night. Pops got us pizza and hot wings. A spread big enough to feed a whole baseball team. He was feeling sorry for us again, I guess. Big Time stood at the end of the table rubbing his hands together. Practically drooling. I remember thinking we looked so ragged, the pair of us. He still had bruises all over his face. And so did I. My head swam. Barely even present at the table.

Pops thought *pizza* and *hot wings* would fix what he'd done.

He said, "You want pepperoni or sausage?"

And I started to sob.

Pops was like, "What's wrong?"

And I had to tell him: I had no damn clue.

Outside the principal's office, it hits me again. A secretary looks up at me. She makes a face like she might cry, too. Asking me if I'm okay and calling me *sweetheart* and handing me a box of tissues. And I'm like, *I don't know what's wrong with me.* "Four-wheeler wreck," I say, as if that explains it.

She says, "Are you okay?"

I nod my head yes, but I am still crying. Hiding my eyes. Wishing like hell I could get up, run down the hallway and out the front doors.

Why am I gettin' called outta art class?

Principal comes back. Says, "Come this way, Crawford. Are you okay? You can bring them tissues with you."

I bring them.

He leads me to a back room. There's a woman sitting at a table. Brown dress. Brown hair. Brown eyes. She's even got a little brown folder on the table in front of her to match, and it's like, *Really*. She says, "Crawford Cope?"

"Yes, ma'am."

"I'm Donna Melton with the Department of Human Services. I work in Child and Family Services."

"Okay."

Donna opens up her folder. Takes out a yellow legal pad and clicks open a pen. She touches it to the page and says, "I want to talk to you about a few things that happened recently, if that's okay? Why don't you sit down."

"Okay." I sit. Clench my fists in my lap. Looking down, I notice how beat-up my knuckles are. Like maybe I scraped them on the ground. Or maybe I busted them a time or two over Pops' head. I tuck my hands under my legs to hide them, praying to God this lady hasn't noticed. I'm getting numb. Head fuzzy. Like my soul has one foot out the door. Say one more word I don't like, and it's gone.

"Let's start with you, Crawford. Can you tell me how you got those bruises on your face? What about your hands? How did you hurt your hands?"

"What bruises?"

She puts the pen down. Stares straight into my eyes. Lets the moment get awkward. Then she says, "Crawford, I am here to help you. But I can't help you if you don't talk to me."

"What is this about?"

Donna's eyes never leave mine. "Your father, Crawford. We received a report."

A report? My soul takes that last step out of my body. Kills the lights and shuts the door. And I am watching everything from far away. Blurry tunnel vision. Donna Melton in the center. Asking her questions.

"Who gave you the bruises on your face?"

"Four-wheeler accident."

"Did you go to the ER?"

"No."

"Why not?"

"It looks worse than it is."

"What about your brother? Who blacked his eye?"

"He got hit by a baseball."

"Did he go to the hospital?"

"No, but I sat up with him in case he was concussed."

"Why didn't anyone take him to see a doctor?"

I look down at my sneakers. I should have. This is my fault. Just like everything else. I should have taken Big Time out of there. But I was too scared we would get separated. And now, this woman is here. And I know she means to break up our family.

"I didn't know what to do," I tell her.

She writes something down. "Are there any guns, alcohol, or drugs in your home?"

"I don't know."

"Why don't you tell me what happened on Saturday?"

"I don't know."

"Did you attack your father to protect your little brother?"

"I didn't attack nobody."

This feeling in my heart is like the earth splitting. There is only one person I can think of who could put all these questions on this woman's lips. One person who knows enough about what happened behind the scenes at our house to make this hotline call.

Hannah.

"Crawford," Donna says. "You aren't in trouble. I just need your help."

Hannah told them to check in on me. Hannah kept saying to me I should talk to someone, I should tell them what I'm going through. And after seeing me busted up so bad in my bedroom, she must have taken matters into her own hands.

Goddamn.

Tears roll down my cheeks. Breaking free at my chin. Splattering like raindrops on the wood grain table.

I am crying again.

Only this time, I know exactly why.

THE SEASON
ALL GET OUT

My soul checked out of my body the entire time Donna Melton asked me questions about Pops. And adios, because it hasn't come back. Standing on the pitcher's mound. Twiddling a baseball behind my back. Can't even read Luis's sign. My brain is too far gone. My body like the husk you yank off a corn cob. Withering right here in the open in front of everybody.

Snap back into the moment. The batter's eyes narrow. Some little hamster in my head jolts on his wheel, and it's like, *Oh yeah, we got a game to win here. Lake Village. Number one team in the state. Conference rival. A must-win game for conference seeding. A chance for me to show what I can do against good hitters.*

Coach Rodriguez steps out of the dugout, hands on his narrow hips. He calls time. Luis rises from his haunches and trots toward the mound. I let out a deep breath. Feel that brain hamster lose its footing and go sailing off the wheel. My head soaring back out to the cosmos. Luis says, "Hey, you alright?"

I don't look him.

Barely hear him.

I manage to nod my head yes.

All day leading into the game, folks been asking about my face. Asking about my hands. I have said "four-wheeler accident" over and over again. I can hardly stand saying it anymore. My whole world is coming apart. And here I am in some stupid baseball game.

Pops sits at the top of the bleachers, Big Time beside him, eating a box of Cracker Jacks by the handful. He's got four boxes lined up on the bench next to him. Pops' face is unreadable behind his sunglasses. But I know he isn't happy. Whole place keeps looking back at him. Then looking at me. Like, *This is the pedigree of Hunter Cope, the best baseball player to come out of Quiet County?*

Cope Field

A man walks up the bleachers. Baseball cap on. Shades. Blue-and-white windbreaker jacket. Clipboard in one hand. He waves at Pops, who stands to shake his hand. And for a second, I am crystal clear in the moment. Who is that guy? Why is he here? He turns, still talking to Pops. They look right at me, and I see the front of his windbreaker.

A Royals logo.

And all at once, I remember what Pops said before school today.

That scout is coming... so it's real important you show up.

My heart sinks straight into my stomach. My knees go weak. I have to grab on to Luis's shoulder to keep from falling. The baseball I was holding falls to the dirt and rolls down the hill into the grass.

I completely forgot.

"Whoa," Coach Rodriguez says, approaching from the dugout. He eyes me up and down. "Crawford, are you sure you're alright?"

I shake my head. "Rolled my four-wheeler."

"Yeah, you said that."

"I'm good."

"You don't look good. You sure?" His eyebrows rise. He wants an honest answer. But I got no honesty left inside me. I tell him I'm fine. Let's get this bread. Let's win this game. I'm fine. I'm fine. I'm fine. Because this is my shot. This is one of those moments where you need perfect timing. The kind of *dig deep, overcome it all, do the right thing when it's hard* moment Pops is always telling me about.

"I got this," I say. I say it over and over. Begging myself to believe it is true. "A scout is here. I *have* to be fine."

Luis looks over to the bleachers. "It's a lot of pressure, huh?"

I stare past him at Pops. At the scout from the Royals. Then, I see her.

Over by the visitor's dugout, where she always sits. Hannah Flores. Here to watch a little baseball game. After ruining my world.

I stare at her so long Coach Rodriguez waves his hand in my face again. "Hey."

He shares this look with Luis. Like they are talking with psychic powers. Then Coach says, "Crees que está bien? Debería sentarlo?"

Luis shrugs. "A lo mejor, pero tal vez dale una oportunidad."

Coach Rodriguez nods slow. "Alright, Craw," he says. "You got nine more pitches to turn things around. Then I'm pulling you."

I don't say nothing.

Coach Rodriguez says, "Yes, sir?"

I still don't say nothing. Just stare across the field at Hannah.

Coach says it louder. "Yes, sir?"

But my mouth is shut tight. Coach lets out his breath. He says, "Alright, fine, Craw. Get on the bench."

Then he leads me by the arm off the field.

Whole crowd reacts. People talking. Gasping. Booing. But above them all, there's Pops. Cussing up a storm. Thundering down the bleachers. Leaving that MLB recruiter behind him with red cheeks. I go inside the dugout. Sit in the corner. Lean my head against the wall. Refuse to look at anyone.

There are five innings left in the game. Keep expecting Pops to come tearing around the corner. What would he say? *You quit on your team, Craw.* Disciplining me. Coaching me up. Teaching me what I done wrong. Yelling right out loud what everybody already knows. Thing is, it won't be about me. It's not about me going professional. Not about opportunities for success. Not about never having to worry about my future. No. This is all about him. And that is something I am seeing more and more clearly. It's not about me doing bad at a baseball game for *baseball's* sake. It's about *Hunter Cope's son* doing bad at baseball and just what exactly does that mean about Hunter Cope?

Lord.

I don't even want to hear his speech on what kind of opportunity I blew today in front of a scout from the Kansas City Royals.

I got to get out of here.

I tell Coach Rodriguez I gotta take a piss. He eyes me for a long minute, then says to hurry back. But I am not coming back. My plan is to hustle to my truck and drive that thing until I am out of gas. Maybe right off the side of a mountain. Blow up in a big fiery crash.

I walk to the edge of the building and peek around. I look up and down the stands, looking for Pops. Looking for Big Time. But I don't see either of them. Which is weird. There is *zero chance* Pops is not lurking around somewhere like a vampire, waiting to pounce.

"What are you doing?"

I jump, half expecting that Donna Melton woman. But it's Hannah.

"Nothing," I say. "What do you want?"

"What do you mean, 'What do I want?'" she says, looking like a little wounded bird.

Cope Field

Well, who cares? Because what did I look like sitting in that office with Donna? A crying little baby, that's what. And *she* made that happen. She took it upon herself to send a big wrecking ball through my whole world. And it's not about Pops anymore. Not for me. I don't care what happens to him. It's about Big Time. Big Time don't understand. He don't got a clue. Because this whole time, everything that's happened... it's all he's ever known.

If they break up this family, he might not ever forgive me.

Especially if they put him in foster care a hundred miles from anyone he knows.

"I mean why are you here, Hannah?" I look past her. Back around the building. Scoping the place out for Pops.

"I have been to almost every game since we met. What do you mean, '*Why are you here?*'"

I don't say nothing. Just keep looking around.

"Crawford," she says.

But I'm not talking. Not to her. Not anymore.

"Leave me alone," I say. I can hear Pops in my voice. It makes me sick. But I can't stop. I push past her, making my way a little farther into the ballpark. I can't quite see the concession stand from here, but if Pops and Big Time aren't waiting to yank my ass in twain, they're probably there getting more Cracker Jacks or some nonsense.

Hannah says my name again. She puts her hand on my wrist. I recoil like she's some spindly spider.

"Do not," I say.

And even though there is heartbreak on her face, she doesn't bite back. Instead, she looks me straight in the eyes and speaks slowly. "Crawford, what's happened?"

"Will you stop?"

"Stop what?"

"Stop asking a million questions. If I wanted you to know, I'd tell you."

The game behind us resumes. The metal clang of a base hit. The sound of the crowd. Everything was good before I met Hannah Flores. I had it under control. I was fixing my anger problems. And we were gonna make this work. We just needed more time. We needed to circle the wagons. But Hannah tricked me. She tricked me into giving her a peek inside. And she don't understand. Don't know all the history. She don't see the good. Just the bad. Then she goes off and does what she always does.

Runs her mouth.

Hannah's eyes get wet with tears. But she doesn't cry. "Why are you saying this?"

"All you ever do is talk. I am *done*." I yell it. Belt it out. Full-on Pops mode. My stomach eating itself the whole time. But I don't care. Hannah has pushed me and pushed me. And I have said things to her I ought not to have said to nobody. I see that now. I see why Pops always warned me to keep my mouth shut. A small crowd forms around us. Elsewhere, baseball is happening. An umpire yells *yer out*. I hear the other team's coach arguing the call. Two fights on the same field. Worlds apart. Her expression shifts right in front of me. Surprise. Anger. Hurt.

"We were going to that punk show," Hannah says, her voice tiny. Broken.

I speak slowly. Deliberately. Aiming my words like a fastball. "You are stuck here, Hannah. I am going places. But you are stuck here. So stop trying to hang on."

She opens her mouth to speak. Then closes it.

Then, something else.

Complete void.

She is cutting me loose. Whatever part of her heart that held on to me. She cut it in that moment.

Good.

She wipes tears from her face with the sleeve of her battle jacket. She says, "Okay." Another deep breath. "Okay. Fine. I guess I am disappointed. But I cannot say I am surprised."

She turns. Pushes through the crowd and walks the long, lonely path back to the parking lot. She looks at me over her shoulder. Stops for a second.

"Hey, Crawford," she says.

Our eyes meet. The storm inside me going buck wild.

"I know I said you were the strong silent type."

I just stare at her.

"But I'll take loud and honest every day. Every damn day."

She waits a second. I guess hoping I will respond. Maybe giving me one chance to apologize. But I keep my lips sealed.

Hannah laughs to herself. Lets out a long breath and shakes her head. "Lose my number, Crawford."

I scuff my cleats on the ground. Already, that belligerent part of me is dying down. Hannah hurries through the crowd, shouldering a kid out of her way. He turns and cusses at her. But Hannah don't care. Let the cusses fly, kid. She pulls her hood up, pops her earbuds in, and stuffs her hands in her jacket pockets.

Some voice in me says I should go after her. Tell her I'm sorry. Tell her everything floating around inside me that I do not understand. Tell her there's just one person on this whole planet can make it better. And it's her. And I *do* wanna go to that punk show. I want to tell her I am scared.

That's what this is really about.

I'm *scared*. I'm *hurt*.

And I don't know what to do about it.

A woman's voice comes from the crowd. Calling my name.

Donna Melton.

"Crawford, I need you to come with me," she says, pushing through the crowd toward me. All brown. Folder still tucked under her arm. She holds out her hand. Like I'm gonna take it. And it's like, *Lady. The world is ending. And I am not running for cover with you.*

But I am running.

Away.

Because there is nothing here for me.

I bolt alongside the dugout. Down past the concession stand and through the parking lot. There are tears coming from my eyes, and the moment I climb into the truck it all comes out. I fire up the engine, full-on sobbing, and squall tires as I drive past Hannah, who has made it to the sidewalk outside the park.

I floor it, watching Hannah get smaller and smaller in my rearview mirror, her arms crossed around her body, her face obscured in the shadows of her hoodie. She never looks up. I watch her as I drive away. I watch her until I can't see her no more.

ON SOME EMO SHIT
BLINK-182

I fly around the unpaved back roads. Driving like I do not care if the tires explode. Like it'd be a good thing to roll down the embankment and into the valley below.

They would not find me for weeks.

They would not find me until I was a festering skeleton in the woods. Trapped upside down. My mouth hinged open. Probably a little family of squirrels moved in, setting up a little homestead inside my vacant skull.

There is nothing in my rearview mirror but billowing clouds of dirt. Without even trying, I end up at the creek where me and Hannah sat with our feet in the water. I get out and stand on the bank. Watch eddies swirl around jutting rocks, the sound of trickling water like people far off whispering. I lower into a squat, my elbows on my knees. And all I can think is, *What have I done?*

Hannah told me to lose her number.

I take out my phone. Think about texting her. Think about her on top of me. Think about her kisses. About the simple fact that when I went off the deep end at the ballpark, when I let meanness come out of my mouth and land on her, her first reaction wasn't anger. She didn't get defensive. She didn't strike back. Her first reaction was to see through my nonsense. To see that I was hurt. She wanted to help.

And how did I repay her?

I put my face in my hands.

What have I done?

I take out my phone. Thumb through the contacts until I find hers. Delete her number just like she wanted. Then, I take one last read through all our messages. It takes a couple hours. All those texts asking how I was. At the time, I thought it was just her being polite.

Folks ask folks how they are doing. They mean it more like, *Hello.* They don't really want to know.

But rereading these...

Hannah wanted to know.

She really wanted to know.

She saw that boulder I was shouldering up the hill. And even though she had her own boulder to deal with, she wanted to help work on mine.

That's the problem with me, I guess. Pops is always saying it: I got to be tough when things get tough. My timing is so bad. I get in my own head. And when it matters most, I don't do good. You can strike out all game but hit the winning grand slam. But the opposite is true, too. You can be the best pitcher in the state all season but blow it when a scout is watching. And how you respond under pressure says a lot about how you will play in the majors. It says a lot about how you are in your whole damn life.

Pops was right about me.

He was right the whole time.

And that's exactly why I am no good for Hannah.

Or for anyone.

She wanted something real from me.

But all I can give her is fake.

I delete her text messages. Let myself cry for a little while. Hear her voice in my head when I do.

Lose my number.

Lose it.

I never did deserve this girl. So this is the universe self-correcting. One touch with my thumb. A little confirmation screen. *Are you sure?* And it's done. The whole cosmos barrels on like it oughta. No concern left for little Crawford Cope who had a fleeting moment of gladness in his heart. God's like, *No, sir, we can't have that.*

BACK HOME
YELLOWCARD

I know Pops is waiting on me back home. But where else can I go? I drive slow. Brain melting.

I pull into the driveway. I start to get out of the truck. But my hand freezes on the knob. I sit there for God knows how long. Just staring straight ahead. My soul completely checked out of my body. After a while, I shake my head. Pull myself together. Then I get out and walk up the steps.

I stop at the door. Listening. I don't know what for. The house is dead silent. So I slip in as quiet as I can, thinking maybe I can sneak to my room. Lock the door.

I creep through the den. Down the hallway. But I got to walk past the entryway to the living room, where Pops likes to sit watching old baseball games. I can hear one now. Another one of Pops' old games. The low murmur of the announcers, saying his name. Over and over. *Hunter Cope. Hunter Cope. Hunter Cope.*

I take a quiet step into the open. Pops' head is tipped to one side, facing the television and away from me. I take another step. Pops moves. Just a little. He says, "That you?"

I stand silent.

Pops lowers the leg rest of the recliner. He wobbles to his feet. Then falls backward into the chair cursing. Drunk. Or stoned. Or both. My heart sinks to my belly. I think about bolting back through the front door. But he jerks to his feet like a zombie from a horror film. Sudden, alarming speed. He turns and says, "What are you doing here?"

"I live here."

"You . . . you ain't s'posed to be."

"Pops."

"You . . . ain't s'posed to be here."

"Where's Sutton?"

Cope Field

"That woman . . ." His eyes are wild, glistening. His nose is red, like he has been sobbing. There is no fight in this man. And that puts a little calm in my stomach. Enough where I can interact with him without thinking it's about to come to blows.

I help him back into his seat. "What's going on?"

He doesn't seem to hear me. He groans. Puts both hands on his eyes. We sit in silence for a long time. Feels like I am beside his hospital bed, and he's dying from cancer or something. Feels like I ought to hold his hand. But no. Me and Pops don't touch like that much.

Eventually, his expression shifts. This slow-growing grin. Like he is remembering something hilarious. Or else cracking completely. He says, "I was so pissed about the field, Craw. You have no idea."

"I got some idea."

"And I knowed right away it was you."

He's still smiling. Given the topic, it's a little scary. I start to think I ought to leave again. Just go back to my car and drive away.

His hand closes on my wrist. Tight. "But the more I thought about it," he says, "the more I realized it was a blessing."

"A blessing?" I try and pull my hand away. But his knuckles go white.

"We gonna turf the field. Put in drainage. New dugouts. New everything."

I am dumbfounded by the idea of turfing a little league baseball field in the middle of nowhere. But my head goes straight to painting the old dugouts with Hannah. The little freckles of white paint on her cheeks and nose. Our first conversations.

"I painted the dugouts," I say.

"Sure. And now there'll be even better ones."

I try my wrist again. He still won't let go. So I say what I think he wants to hear. "It sounds fantastic, Pops. Just fantastic. Just what all the hillbillies out here need."

He laughs and lets go of my wrist. "You're making fun. This whole thing gonna cost about thirty grand. Already talked to an architect, looked at some blueprints, and everything. And I got a contractor hired with a whole crew. They gonna knock it out lickety-split. I paid extra for that 'cause I want it done by summer. This is no small thing, Craw. People will come from all around to play on this field. And if it's going to have my name on it . . . if it's gonna have *my* name on it, then it has to be the best."

I get up and walk to the kitchen. Pops' eyes follow me. I get a soda. Crack it open. Nearly kill the thing in one swig. Then I rummage through the cabinets and start stuffing chips and corn snacks and whatever else I can find in my mouth. Stress-eating like Big Time. Then I walk down the hallway and try Sutton's door. It swings open to an empty bed, and I stand there staring at it. It's early enough he could be somewhere else in the house. But the sickness in my stomach says he is not.

My hands start to tremble.

I walk back out to the living room. "Where is Sutton?" I ask, and Pops rolls his eyes. But they stay rolled away from me. The old man won't look my direction, so I repeat myself. Slower. "Where is *Sutton?*"

Pops' eyes crawl back toward me. "Crawford," he says. My name coming out like a rasp. "I am so, so sorry for what I done." He pauses, cries into his hands for a few seconds. Then he rasps, "Your momma was the most beautiful woman in the world. She would be so... so *hurt* by this... by what I've become... by what I've done..."

I swallow. We don't talk about Momma much. I am shocked he's gone there.

"You know how proud of you she was, Craw?" he says. "She'd always tell me *baseball is not everything.* We'd lose a game, or you'd do some boneheaded nonsense on the field, and she'd say *he's just a little boy, Hunter.*" He laughs. His eyes somewhere distant. Remembering. "Mommas are supposed to say that kind of thing. I *needed* to hear it more than most daddies, I guess. I just... I just wanted everyone to see what I saw."

"To see what, Pops?" I choke the words out. They snag in my throat. But I get them out.

His eyes fall on me, his stare hot in the dark of the living room. "Your greatness, Craw. Better'n I ever was. And that's—" He pauses. Starts to cry again. "That's on and off the field. Especially off the field."

"Pops."

"What?"

"Where is *Sutton?*"

Pops sobs. His chest jerking up and down. He shakes his head like, *No, no, no.* He says, "It shouldn'ta been like this."

"Like what?" My blood turns to ice. Feels like I am freezing to death. I scream this next part. Because I need him to know I am serious. That he cannot drag this moment out any longer. "Where is Sutton?"

Cope Field

His eyes drift to mine. Streaked and red around the edges. His lip trembles. "They took him away from us. Just like I told you they would."

IN TOO DEEP
SUM 41

Pops says he came down from the bleachers after Coach Rodriguez benched me. Says he was going to lay into me for not taking my opportunities seriously. How many baseball players in this damn country would kill to pitch in front of an MLB scout? He was going to lay into Coach, too. Lay into everybody on staff. Because: "One, yes, you was not pitching a great game. But two, they oughta give you a chance to turn things around. Coach knew you had scouts in the crowd. But Coach cared more about his precious winning record than he cared about Crawford Cope's future. And you know what I say to that? I say don't coach high school ball you feel that way."

Pops says he got halfway to the dugout when someone called his name. He stopped, figuring it was a fan or some old fogey wanting to give him hell.

But it wasn't a fan.

I already know what he's about to say. It was Donna Melton. And Pops says she had two police officers with her. "She said they's been a report made against me, said she needs me to come to the office, make a statement, to which I said hell no, not without my lawyer. And then she tells me they are taking the boys away from me until this thing is resolved. Like *right now*. Big Time had no idea what was going on. She started using this baby voice on him. Saying, 'You're going to come with me for a little while. Don't worry. Everything is gonna be fine.'"

I have a lump in my throat thinking about it.

Pops says he fought and argued and asked her why. Over and over: *Why are you doing this? Why here? Why right now?* "You know what she tole me? She said, 'Right here, right now, so you can't make a scene.' Then she pointed over by the gate, and there was two patrol cars parked out front, more officers standing there, waiting in case things got bad. So I . . ." He struggles to get the words out. "So I got down on my knee and hugged Big Time. Tole him I was sorry. Said he needed to go with the lady. Said for him not to worry none. That it'll work out."

He stops for a long time. I listen to the soft sound of him weeping.

"I couldn't do a damn thing about it, Craw. And she was supposed to round you up, too. That's why I said you shouldn't be here. They probably got officers out looking for you right now. Hell, Craw. They probably driving past our place. Making calls. About to come up here and kick down the door."

"What should I do?"

Pops shrugs. His eyes drift away from me.

"Pops?"

He lets out a long breath. Reins in his tears. "You ever feel cursed, Craw?"

"Cursed?"

"Like God don't want you happy? And you gotta pay tenfold for whatever good you ever had in life?"

I love and hate this man at the same time. And it is emotional whiplash trying to discern which side I am sitting in right now. I want to make him happy. I want to fight him. I want to go get in my truck, find Big Time, and never come back to Quiet County.

I walk to the den and peel back the curtains, peering into the dark. Our house is a long way from the main road, behind a gate and at the end of a long driveway. But I can glimpse the highway through the trees. There is nothing but dark, but I still feel like there are eyes on me. Like there are patrol cars cruising in the distance, their radios chattering my name.

I slink back into the dark. Feeling like a criminal. A little fragment of my brain says, *It's not you that done wrong, Craw. Holler his name through the woods. Get the attention of Donna Melton. Tell her every secret you've hid until they run their pathetic hero Hunter Cope straight outta Quiet County.*

And still there's this other part of my brain saying, *No. No to all that.*

This is my family.

For all that means.

For all the hurts that come with it.

This is my family.

I take ten deep breaths. Trying to calm my racing heart.

Then I remember: When Pops saw me tonight, what was the first thing out of his mouth? It wasn't telling me straight away what happened. It wasn't talking about how we could get Big Time back. It wasn't wondering how Big Time is doing or asking if I thought he was scared.

No.

The main thing on Pops' mind, with his son taken into state custody, was the status of a dilapidated baseball field in the middle of nowhere with his name on it.

Artificial turf. Fake grass. Fake everything.

Fake as my VR meditation videos.

I separate from my body again. Walk back into the living room. See Pops now opening a beer can. He takes a long swig, then plummets backward onto the couch. Hits it so hard the entire thing rocks back and slams to the hardwood. Pops lies there, laughing at himself. But it is not funny. Not even a little bit. He sees the look in my eye, takes a defensive expression and says, "What're you looking at?"

"Nothing."

"Ain't you gonna help your old man up?" When he sees I'm not inclined to help, he pulls himself up on the wall. His legs limp and wobbly. Then he stands there for a second, looking like he might throw up.

I start to walk past him, toward my room. I'm gonna pack a bag. Gonna find Sutton. And we're gonna make a real life for ourselves. I shoulder Pops on the way. Half accident. Half not. He springs to life like a coiled cobra. Grabs me by the neck and slings me in a circle against the wall. My backside punches a hole through the plaster, and for a terrifying second, he's got his hands closed around my neck. We lock eyes.

And there is nothing there. Just empty void staring down at me. And it's like:

I got to get out of here.

Away from him.

Because it's clear now. Every bad thing in my life, every molecule of anger inside me, got put there by him. He is making me into a statue of himself. Chipping away little flecks of who I am supposed to be. Until all that's left is a little withered statue, formed in his image.

I shove him as hard as I can. Put everything I have into it. Drive with my legs. Roaring and grunting like a wild animal. Pops tumbles backward over the tipped couch. He hits the far wall so hard the house shakes. And above him, that seventy-two-inch television—still showing clips from one of his old games, his own young face grinning the entire time—teeters off the mantle and crashes down over his head. He cries out in pain. But I am not hanging around to see the damage.

I hurry through the front door and jump in the truck. And before my heart rate has calmed down, I am on the highway, my foot all the way to the floorboard, all of the Ozarks a blur past my window.

DEAD!
MY CHEMICAL ROMANCE

I drive without thinking. Letting the road pull me along. Following my headlights. But I am not surprised where I end up.

Cope Field.

I stop in the middle of the highway. Get out of the truck and stand in the dark. Below, I can see the old, dilapidated field. The dugouts, newly blue and white. And the ruined patch of grass in the middle, where I pulled donuts the other night.

The stars are vast above me, glittering like the eddies of a creek bed on a summer afternoon. Makes me think of Big Time. All his outer space nonsense. One time, on another night like this, looking up at a similar sky, he said to me, "Did you know there are like nine thousand stars visible to the naked eye?"

"I did not," I said.

"You can only see about two thousand at any given time on Earth."

I didn't say anything. And because Big Time hates silence, he kept on.

"Did you know there are one hundred billion stars in the Milky Way? And there are more stars in space than grains of sand on all the beaches in the world? And it would take you a hundred thousand years to travel across our galaxy, and there are at least a hundred billion galaxies total in the universe? And we are all made out of the dust of the Big Bang? And the universe is expanding? And some scientists think it might even shrink again one day and everything you know and don't know will smash into each other? They call that right there the Big Crunch."

Back then, I did not think hard upon it.

But right now.

I am small.

And in control of nothing.

Cope Field

The universe outside us is infinitely complex. And so is the one inside us. Complexity upon complexity. It is staggering, and I cannot breathe. I stumble back into the truck and slam the door. Sit there for a long time, my hands pressed into my eyes. No clue where I should go. But knowing deep down where I *want* to go.

I look up at Hannah's house. Dark on the hill.

I have to apologize to her. Even if she don't ever want to be friends with me, I want to tell her I am wrong. That it's me who messed up whatever good thing we had going. That I cracked under pressure. That I wish I'd just pulled her into my arms. Held her. Told her I was scared. That even if she did make the report, I know she only did it because she cared about me.

I put the truck in drive. And before I can stop myself, I drive all the way up to her front porch. I stop the truck, get out, and stand there looking up at the windows, wondering which one is hers. Thinking maybe I'll tap on one and sneak inside. Like she did for me.

I've never been inside her home. I have no clue which window is hers.

But I am brave tonight.

Or crazy.

Already threw hands with Pops. Might as well keep this disaster going.

I walk up on the front porch. Cup my hands and peer through a window. There is a couch against the far wall. Fabric torn with stuffing poofing out from the edges. A small box television, the kind you see in old movies about the '80s. The coffee table is loaded with soda and beer cans, cigarette cartons and magazines. Whole thing gives me the creeps. A liminal space. A peek into a world where I do not belong. Rich boy, go home.

Movement catches my eye, coming from one of the back rooms. And I am stupid enough to think it might be Hannah. But the tall, rangy shape, the gleam of light reflecting on a bald head, wises me up right away. I back away from the window. Hold my breath. Pray to God Shotgun didn't see me.

But the door cracks open. And the long slender end of a rifle emerges from the darkness.

Shotgun's face appears from the shadows. His eyes hidden in the dark. He says, "You trying to die?" His voice calm as a pond in the dead of winter.

"I was hoping to see Hannah."

"It is one in the morning."

"I'm sorry."

Shotgun steps into the moonlight. He lowers the end of the rifle and quietly closes the door behind him. I catch a glimpse of that skull tattoo on the back of his head as he does. Then he turns and leans against the porch railing. Props the weapon up beside him and dips into his pocket. He takes out a box of cigarettes, taps one out, and sticks it into the corner of his mouth. Then he cracks a butane lighter and dips the cigarette into the dancing flame, his face glowing orange. I watch all this in silence. Not sure what to think. He looks up at me over the flame. Says, "You want one?"

"I do not. Is Hannah awake? Can I talk to her?"

He shrugs. "She's not here."

"Where's she at?"

He shrugs again. "She runs off sometimes. I can't stop her no more. So I don't try. Anyway, I ain't sure she wants to see you, Craw."

"Why not?"

"She come home crying earlier. Which I reckon has to do with somethin' between y'all. So my question to you is: Why are you on my front step at one in the morning? You come to say sorry? Come to try and smooth things over with her?" He takes a long drag on the cigarette and breathes smoke into the night sky. "Hannah don't cry easy. I'll tell you that. She don't forgive easy, either."

There is something about his eyes I hate. They bulge out too much. And they're too wet and slimy looking. And the smile on his mouth don't touch those eyes. Nothin' in those grimy marbles but malevolence. I take a step backward toward my truck. Feel uneasy with that gun sitting there. Even if it isn't in his hands.

Shotgun says, "Why don't you stay a minute?"

"I think I should not have come here."

"No, you really should not have."

A white truck drives past the house. Lights throwing shadows across the lawn. We watch it until it disappears around the bend. Shotgun's house is a good distance from the highway that separates it from Cope Field, but it's still in clear view of the road. It's tough to see good in the dark. But for a second, I have this horrible thought: *That's Pops' truck. Looking for me.*

"I called in that report on your Pops," Shotgun says.

Cope Field

It is so unexpected my mouth falls open. "What?"

Shotgun watches me closely. And I feel naked. Exposed. Like this man has pulled back my shower curtain.

"Craw, I been around your family off and on ever since you come back to Quiet County. Did you know that?" He inhales smoke. Lets tendrils come from his nostrils. I guess he's trying to say he's been Pops' dealer all along. From his tone, I think he believes this will come as another shock. But it doesn't. Because I think Pops did get clean for a while. But then he fell back into it. And like that on repeat. My whole life has been a mashup of two versions of him. Stoned. Not stoned. But it don't matter. Not really. Because remove Shotgun Sam from the equation, and there'd be some other walking scarecrow more than willing to push pills on my father.

"I like you, Craw," Shotgun says. "We're survivors, Craw. *Survivors.* One and the same. You ain't the type to lay down and take it. Not the type to call out for help. You're gonna do whatever you gotta do to survive."

I try to keep my face steady.

He points the glowing ember of his cigarette at me. "You put forward a pretty picture. Paint up that hero daddy of yours nice and good. Keep quiet and keep the bullshit hidden. But I know it's all fake. You got a mean streak hidden in there. Just like your daddy. I can see it. Even if nobody else does. I can see it 'cause I got one, too. I'm what you might call the loud, angry type. The *I'm gonna make it your problem* type. But it's all the same thing."

He laughs at my expression. Because it's clear that I am not following. Like any of this is funny.

Then his laughter catches his throat, and he coughs a loogie into the grass. "I seen them welts on your kid brother. Seen you all swollen up. I knowed right away it weren't no baseball. Weren't nothin' else you might make up, either. Them's lies you cook up to explain why your life is like it is. Because it hurts too bad for someone to know you ain't what they think you are. You ain't lucky. Ain't the golden boy of Quiet County. You're white trash. Like all of us."

"I'm not."

"You are. And it's okay that you are."

"Pops takes care of me."

"Does he?"

"He's hard sometimes. 'Cause it makes me better."

Shotgun shakes his head. We sit in silence for a while. Listen to the crickets.

Eventually, he says, "My old man used to whoop on me, too. I know what it's like. Vowed to myself I wouldn't ever put my hands on any kid of mine. But I don't want you mixed up about me, either. I ain't make that hotline call outta goodness. Or because I wanna save your life or nothing like that."

The crickets go silent. Somewhere far away, I hear cattle braying. My whole body is hot listening to him. Fearful. Like he is holding the truth to my whole life. And if I can just coax it out of him, I can go back to fixing everything.

"Why did you?" I say, my voice quiet. Barely louder than the AC unit buzzing from the side of the house.

"Revenge, Craw. Pure and simple."

"Revenge?"

"Your old man pointed that gun at me. But it was bigger than that moment. Bigger than just a gun. That was a betrayal of trust, Craw. I helped your pa do all kinds of things he ain't had nobody else willing to help him with. I helped him when he needed it most. And he thanked me by pointing a gun at me. Threatenin' to kill me."

"Jesus Christ." This is full-on meth head speak. Makes no sense.

"I'm not a good person, Crawford. I ain't never pretended otherwise."

The sound of cicadas mixes with some far-off hound dog hollering *arooooooo*. And me and this villain. Alone underneath it all. Another truck drives past on the highway. Again, my heart in my throat. Scared to death it is Pops, out patrolling the county, looking for me.

Shotgun blows smoke straight into the air. Then he finishes his cigarette, stubs it out on the deck railing, and goes about lighting a second one.

"My old man was like half grizzly bear, half teddy bear," Shotgun says. "A tender hand one second. Claws the next. You never could guess. Liked to get real drunk and bust up the house. Locked me in a bedroom closet for a whole day one time."

I don't want to know about this. But I don't see a way out.

"The worst thing was myself. How I thought about it. The reason I thought he done all that to me."

"He was hard because he loved you," I say, almost automatically.

Shotgun smiles. Little nubbin teeth flashing in the light of his cigarette. "See, Craw?" He lets it hang in the air for a moment. "We are the same."

The sounds of the cicadas rise in unison. Like they are at the most important part of whatever song they are singing. It settles in the pit of my stomach. I swallow. Wipe sweat away from my eyes.

"You want I'll kill him for you," Shotgun says, not looking at me.

A breeze whips through the yard.

"All you have to do is never say a word about it. You were never here. And you don't know what happened to him or who coulda done this."

The cicadas fall silent. My heart thuds in my chest.

"Every red cent of his money is yours the moment he dies. Think of what you could do for yourself with that money. What you might could do for that little brother of yours."

A long time passes.

I don't know how long.

My brain unable to process what he has said to me.

Shotgun finishes his cigarette. Then he laughs and claps a hand on my shoulder. "I'm just fucking with you, Craw. Jesus Christ. You shoulda seen your face. You were actually thinking about it."

"I wasn't," I say.

"Well, ain't you a dandy."

"Shotgun," I say.

He stares at me in the dark.

"When did you get that tattoo?"

His hand goes to his scalp. "This? Oh, well—" But he doesn't finish his sentence. He stops. Head inclined toward the road. Listening. Then we both see that white truck come crawling down the highway from the opposite direction. No question it is the same truck. And I see:

It *is* Pops' truck.

It hesitates at the end of the driveway. Shotgun says, "We got company," and he takes a step toward the rifle.

It all happens so fast I cannot take it in.

Pops floors it, roaring up the gravel road toward the house. Shotgun picks up the gun but barely has time to shoulder it. The truck door hinges open. Gunshots set my ears ringing.

I fall to the ground, curl into a ball, my hands over my head. Start calling out *Jesus* over and over and over. And I am not being at all profane.

Shotgun hits the ground beside me. The rifle clatters down the steps and into the grass. He groans, his hands clasped across his belly. He tries to sit up, but he can't. He looks at me. Eyes wild. Scared.

He whispers, "Help me." His voice wet. Raspy. And small.

Pops appears at the bottom of the stairs. Pistol still in his hand. He says, "Get up. Come with me."

I have no choice.

I get up. Walk down the steps and stand beside the truck.

Pops walks up the steps. His footfalls loud in the quiet dark. From behind, I watch him point the gun at Shotgun. He pulls the trigger. One. Two. Three times.

YOU
BAD RELIGION

I puke in the grass. I cry and scream so loud, Pops has to smack me across the face to get me to stop.

He says, "Craw, stay with me here."

And I'm like, *Stay with you where? You shot a man four times right in front of me.* And beyond belief, he isn't dead yet. He's lying there, arms still posturing. Rasping through wet lungs. Shotgun's eyes drift toward mine. Little flecks bright red on his lips. He wheezes for a while. Then spasms. His eyes roll backward in his head, and his entire body starts jerking around. I watch his hands. For some reason, I can't stop staring at them, clenched in the air in front of him like he is wrestling with some invisible creature.

Then he is calm.

Perfectly calm.

I keep expecting him to wake up. Like the killer at the end of a horror flick.

But I am watching a life leave a body.

I will never forget it.

Pops shakes my shoulders. "I need you to listen to me. Right now."

I nod my head a little. Thinking, *Go on, old man. Fix this.* Knowing there is no way. The trajectory of my life is forever altered. Through and through. Like all of the cosmos turned its slate face downward at me and screamed, *It's over, kid.*

I am all the way out of my body. Pops saying, "I need you to back me up, Craw. When the police come up here, you got to tell them he had that gun pointed at you. Are you listening to me?"

I am.

And I am not.

My eyes won't focus. My brain won't stop spinning.

He shakes me again. I feel like a limp doll in his hands. He is yelling at me now. "Please, Craw. They already think I beat you kids half to death. They ain't gonna believe I shot him for some kinda self-defense if you don't back me up. It's God's truth, Craw. He had that gun out. Instinct took over. I'll tell them I had to do it to save your life. And you gotta back me up. Don't say anything. Just say what I said is true. That he was gonna shoot you with it. And I had to shoot him first."

He's so desperate.

So shaken.

And the part of me that *is* him wants to help him so badly.

I swallow down every inch of that swirling toilet bowl inside my head. Look him straight in the eyes and say, "I won't say a word."

Pops gets on the phone right away. Only he don't call 911. No, he calls a deputy straight on his cell phone. One of the fellas from his old state championship baseball team. Calls him by his first name. "Evan, I think you oughta get out here to Jerusalem... that white house across from Cope Field... yeah... Sam Ledbetter... yeah, that's the one... Listen, Evan, listen, I gotta tell you something..."

I sit in the grass, my knees pulled up to my chin, looking at Shotgun. His eyes are stuck open. Staring straight at me. Unblinking. His expression blank but somehow accusing. Like, *How could you? How could you let this happen to me?* Once upon a time, he was somebody's little baby. It is terrible to think about. Was he like Big Time? Full of possibilities? Until that daddy of his squashed everything good out of him? Was he like me? A good baseball player? Pops said they was on that team together. What went wrong? What in the hell went wrong?

My eyes shift back to Pops.

"Came up here looking for my son... he been seeing Sam's daughter, you know, so I figured he run off up here... yeah, yeah, I know DHS is looking for him... all I meant to do was find him and then give them a call... Evan, you gotta listen to me for a second and stop asking questions..."

My stomach turns. I lean over and dry heave in the grass.

"He had my boy up on the porch with a rifle," Pops says. "Pointed it at him. I didn't know what to do, so I got out of my truck with my pistol. I shot him, Evan. He's dead. I done it to save my boy... yeah, no... the boy is in shock... I don't blame him... I know... I know they'll want to talk to him... but listen, Evan, if you could... go easy on him. He's been through a lot..."

My belly feels turned inside out. But it's not done spasming in my gut. I dry heave some more. Both hands on the ground. Then I start sobbing, falling over to my side, pulling my body in tight. Pops stands over me. Still on the phone. "We'll wait right here for y'all... yes, of course... yes... yeah, Crawford will tell you the same thing... yes... I'll see you soon, Evan."

Then he hangs up. He looks down his nose at me. For a second, I think he might kick me in the ribs. He shakes his head slowly. Says, "Pull yourself together, Craw. This is important."

WHERE IS MY MIND?
PIXIES

Donna Melton. All the way out here at Cope Field. Along with the Arkansas State Police, the county sheriff, and who knows who all else. A detective asks me to come sit with him inside Hannah's house. He's got on a suit. Badge on his hip. I follow him through the front door and to the kitchen table, where he's already got his things: a cup of gas station coffee, a notebook, and an ink pen. I sit down, and he puts a little recorder on the table between us.

Pops is nowhere to be seen. Donna Melton sits beside the detective. She's got her own recorder and her own notebook. No coffee, though. This time, she isn't all brown. She's got on pink. Pink shoes. Pink skirt. Pink blouse. The detective says his name is Louis Brawner. Says he just has a few simple questions.

"Oughta be no problem," he says. "We can put this thing to bed lickety-split."

I sit with my arms folded across my body.

"You can start by telling us where you went after the baseball game yesterday," he says, picking up the ink pen.

Donna leans forward. But I don't say anything. I'm having these heart palpitations. All this electric anxiety screaming at me. Saying, *They think you helped kill Shotgun. They're blaming you.*

"Craw, we just want to know what happened. But you got to walk us through it," Donna says.

"Am I in trouble?" My voice sounds small and broken in my own ears.

"Are you?" the detective says.

I don't say nothing.

"Start with where you went after the game," Brawner says. "Tell me everything you can remember. All the way up until we got here."

Through the side window, I see them put a sheet over Shotgun's body. A man stands nearby taking photos. The flash bounces through our windows, illuminating the entire kitchen. I look around at Hannah's house. Her *home*. Locks on the pantry drawers, just like she said.

"Take your time," Brawner says.

But no words will come out of my mouth. Not one single sound. The detective's eyes stare straight into mine. But I am not here. I am a million miles away. Somewhere that is nothing like this place. Where nothing hurts, and nobody is asking me any questions. I am thinking about floating over mountains. Taking deep breaths. Thinking, *If I don't speak, then Pops will speak for me. And he'll speak our way straight out of this. Just keep your mouth shut, Crawford. Keep it shut tight, and don't never tell nobody what you know.*

"Are you afraid of your father? Are you often afraid of him?" he says.

Another flash. Our shadows thrown against the wall. Brawner takes a sip of coffee, then gets ready to write whatever I say.

But still, I keep silent.

Brawner waves a hand in front of my face. "You okay in there, kid?"

"He's been through a lot," Donna says.

Brawner thinks for a beat. Then says, "Listen, it's my job to catch the bad guys. I am not saying your pops is a bad guy, but in order to rule that out, I need you to talk to me. I can't do my job unless you talk to me. I will sit here as long as you need me to sit here."

Donna says, "He's in shock."

Another flash. White. Black. Dark. Light. My hands tremble. The scabs still hurt if I touch them.

A long silence. The sound of an ink pen scratching on paper. Donna says, "You're very brave, Crawford."

I don't say anything.

"It's going to be okay," Donna tells me. But her eyes tell me the opposite. It's not okay. It never will be okay again. I am not brave. Not one little bit brave. Pops' words come drifting to me from outer space. One of his many baseball life lessons. A thing he used to say about timing. *It don't matter if you strike out all game if you hit the walk-off grand slam at the end.*

Do the right thing.

At the right time.

This feels like one of those moments.

Outside, the flash. The dead body. The endless dark through the bottoms of the trees.

Donna says, "Why don't we let him rest. Try again tomorrow?"

The detective frowns and turns off the recorder.

POISON HEART
RAMONES

That same night, they load me up in the back of a vehicle. I'm so checked out, I more or less let it happen. Donna gets in the driver's side, starts the engine, and backs out of the driveway. I keep thinking she is driving me home. But after a while, I realize she is heading the wrong direction.

"Where are you taking me?" I ask.

She looks at me in the rearview mirror. "Don't worry about anything, Crawford. It's going to be okay."

"Where are you taking me?" I ask again.

"You're in state custody."

"What's that mean?"

Her eyes cut back to the road. "You'll be in a foster home for a little while. Don't worry about it, okay? You'll be cared for while everything gets sorted out."

"Is my brother there?"

Donna's eyes look sad. She says, "Why don't you rest. We'll talk more after you have some rest."

I want to scream. I want to kick out the window. Because I know already why she don't want to talk about it. She don't want to tell me that all my fears come true. They separated us. Broke up our family.

I lie down on the seat. Watch the stars through the window.

Cry softly for myself.

Nothing is good anymore.

Not one thing.

She drives me for almost an hour. Until it is almost morning. A man greets us outside a house. Donna speaks to him in hushed tones. He leads me to a small bedroom in the back of the house. The man says, "You can sleep right here. Sleep all you want. I know you been through it."

Then he leaves, snapping the door closed behind him.

Donna comes in soon after. She says, "This is temporary. We'll get you someplace more permanent as soon as we can."

"Where is my brother?"

Donna looks like she wants to hug me. But she heads back to the door. Before she leaves, she turns and says, "You'll see him again, Crawford. I promise."

Maybe I sleep a little. But I keep waking up. My head full of nightmares. My phone is dead, and I have no charger. And I can't bring myself to get out of this bed and step through the door. I don't want to see what is on the other side. Don't want to find out answers to any of the questions rolling around my brain.

A roach crawls across the ceiling. Meandering around pointlessly. I watch it walk the full length of the wall then disappear beneath some paneling.

Someone knocks on my door. I don't say anything, hoping they will leave. But the door cracks. And Donna's face appears in that small space. She sees that I'm awake, clicks on the light, and comes in. "Crawford, are you feeling okay today?"

"Yes."

"Would you like to talk some more about what happened last night?"

"No."

"Crawford, this is my house. You are welcome to any food in the fridge or in the pantry. You can watch television in the living room. Whatever you are comfortable with, okay? You're here for a couple days."

"Then where?"

"That's being decided."

"With Sutton?"

"Crawford, I don't want to promise you anything, but the state does try and keep families together. It doesn't always work out though."

I feel panicky again. This room is small. I bet this whole house is small. They got no right to uproot my family like this. I coulda watched Big Time at our home. I coulda kept him safe. Coulda drove him to school and kept his life normal.

But I bet he's in some roach home, too.

Probably scared.

Probably crying himself to sleep.

I hate it. Want to pull my hair out thinking about it.

I pull the blanket over my head and roll away from her. She stands there a long time. "Look, I'm just going to be as blunt with you as I can. Because I think you need to hear this. I know you've gone through a lot, and I know it's scary, and I know you are confused, but you need to think hard and decide what is best for you and Sutton. Because I can promise that's telling the truth about what happened. I know it's hard. I know you love your father, but that's the situation you are in."

She leaves me with that thought. And I don't see her again for hours, until she knocks on my door to say there's dinner.

I don't come out for that, either, so she comes back with a plate of two slices of pizza, plus a Cherry Coke.

"I don't like any of this," I say. Even though my stomach is growling.

"You want a different soda?"

"No, I don't like any of this."

She leaves the pizza on a dresser nearby. But I don't eat it.

We go on like this for another day. I come out of my room to use the bathroom. But then I am right back in. Donna checks on me sometimes. But I don't talk. All I want is to get out of this place.

That night, she makes Hamburger Helper. I eat it alone in my room, because I am damn near starving to death by this point.

"Glad to see you eating," Donna says from the doorway.

I just chew.

"I got some good news," she says.

I chew some more. Don't talk. Don't even look at her.

"They are gonna run by your house to pick up some things for you tomorrow. Try and write down everything you need, because there won't be another chance to go over there for a long while." She hands me a pocket-sized composition notebook and a little felt-tipped pen.

I open the notebook and stare at the blank pages.

What do I need?

It feels so stupid to be in this situation.

"I need my whole house. How about that?" I say.

"Nice try. We can't bring everything, so just pick stuff that's most important."

I touch the pen to the page. Watch the ink bleed out. Then I write:

playstation
nolan ryan poster

Donna looks at the list. "That's it? What about clothes?"

So I add:

jordans
whatever clothes
my truck

"There we go," Donna says. "I can't promise they'll get everything. But they'll try. Okay? And I have more good news, Crawford."

I look up at her.

"You're going back to school on Monday. And after school, I'll pick you up, and all your stuff will be waiting for you at your permanent placement."

That doesn't hit me like good news. I keep thinking I can't sink any lower, can't feel any worse. And then words come out of this woman's mouth, and I find a way to get there. "Permanent?"

"I mean more permanent than this."

Then a small hope rises in my chest, like a beam of sunlight breaking through the forest. "Will Sutton be there?"

Donna Melton smiles at me. And I have hated this woman, but this is for sure the best smile I have seen in a long, long time.

HOUSE IS NOT MY HOME
ZEBRAHEAD

Donna Melton picks me up after school. She asks how I'm doing, if I'm feeling any better, if there's anything she can do to help me. But I keep my mouth shut, shaking my head no to each of her questions. She drives us through Hosanna proper, which ain't much, then pulls off into this tiny neighborhood, a buncha *Little House on the Prairie* lookin' houses and mobile homes. We drive down that gravel road for a while, then she pulls into the driveway of a small brick house, bigger than most the houses we've driven past, but still small.

My truck is already parked in the driveway, which I am happy to see.

There's a house right next door, sharing a fence. A woman on the front porch, snapping green beans into a silver bowl. She looks up through her giant bifocals when we pull in, I guess wondering who the new kid is gonna be at her neighbor's house.

Before I get out of Donna's car, she says, "Hold up, Crawford."

So I do.

"Have you thought anymore about talking with the detective? With me? About what all you've been through and what you saw that night?"

That question puts so much anxiety in my heart. I start looking for the door handle.

Donna says, "Take a deep breath, Crawford. It's okay. We have time. Just calm down."

But I am out the door. Standing in the front yard.

The woman on the other side of the fence calls out to me immediately. Her face is a map of lines. But she is smiling. "Welcome, young feller. Where are you in from?"

I stand there with my heart beating fast. Tell her, "Nowhere."

The old woman laughs. Goes on snapping green beans. "You let granny know you need somethin'."

Cope Field

Up at the house—my new home, I guess—a woman steps through the front door, pushing a man in a wheelchair. They take a ramp down to the yard, and Donna gets out and greets them. They talk for a while, and I go check out my truck. The cab is filled up with some things from my house. But I don't see my PlayStation. Just some clothes. A couple pairs of Jordans. And rolled up with a rubber band on the floorboard, my Nolan Ryan poster.

"Crawford," Donna calls out. "Come say hello."

I walk over. Shake hands with both of them. Because it feels like the right thing to do. "Where is Sutton?" I ask.

"Inside," the woman says.

Donna says, "This is Beth and Adam Wooster. They'll be taking care of you."

"Can I go see Sutton?"

"Of course," Adam says.

But when I look up, Big Time is standing in the doorway, his face bunched up in a grimace. Like I make him sick to his stomach to look at. I am so glad to see him. I want to throw my arms around him. I halfway want to throw him in my truck and run for it. But that look on his face... it freezes me in place.

"Hey, Big Time," I say, my voice cracking.

"What are you doing here?" he says.

My heart hurts hearing that.

Donna says, "He's moving in, Sutton. Isn't that great? You're together again."

Sutton shakes his head. Says flatly, "Yeah. Great."

Then he disappears inside. The screen door slams shut with a rattle of glass.

⚾

Every time I drive through our new neighborhood, I'm reminded how weird everything has gotten. Some kind of new normal. But I can't get used to it.

The only person here I like talking to at all is that old woman who lives across the fence with the thick bifocal glasses and a perma-perm. By which I mean never not permed.

She hangs out on her front porch all day doing old lady stuff like that thing where you twiddle needles with some yarn and end up with a whole damn blanket. She waves at me when I pull in the drive and hollers, "Hey there, Craw."

I ask, "Whatcha making there?"

"An afghan for that baby brother of yours." She rattles her needles together. Doing stitches or whatever in the hell you call it. "That child sure loves him some cheese singles."

I guess she's made friends with Big Time, too. Which, good for her. Because he still won't hardly talk to me.

"He'll eat 'bout anything you give him," I say, before heading inside the house. It's this small three-bedroom. No pool. No Baseball Dungeon. No nothing. These people don't even got a television. Who doesn't have a TV these days? Big Time is making the best of it, I guess. Inside, I can see him through the back kitchen window. He's sitting in one of those little inflatable swimming pools. The kind you get for toddlers to splash around in. Thing is made to look like a slice of watermelon. He's got his butt down in the water and his arms and legs out over the sides. Bag of fun-sized Cheetos on his belly. Looks like a flipped turtle sitting there. I head out the back door, hoping enough time has passed he will talk to me. He glances at me through his shades. "Ain't the same, Craw," he says. "Ain't the same *at all*."

His cheeks and nose are about as red as some 1950s Santa Claus. "You got on sunscreen?"

"No."

"Why not?"

"Too tough."

"You'll think tough tomorrow when you wake up."

"I'm in a battle of wills."

"Against the sun?"

"Yep."

"Big Time, you can't win that one."

"Watch me."

I go inside. Beth is in the kitchen, just standing there with her hands on the countertop looking down at some papers, which I guess are all the medical bills she gotta figure out some way to pay. The silver cross necklace around her neck dangles down. Catches some light.

"Where do you keep the sunscreen?" I ask.

"Little basket under the bathroom sink."

I start to leave, but she calls my name. Asks me how my day was. "Folks still treatin' you different?"

"Yep."

"We can transfer you someplace else. I don't mind driving you."

"And miss out on the state tournament? No thank you."

She smiles. Says, "You're a tough kid, Crawford."

I'm not sure if you're supposed to say thanks to somethin' like that. But I do just to be safe. Feels awkward, so I walk down the hallway, grab the lotion, and take it back out to Big Time. He's already wallowing around in protest by the time I'm out the front door. "Get that stuff away from me."

"Will you stop being a little idiot?"

"I will not."

I pop the cap on the lotion and squeeze a rope of the stuff out across his chest. Way too much. Like a glob of pancake batter on a fried piece of ham. "Rub that in."

"Jesus, Craw. Look what you done. Pops never woulda done this nonsense to me."

I let that slide. As if wearing sunscreen is the worst thing a person can have done to them. "Use the extra on your arms and cheeks."

I leave him out there cussing up a storm. Loud enough Beth goes out there to scold him. "We don't talk like that here," she says. "No, sir."

Later in our room, Big Time sits on his twin-size mattress opposite mine, chubby red arms folded across his chest. He looks at me with the fury of a man who has lost everything and says, "I will never forgive you, Craw. You know that? Never."

And it is pretty clear to me he is *not* talking about the lotion.

That night, we eat dinner around the table. Beth holds hands with Adam, who sits in his wheelchair at the end of the table, while we bless the food. Something we have never done with Pops. Maybe I done it some with Memaw back in the day, before she finally croaked. Big Time and I look up at each other at the same time like magic. Everybody got their eyes closed except us. "Bless this food for use of our bodies and our bodies to serve you. Amen."

Then it's off to bed. Because we got school tomorrow.

Something else that's foreign to us.

Bedtime.

Pops never cared when we went to bed, regardless of what day of the week it was. All he cared about was that I got up early enough to drive me and Big Time to school. So of course, neither of us is tired. I scroll through my phone for a couple hours while Big Time thumbs through this baseball stats book he picked up somewhere. He says, "Hey, look," and he shows me a page with a huge picture of Pops right in the center.

"Where'd you get that?" I ask him.

"Adam had all this in a trunk in his office."

Adam works from home, and his whole office is done up in baseball stuff. So I guess I am not surprised he's got a trunk full of extras somewhere.

"Did you ask?"

Big Time says no he didn't. And he says there was all kinds of Hunter Cope stuff in the trunk, too. Posters. Baseball cards. Even a Kansas City Royals pennant signed by Pops. And I'm like, *Great. We get away from Pops only to find ourselves with Pops' biggest fan.*

Big Time stares at the page for a long time. He touches Pops' face. Finally, he says, "Did Pops really shoot that man?"

"He did."

"Why?"

"'Cause."

"'Cause why, Craw?"

And I got no clue what to say. I guess deep down there is a part of me that doesn't want Big Time to know that Pops is a killer. There is a part of me that wants him to stay naive about it all. To still love Pops like he's always loved Pops. But the truth is the truth. I just don't know how to say it.

"Kids at school said the news called him a murderer," Big Time says. "Ain't nobody what knows him believe that. So what did you tell them, Craw? What did you tell them that made the news think he is a murderer?"

I take a long time to answer. There's no way to say it. No way to fix all the bad that's happened. Nothing I can do to make him feel better. Still. It feels rotten to break this already broken kid further. I can't tell him his favorite person on Earth rolled up and gunned this man down right in front of me. So I tell him my small version of the truth. "I didn't tell them nothing," I say. "I swear to God, I didn't tell them nothing."

He seems to relax. "Good, Craw. That's good."

A long time passes. From somewhere else in the house, I can hear country music. Dolly. Like Momma used to sing when she was happy.

I close my eyes. Feeling heavy in my chest. Begging my brain to go to sleep. To turn off these thoughts. To float away from this moment.

Big Time says, "I can't wait to get out of here."

"Yeah."

"To go back up to the house."

"Yeah."

"Me, you, and Pops. Together like we is supposed to be together. Hell, Craw, I bet he'll throw us a big ole party, he'll be so happy to see us. I know I'll be happy to see him."

I stare up at the ceiling. Wordless. Tears stinging my eyes.

THEY PLAYED BASEBALL
THE BASEBALL PROJECT

The morning of my first game since Pops was arrested, Adam rolls into my room with a baseball in his hand. He soft tosses it to himself and says, "You're quite the pitcher, I heard."

I am bracing myself to be compared to Pops.

But Adam says, "Do you know how to throw a knuckleball?"

I let out a breath. Glad to move on to something safer. "No."

Adam rolls closer. "There's no spin on a knuckleball."

"I know what a knuckleball is."

Pops hated the knuckleball. Called it a gimmick. Said he wouldn't be caught dead seeing his son throw one. Looking back, I bet Pops didn't know how. He was always making up reasons to explain his own ineptitude.

Adam holds up the ball and says, "Dig the ball in your palm far as you can. Then dig your fingernails into the leather." When I reach for the ball, he has the absolute audacity to add, "Oh, you bite your nails. Maybe you ought not do that, if you want to throw a good knuckleball."

Like, *What?*

Turns out, knuckleballers dig their nails into the leather to help stop the spin. I don't know. I zoned out a bit. I got zero cares about learning to throw a knuckleball. But lowkey, I'm impressed he knows so much about it.

After that, we load up and Beth drives us to the ballpark. Her driving. Adam in the back of the van since that's where his wheelchair lift is. Big Time stayed back home with the next-door neighbor, watching soaps. It's not a long drive compared to where we used to live. Adam has a scorekeeper's notebook and a camera bag across his lap. He says he likes to keep stats and take photos for small schools and send them to the state paper, but they almost never get published. Usually, he and Beth go up into Abner County, where he's got a nephew who plays ball.

"Nobody in sports media cares about the little guy," Adam says, as we bounce down uneven pavement outside the school. "But I think it's all important."

We pull into the park. Beth drives around back to the parking lot. I'm looking down at my phone, hoping I can pick up the school's Wi-Fi for a second, since I am all out of data. Then Beth says, "Oh no," and her tone makes my heart sink into my guts.

I peek up through the window.

There are four media vans parked in the back lot.

Several men already have cameras on their shoulders. A few well-dressed news anchors stand around chatting, their press credentials gleaming in the late afternoon sunlight.

They aren't local, either. It's national news. Borderline tabloid types. Beth drives a full circle around the park and lets us out at the gate. Which seems to evade them, at least for now. I hustle inside with my head down low, my cap pulled close to my eyes. Then I slip into the dugout, sit down, and bury my face in my hands.

I cannot do this.

Cannot answer their questions.

Cannot pitch this game with this weight on my shoulders.

Pops always said the great ones rise to the occasion. But I am coming to terms with some facts: I am not great. I never was great. I do not rise to the occasion. Ever. I break under it. I shrink. And disappear. And swallow it all down. Until I am nothing.

That is who I am.

"Yo, Craw," Luis says, plopping down beside me.

I look up at him with one eye, still hiding my face in my hands.

"Bro, you look awful," he says. He thumps a hand on my back. "You okay?"

My body wants to lock up. To tell him *I'm fine*. Tell him not to worry. Get his glove so we can warm up. That I am solid as a rock. But I'm too tired. Too beat-up. I shake my head no. Luis doesn't move his hand from my back. He considers for a second. Then he leans forward, so we are a little closer.

"You worried about everything?" he says.

"Something like that."

"Well, look, I know we don't know each other that much outside baseball, but I'm here if you need to talk. No judgment. But don't worry so much. Your padre ain't going to prison or nothing. We all know he saved your life. And this whole investigation is just a formality. That's what I think. They just gotta do it because it's their job. But they already know the truth, too. Hunter Cope is a hero. And who knows what mighta happened to you if he hadn't showed up."

I stare at a spot of concrete on the floor between my cleats. A teardrop breaks free and hits the ground.

"Luis," I whisper. All my insides raging. I should tell him. Tell him Pops really did kill that man in cold blood. I got to get this weight offa me. Gotta make it stop hurting.

I open my mouth.

"What in the hell are you doing?" Coach Rodriguez says, appearing in the door.

"What?" Luis says, throwing up his hands.

"The game starts in ten minutes! *Crawford*, you're starting. And neither of you are warmed up."

That puts a different kinda panic in my brain. A shot of adrenaline. "Aw, shit!" I yell, jumping to my feet. I grab my glove and head to the bullpen. Luis trundles after, pulling on his helmet.

I look up.

All those media cameras lining the fence, pointed straight at me.

There is no such thing as ignoring them.

It is the last game of the regular season. If we win here, we lock up the number two seed in the playoffs. Coach Rodriguez says that's good for us because it puts us opposite the team that beat us earlier this year. Meaning we won't face them until the semis, assuming we both keep on winning. Today, we're playing the Luxburg Bulldogs, one of the worst teams in our conference. So as long as I don't lay an egg, we oughta be fine.

The first batter walks to the plate, goes through his whole routine. Adam sits behind the backstop with Beth, where I can see them every pitch. The media cameras move down the fence line, pointed straight at me. I don't know what they could want video of me pitching for. I guess to intercut with some broadcast talking about Pops and how he was famous for pitching and how maybe one day I am going to be famous, too, unless my life gets completely derailed by current events.

I get it. That's good TV.

Cope Field

But I can't think straight looking into the lifeless eyes of those camera lenses.

And something else is bothering me, too.

If there's so much media buzz around this, how come I haven't seen one newspaper?

I could Google it, I guess. But that's a bit like looking up stuff about Momma. I am not sure I really want to know.

Luis calls for a heater. I sling it on a rope, staring straight into the eyes of the batter. It flies low, and Luis has to block it with his knees.

Ball.

My heart kickstarts in my chest. I can feel those cameras zoom in on me. I swear to God.

"It's alright, Craw," Luis calls out, tossing the ball back to me.

He signals another heater. Like, *Let's get this one right. Get you comfortable. Get you in your element.* I nod. Go through my routine. And sling it hard. It flies funny. To the right. Luis has to reach outside the batter's box to catch it.

Ball.

I shake my head. Wipe sweat from my eyes. Catch the pass from Luis, then turn my back on him. On Adam. On Beth. And on all those big, expensive cameras.

I look over at the spot where Hannah used to sit.

Empty.

God, I miss her.

Chatter picks up in the crowd. A low murmur. These folks have seen me self-destruct live before. So now they are expecting it. I pick up little snippets of conversation. *Here we go again... It's too much for the kid... He ain't got it... Not like his daddy, I'll tell you what...*

But then another voice rises from the crowd.

"Have fun, Crawford."

Adam.

Our eyes meet up.

A little smile on his face. He nods. Says it again. "Have fun."

Have fun.

It rattles around in my head. Like, *No duh.* But at the same time... eureka. The one thing I forgot about baseball is the whole point. Silly but not so silly. This game has been pressed into me like a hundred thousand stones. In the world of Hunter Cope, fun was never the point. But I am starting to realize something about Pops...

He got it wrong.

He got a whole hell of a lot wrong.

Luis calls the heater again. I give him a curt nod. Then I wheel through my motion and turn the ball loose. It smacks Luis's glove. A strike. I hurl two more heaters right behind it. Out. The kid walks back to the dugout, his head held low. Adam cheers and claps and hollers from his spot behind the dugout. Even Beth yells out, "Way to go, Crawford!"

I strike out the next two batters in six pitches. And Adam doesn't stop carrying on. He's excited. Whooping. Hollering. We lock eyes again as I walk back to the dugout. He makes a little fist with his hand and nods his head. Like, *Aw yeah.* And I can't help it. It makes me laugh. Despite everything. The media. Pops. Big Time. Hannah. Despite all those things gone wrong.

Baseball still made me get good feelings.

Later in the game, with us up 6–0, a kid lays down a bunt and reaches first. I walk another because my arm is wearing out. Coach Rodriguez pulls me, says, "Good work," but I go and sit on the bench feeling panic anyway. I put my hand on my chest. And like that, all those good feelings I had are gone.

I can't believe I walked that kid.

Pops ain't even here, and I can feel the heat of his wrath on my shoulders.

Deep breaths, Craw.

Deep breaths.

"You're one hell of a pitcher."

I look up.

It's Adam, rolled up to the chain-link fence near the dugout. I manage a *thank you*, expecting him to bring up the other part, the part where I screwed up. But that's all he says. And it feels like God himself told me I am a good person.

We record the final outs of the game, and I smile when we tell the other team good job. I smile when Coach Rodriguez talks to us after. And I smile as we walk to the front gate, where Beth is waiting.

Then some news media folks ambush us near the van, pressing their microphones our direction, shouting out questions. And the commotion starts to draw a crowd of lookie-loos.

There's so many voices, I can hardly make out any of them. But I hear a few.

"Do you miss your father, Crawford?"

"Is your father your hero, Crawford? Did he save your life that night?"

"Was it hard to focus on today's game given everything going on?"

One of them even says right out loud, "Did Hunter Cope abuse you and your brother?"

That last one draws a reaction from the crowd. People start rushing forward. Yelling. One man, a teammate's father who I barely recognize, grabs the reporter by the front of the shirt and yanks the microphone away from him. I hear him say, "What is wrong with you?"

Somebody else yells out, "Tell them the truth, Craw!"

I start to feel sick, but Adam yells out, "No questions!" and we load up in the van as quick as possible. I sit there with my heart racing, trying not to throw up, unable to believe that this is what my life has become.

Beth starts the car and leaves the parking lot. We drive in silence for a long time, everyone processing what just happened.

I am so glad Big Time was not here for this.

After a while, Adam says, "What a mess," and I know he means the media circus.

Beth touches my hand across the center console. She smiles weakly. "It's going to be okay," she says. "I promise you."

HIGH SCHOOL NEVER ENDS
BOWLING FOR SOUP

No one knows how to talk to me anymore. Maybe that's 'cause right from the start, I told every person who brought up Pops I wasn't gonna talk about it. Sometimes I'd make it a joke. Say something like, "My agent advised me against talking about that right now."

Other times, I just used my Pops voice to say *not interested*.

Worked most the time.

Except on Luis.

Jokes don't work on him.

Pops' voice don't work on him.

But whatever.

I can handle a little bit of talking from Luis.

Walking into high school now, a place I have been a thousand times, feels like walking into a haunted house. Like coming back for your backpack with half the lights out. Folks smile to see me. Ask me how I've been. But there's this look in their eyes. And I can't help but think it's 'cause now they know the real Crawford Cope. They got a look behind the scenes. And they are just as mixed-up about it as I am.

Luis sits beside me in our journalism elective. Coach Rodriguez has us watching old World War II documentaries. Luis says, "We been praying for you at church."

I say, "Thanks." Because I guess I need prayers.

We watch some old-timey soldiers talk about how they stormed the beaches of Normandy. They all got this far-off look. Like they hate remembering this. And I feel like it is so wrong to make them talk about it.

Luis tugs my sleeve. I look at him.

"We been prayin' for your padre, too."

"Pops?"

"Yeah. It ain't right, these lies they telling about him all over the

Cope Field

news. I know that's hard for you, but it'll be all cleared up. My dad is saying the whole thing is gonna get dropped here soon."

I almost forgot Luis's dad is a lawyer. So he might know about this kinda thing. I feel a little like I might puke, so I make a motion with my head like, *We better pay attention*. For a minute, it works. Then Luis tugs my sleeve again. "You going to the dedication ceremony Saturday?"

I raise both eyebrows. "The what?"

"The dedication ceremony. For Cope Field."

"How can there be a dedication ceremony for a field named after a man in jail?"

Luis looks confused. "What do you mean? Hunter Cope isn't in jail. They released him. He's gonna be at the field for the ceremony, Craw."

I stare at him a long time, unable to process what he just said to me.

"That's what I heard anyway," Luis says.

I raise my hand.

Coach Rodriguez says, "What's up, son?"

"I gotta get outta here a minute."

Coach thinks a second. Then he says, "Ten minutes. Take a hall pass."

I walk down the hallway toward the music lab. Stop at the trophy case, where Pops' jersey and the state championship trophy he helped win are kept. There's a sign on the glass, handwritten in red, white, and blue markers. It says:

HUNTER COPE IS A HERO.

I stand looking at it for a long time. Then I pull it free from the glass.

"We put that up for you," a voice says.

I look up.

LeAnne is a few paces down the hallway, her backpack slung over one shoulder. She smiles. Looks sympathetic. "We all know the truth, Craw. So you ain't gotta worry. My dad says him and the detective talked the other day, and he told me not to say nothing to nobody yet, but I wanted to tell you anyway. That detective told my dad they was gonna close the case soon and not press any charges. They just gotta tie up the loose ends first."

Panic in my heart. I try not show it. To keep my voice calm. "I don't want to talk about Pops," I say.

But it's like she don't hear me. She walks closer. Almost right up to me. "Me and the other cheerleaders put them up all over town. Especially after we saw him make his statement."

I blink. "Statement?"

"He spoke, Craw. On the news. Ain't you seen it? Spoke right to you and this whole community. He was real tore up and sad. I cried the whole time watching." She hesitates. Touches my shoulder. "I felt real bad for you."

I shake my head, unable to process anything. LeAnne slides her arm around my shoulder and pulls me into a side hug. Then her other arm goes around my neck. And I just stand there taking it, feeling ten thousand miles away.

"What's he saying?" I ask, my voice so small and broken-sounding in my own ears.

"That he loves you. That he was protecting you. That he can't wait to get back to normal once this is all cleared up."

My shoulders tense up. My fist closes on the paper sign in my hand, crunching it into a ball. LeAnne don't seem to notice. When she turns me loose, she says, "You let me know if you need anything?"

I nod, unable to hold eye contact with her.

She smiles. Hugs me again, her lips briefly brushing against my cheek. Then she walks back down the hallway, leaving me alone in front of Pops' retired jersey and state championship trophy. I stare at them for a long time, thinking I oughta break the glass. Shatter that damn trophy. Rip that stupid jersey to shreds.

I drop the wad of paper on the ground. Flatten it with my foot. And then, 'cause nobody is looking, I full on stomp on it three or four times, scoop it up off the floor, and huck it as hard as I can down the hallway.

I cannot believe this. I didn't look up Pops online on purpose. But it was stupid of me to think he was gonna lay low.

I hurry down the hall to the music lab. It's dark inside. But I am hoping to find Hannah hidden away in her secret cave.

I throw open the door, but the room is empty.

What I wouldn't give to hear her voice right about now.

She would know what to do.

And if she didn't, she would at least listen to me talk about it.

I close the door and head back through the dark. But instead of going to class, I walk outside, around the building, and down the sidewalk until I get to the baseball field. I stand there for a long time,

Cope Field

looking across the perfectly manicured grass and dirt. Practice is in a few hours. But my heart isn't feeling baseball at the moment. I hop the fence and head back around to the parking lot.

I get in my truck. Start the engine. Bark tires on my way out of the lot.

STRAIGHT TO HELL
THE CLASH

I almost drive home.

And I mean *home* home.

Like... where Pops is, since he was apparently released.

But I catch myself and haul ass back to Adam and Beth's place. I park next to the van and stumble out of the truck, getting tangled up in the seatbelt. By now, the fire in my chest is stoked to an inferno, and it's coming out of my mouth in the form of every cuss word and obscenity I can think of.

I head up the front steps and throw open the door.

It rattles against the back wall, and Beth, who is sitting in a recliner in the living room, nearly drops the book she's reading on the floor. "Crawford?"

I open my mouth.

No sound comes out.

Beth rises from the recliner. "Are you okay? What's happened?" She closes the distance between us but hesitates to touch me. Adam appears from the other room, both eyebrows raised. He and Beth look alien to me. Like invaders in my life. But who else do I have? Where else can I go but here? My shoulders relax a little. My knees go with them. I slide to the floor in a puddle, and pretty soon I can't fight off the tears anymore.

I know I look stupid.

Like I am going insane.

But I can't help it.

Something touches my back. I look up. Beth is on the floor with me. She squeezes my shoulder. Then offers me both hands. When I take Beth's hand, she helps me to my feet. She guides me to the couch, then sits beside me.

Adam shuts the door. Then he wheels around to face us. "Are you okay?"

I take a deep breath. Then another. Then I look right at him. "What is going on with Pops?"

They look at each other. Beth says, "You heard he was out."

"Folks are rallying behind him."

Beth nods slow. "Yes, they are."

"They're still namin' that field after him."

Beth nods again. She squeezes my shoulder. I can tell she wants to pull me into a hug. "We worried this would happen. We don't have television. And we canceled our newspaper subscription. We thought it'd be good to shield y'all from most of this, if we could. But, you know, in today's age... it's impossible. Then he came out and started making statements to the press, and we knew it would get back to you somehow. And you know what? He knew that, too. And that was half the point, I guess... So now they are having that dedication at the field for him, and he's going to be there. He's going to speak at this thing. We couldn't believe it. And we've been beside ourselves about you finding out."

My breath comes ragged. My heart hammering. "Why would they do that?"

Adam thinks for a minute. He speaks slowly. "When people look up to someone, and that someone does something terrible... sometimes it's easier to believe that terrible thing never happened than it is to admit you were wrong about your hero. They won't change their minds about Hunter Cope until they have no other choice."

I look out the window. The sun pokes dappled beams of golden light through the trees. All yellow and gold. And warm. Like every spring afternoon playing baseball with Pops on the lawn. It hurts so bad to think about those memories. How happy they oughta be. How happy they aren't.

"So what happens now?" I ask. Just saying that feels like defeat. Like there ain't one thing I can do about whatever answer they might say back to me.

"Well, the DHS investigation and the police investigation are separate. So far, he hasn't been charged with anything. But from what I understand, both investigations are still open," Beth says.

I lean back on the couch and stare straight at the ceiling. I can see it now. Some police detective getting up on the news and announcing charges dropped. Then Donna Melton coming over here, probably thinking she is telling me something good. *Y'all get to go home, Crawford. Ain't that great?*

Yeah.

Great.

So, so great.

"Crawford," Adam says.

"Yeah?"

"I want you to remember something. You don't owe these people anything. But when you are ready, it is *so* important you tell your story. Take your time. Figure it out. But speak your truth."

I want to ask him why. Why does it matter? Why can't I leave it alone? Let it rot away until it's nothing. Go on living like nothing ever happened.

Adam goes ahead and answers without me saying anything.

"Because you deserve to be heard, Crawford," he says. "Your voice matters."

I think for a long time. Think about Pops. Everything that has happened between us. Think about Momma. I have some idea why she left. But it still hurts. Hurts to wonder why she didn't take us with her. How different my life might have been growing up with her and only her.

I mull it over all night.

Then I find Adam sitting in his office, typing frantically on a mechanical keyboard. He stops when I step through the door. "What do I do if I don't even know my own story?"

Adam pushes away from the desk a little. He leans back. Thinking. Then he says, "Seems like then you only got one option. You find out. You do whatever it is you gotta do to find out."

I watch Big Time sleep. Little line of drool at the corner of his mouth. I pull the blankets up around him. Touch his face with my hand. And then I lower down and kiss him on the forehead.

"You're a good kid, Sutton," I whisper. "Such a damn good kid. Better than me in every way. I mean it. I wish I was half as honest as you. That's so good, Sutton. It's so good, and you don't even know it."

Big Time draws in a deep breath. And for a heartbeat, I am worried I woke him up. Then he turns on his side, taking the blanket with him.

He itches the center of his chest, fingernails raking against dry skin. He smacks his lips. Lets out a fart. Then goes on snoring. I can't help but laugh. Perfect comedic timing. Even when asleep.

I crawl into my bed.

Think about Momma some more.

Then I take out my phone and type her name into a search engine.

My thumb hovers over the screen for a long time. My heart races. My brain saying, *You sure you really want to know?* And me finally answering back:

Yes.

Yes, I really want to know.

I close my eyes. Count to three. And press enter.

MAKE DAMN SURE
TAKING BACK SUNDAY

I'm alone in the truck with Big Time, on our way to the dedication ceremony for Cope Field.

There's this heavy feeling between us.

No space facts. No trivia.

Not even Big Time trying to get on my nerves.

I would kill for this kid to start singing some song about the sun. For him to refuse to stop, even after I threaten to put him in a choke hold. What I miss, I guess, is that smile of love he hides under his orneriness. I reckon he still blames me. But that is okay. I can handle it. His hurt goes deeper. And he won't ever untangle it until he knows the whole truth.

He insisted on coming today. And this boy been told *no* by life so much lately, I didn't have the heart to say it to him again. Maybe I should have left him behind, given the way I am feeling. And the kinda crazy thoughts I got bouncing around inside my skull.

I'm about to do something stupid, I think.

Or maybe genius?

Time will tell.

Either way, I figure I oughta warn him.

But I am not sure how.

"You okay?" I say to him, as we drive down the winding Ozark roads toward Jerusalem.

"Fine." He won't say anything else.

I turn on the stereo. Static. So I link up the Bluetooth. Play that punk rock playlist Hannah made for me. It gets an eye roll from Big Time. But I'm starting to think this is the perfect soundtrack for what I'm about to do. Thing is, if there's one thing this playlist has taught me, it's that sometimes it ain't enough to be *against* the bad shit in this

Cope Field

world. You gotta say something. And if folks won't hear it, you gotta *scream* it.

And if that still don't work...

You gotta burn the whole thing down.

We were not invited to the dedication ceremony. But we're going anyway. Because last night, after I did that Google search on my phone, I started thinking about how Pops is probably gonna give some kinda speech at this thing, gonna spew out more of his lies and his poison. And I cannot stand for that anymore.

I'm not sure what I'm gonna do when I get to that ballfield.

But I know I'm gonna do something big.

Pops is court ordered to stay away from me and Big Time until this whole thing is resolved. But I ain't court ordered nothing. I can go wherever I please. So what happens if I turn up at this thing? Does he gotta leave? Wouldn't that be funny?

When we get there, there are news vans lining the highway and pop-up tents in the grassy area near the field. There are folks standing around with cameras, press badges, and little notebooks to write in.

All here for Pops.

I kill the music and drive around looking for some place to park.

"I hate this," Big Time says, pressing his nose to the window as we pass one of the media tents. "I wish they'd just go away and leave us alone."

I park at the end of the line of cars and vans and turn off the engine. The media hasn't noticed us yet, but I can see that Judge, Brucie Boy, talking with a newsperson up ahead. And there's Pops, laughing it up with them. Looking like it is any given Saturday at the ballpark.

I turn to Big Time and grab his hands. He tries to yank away from me, but I don't let him.

"I'm about to do something," I say.

He wrinkles up his face. "What?"

"It might be stupid, Sutton. It might not make sense to you. It might not make sense to nobody. But I am about to do something. And I need you to know, even if it makes you mad, even if you hate me for it, I done it because I love you."

Big Time finally works his hands away from mine. "Are you going crazy?"

I look past him through the window.

Straight at Pops.

"Yeah," I say. "Maybe a little."

We hop out of the truck. Big Time looks around at all the news people, wringing his hands. "Should we even be here?"

"It's our field."

But he stands rooted in place. So I hold out my hand. He hesitates a second, then slips his fingers between mine. I give him a squeeze. Tell him he can hide behind my legs if he wants. But really, between the two of us, he is the brave one. He will put on a smile. Tell a joke. And folks will wonder if he's not the happiest kid who ever lived. Walking across the highway to Cope Field, I realize that's been Sutton's own way of hiding his hurt. I shut up. He talks too much. But it's all the same. The way I figure it, talking too much is nothing but another way of shutting up.

We walk to the edge of the back fence, still holding hands, overlooking this place our father built. Hard to believe this field looked the way it looked when I first seen it. Nothing is all the way finished, but it looks so much further along than before. There's brand-new blue fencing around the entire park. Out front, there's signs showing blueprints of everything they have planned, and looking around I can see where some of the work has started. There'll be wraparound seats behind the backstop and down the first and third base lines. Plus a mini concourse, with concessions and a place for media, stat keepers. There'll be new turf going down, like Pops promised.

Here, in the middle of nowhere Arkansas, a monument to Pops' vanity.

But I know there will be tournaments here. And practices. And pickup games. Boys will fall in love with baseball on this field. Girls will give their hearts to softball.

So maybe there is some good underneath it all.

Maybe.

No one has noticed us yet. So we walk down the fence along the first base line. A pretty woman with long brown hair stands where home plate will be, speaking into a microphone, a camera in her face. Roger stands next to her. His arms crossed over his giant belly like he's insecure about it. And right next to him, smiling big, wearing a pair of aviator shades, is Pops, waiting for his turn to take the microphone.

Big Time freezes in place.

"Look, there's Pops!" he says. "Can we go see him?"

I give him a serious look. "Do not move from this spot. No matter what."

Big Time starts to protest, saying he wants to go see Pops.

"Sutton. Do not."

I leave him hanging on the fence. Then I march straight toward the backstop, slip through the side gate, and head across the grass to where Roger is talking about the history of the field. Ain't nobody seen me coming yet. But I'm waiting for it.

"This field was built in the '60s, I do believe," Roger says. "And it saw use all the way through the '80s. We are not sure how or why it happened, maybe just 'cause not a lot of folks stayed living out here, but the field fell into disuse. Then Mother Nature took over. As she does."

"Was it your idea to rebuild the field?" the news lady asks.

"Naw, I just got saddled with it." He laughs. Pops laughs, too. "This guy right here is who thought of it. He's who you should be interviewing."

The reporter laughs politely and points the microphone at Pops. "So how does a famous former professional baseball player end up reviving a field in the middle of rural Arkansas?"

Before he can answer, one of the media guys notices me and calls my name. Cameras turn, and I can tell nobody was expecting to see me here.

"Did you have something you wanted to add, Crawford?" one of the media folks says, laughing a little nervously.

I look right at Pops. I can't see his eyes because of his glasses, but his expression is plain enough. He's scared.

"Yes," I say. "Yes, I sure as hell do."

The other night when I finally put Momma's name into my phone and let the stories populate, I spent hours reading all the old headlines.

Star pitcher's wife disappears
No sign of missing woman, authorities say
Cope calls murder accusations 'disgusting'
Authorities dismiss foul play rumors
Six months, no body
Baseball star pleads for wife's return
And the gross thing.

The *gross* thing.

There's a momma missing. Leaving behind two boys in the Arkansas hills. And these headlines never once call her by name. Never once say anything that isn't related to Pops. In most of them, her name isn't even in the first paragraph of the story. The narrative isn't that a woman—with all her own hopes and dreams and desires—disappeared.

No.

It's that the wife of a baseball player disappeared.

I lay awake after that. Staring at the ceiling. Collecting memories in my brain. Her smile. Her singing Dolly Parton in the kitchen. Her touching my face at night when she thought I was asleep.

My thoughts drifted to the night she disappeared.

How Pops told me she run off with that man, said he'd made a missing person report about her, reported her as kidnapped. If he had done that, wouldn't one of these articles mention kidnapping?

But they don't. Instead, they talk about murder accusations.

I thought about that man some more. Standing under the Christmas lights with his jet-black skull tattoo.

I climbed out of bed and crept down the hall. Then I slipped out into the garage and pulled down the attic ladder. Adam appeared in the doorway, which I'd left open behind me. "Looking for something?"

"We got any Christmas lights up here?"

He thought for a second. "What for?"

"I want to test something. Please. It's important."

"There oughta be some up there. Couldn't tell you where though. Should be labeled. Gray container."

I climbed the ladder and poked around the boxes until I found one marked *Christmas*. Inside were coils and coils of Christmas lights. I dug through them until I found a strand of blue lights. Then I climbed back down the ladder.

Adam rolled out of my way so I could pass. Then he followed me to the kitchen table. "What are you doing?"

I didn't answer him. I was too focused on my task. I rummaged through the junk drawer until I found a red sharpie. Then I grabbed one of the medical bills from the counter, flipped it over, and drew a garish red skull on the back.

"Crawford, what is this about?"

"It's hard to explain," I said, tossing him the end of the Christmas lights. "Can you plug these in and hit that switch?"

Adam scooted to the outlet and plugged in the strand. Then he reached up and turned off the overhead light. I looked down at the red skull I had drawn.

Jet-black under the blue Christmas lights.

Roger puts his hand in the center of Pops' chest, forcing him backward and away from me. Brucie Boy and a sheriff's deputy hurry through the gate, and they usher Pops to the far side of the fence.

Even now.

Protecting this man.

I stop walking when I reach the pitching mound. I mean, what will be the pitching mound eventually. I don't know why, but it seems like the right spot for me to stop. So I do.

The news lady closes the distance between us quickly, her microphone pointed toward me. All the cameras swivel to face us. I lace my hands behind my back. And wait.

Soon, there are so many cameras and reporters packed around me, I can barely see past them. But I catch sight of Big Time hanging on the fence where I left him, halfway down the first base line.

"First of all, Crawford, are you doing okay?" one of the reporters says. "This must be hard for you."

Pops stands behind the backstop, where he has watched me pitch so many times before. His mouth is a straight line, his arms folded across his chest.

I stare right at him. Open my mouth.

Shut it again. Jesus.

Now that I'm here, my confidence evaporates. Everything in my head is buzzing, saying, *This was a mistake. You should not have done this.*

But another voice is there, too.

Whispering beneath the buzz.

Speak your truth.

I say it in my head over and over again. Say it until it's the only voice I can hear. Thinking of Adam. Thinking of Sutton. Thinking of Hannah.

I close my eyes.

I picture her. Our foreheads touching in my truck. The driving rain. Her saying to me, *Tell somebody. Even if you can't tell me. Tell somebody.*

Okay, Hannah.

Okay.

I open my eyes. Several microphones inch closer. Another reporter asks, "Crawford, what do you think about this field? About everything that's happened? Are you looking forward to resolution? To getting back to a normal life?"

"What do I think?" I repeat, ignoring the other questions.

Everyone is silent. Waiting on my answer.

"I think... my father used to worry he'd spoiled me. Given me too much. Made it too easy on me. But I'm here to say he was wrong to worry. He didn't spoil me."

The cameras inch closer. I take a deep breath. Steady myself. Stare past the cameras at Pops.

"He *ruined* me. Ruined my entire life. There is nothing in this world that I love that he has not destroyed or tried to destroy in one way or another."

Pops snaps off his glasses, shaking his head. Looks like he wants to come through the fence and let me have it, right here in front of God and everyone else. But Judge Brucie Boy clasps him on the shoulder like, *It's alright, old boy. Don't worry about it.*

The reporters murmur a little. Share stunned glances. Behind them all, I can see Roger itching his belly, his cheeks turning bright red.

One reporter says, "Can you elaborate on what you mean?"

"What I mean is"—and I'm realizing it even as I say it—"it was never supposed to be about you, Pops. It was supposed to be about Sutton. It was supposed to be about me. Maybe this whole stupid backwards county thinks you are some kinda hero. That's good for them. But you coulda been a hero to us. You coulda been *our* hero."

I stop again. Collect my thoughts.

"This is my truth," I say, staring my father down. "Pops. I love you. And I hate you at the same time. And that is not my doing. It's yours. You visited upon me and Sutton abuses both explicit and abstract, hurts so deep I do not have the words for them. You are the worst kind of monster. The kind who pretends to be a hero. All my life you told me to keep quiet, to shut up, to hide the things I'd seen. All my life I thought that was to keep me safe, to keep our family safe. But I have come to realize that you only wanted me quiet for one reason and one reason only: to protect *yourself.*"

The Judge has had enough. He leaves Pops behind and pushes through the crowd. Tries to work his way on camera. But someone holds him back. He says, "You been through a lot, Craw. Why don't you go sit down before you say something you regret. Your father is a good man."

"I saw Pops kill Samuel Ledbetter," I tell him. "I was in no danger. Pops shot him four times in cold blood."

The words fall heavy like a hammer.

Reporters reel off questions so fast I can't pick one to answer. So I just say what's been in my heart as fast as I can. Get it out. "I also saw somebody the night my momma disappeared. Saw them standing in the window outside my home. My father told me never to tell nobody about it. And I never did. But that person is the same person my father shot and killed at that house right behind us. There is not one single doubt in my mind those two things are related."

The reporters hurl another volley of questions. But I ignore them. My eyes dart around, looking for Pops. Looking for Sutton. But I can't find either of them. Fear grapples my guts, and I almost take off running, scared to death Pops done some maniac thing like talk to Big Time. Even though he is court ordered against it, you never can tell with that man. He will do whatever he feels like doing. Because all this time, that's exactly what he's been *allowed* to do.

Then I hear Pops' voice ring out above the commotion. "Bullshit!" He's through the gate, striding across the grass, Roger and a deputy hurrying behind him, panic on their faces. The crowd quiets down, and the cameras pan around to face him. "You always was an ungrateful piece of shit," he yells, veins bulging in his neck. "And listen right here. You never will be better than me, Crawford. And what you done today . . . it's unforgivable. I swear to Christ Jesus, I oughta beat your ass right now."

He freezes. Seems to realize he's said too much.

Judge Brucie Boy and Roger are rooted in place, their mouths hanging open. But that deputy. He's seen enough. He grabs Pops by the wrist and wrenches it behind his back. There's a back-and-forth scuffle, but that officer knows how to do his job. Pretty soon, the cuffs are on, and Pops is forced away from the field, cameras rolling the whole time.

I glance at the fence where I left Sutton.

I still don't see him. And my heart breaks a little, knowing how much what he saw might have hurt him. But the truth is the truth. And he cannot heal until he knows it.

The microphones press a little closer to me. Cameras still rolling. There is a long moment where nobody can believe what's just happened.

"Crawford, what made you come out here today?" one of the reporters asks.

I rub the back of my head. Because I am not sure how to answer that. I could tell them about Adam. *Because you deserve to be heard, Crawford. Your voice matters.* Or I could tell them about Hannah. *I'll take loud and honest every day.* But the story is too long, too complicated, for the moment. I tell them, "Some friends talked me into it."

Because that's true enough.

The reporters ask some more questions, a good deal of them that I can't decipher. And I'm done. This moment is dragging on too long. Even though I know I had to do it, it's like it's the ninth inning and I've thrown a hundred pitches.

I lift my hands up to silence them. Because I got the stage. And one more stupid idea on what to do with it.

"I only got one more thing to say. There was this girl I knew. Her name was Hannah Flores. And she was the only person on this entire planet who gave enough of a damn about me to try and see through the lie I was living."

"Where is Hannah now?" someone says.

"I don't know. But if someone out there knows, can you tell her I am sorry? Tell her I done a whole lot of stupid and bad things. But the stupidest thing I ever done was hurt her. Tell her I was just scared. I was stupid. And nothing I said to her that day was true. She's not stuck here. It's me who was stuck. I just couldn't see it. Tell her I know why she don't want to see me anymore. And I get it... it's what I deserve. But I—"

I can't get the words out.

I look at my feet for a long time.

The cameras push toward me.

But I am done.

I walk away from the pitching mound. Walk back through the gate to where I left Big Time hanging on the fence. He isn't there. But I find him sitting on the tailgate of the truck, his arms crossed across his belly, streaks of dried-up tears on his cheek.

He won't look me.

PLEASE, PLEASE, PLEASE LET ME GET WHAT I WANT
THE SMITHS

Things have been weird since I done what I done.

At first, people weren't sure how to act around me.

I made people nervous.

Like, they weren't mean. They just didn't know what to do or say.

Luis hugged me straight away, though. That kid. I swear to God. Threw his arms around me and said, "Hell, Craw. That is some bullshit."

And all the tension I'd been carrying in my shoulders just melted. We went right back to catcher and pitcher. Right back to friends. Right back to shootin' the shit in the bullpen.

At school, I walk to all the usual haunts at school looking for Hannah, hoping she saw me pour my heart out on the television. Hoping that might do some good by way of fixing the gulf I put between us. That maybe, if I am real lucky, she will accept my apology. I check the stairwell. The library. The unused classroom in the back of the music room, where she liked to study during lunch.

No Hannah.

Today, I stand in the music lab for a while, listening to a girl play the piano. A sophomore, I think. And actually, it's killing me I do not know her name. She's like Hannah. On the outskirts of the who's who at our school. Which is super stupid when you sit and think about it. I'm at the top of the social ladder at one of the smallest schools in the state, which is one of the smaller states in the whole country. Who are we to tell anyone they do not belong?

I listen to this girl play jazz music, her eyes closed. I hate to interrupt her. But I am here on serious business. "Do you know Hannah Flores?"

She opens her eyes. Looks repulsed at the sight of me. Like, *Ew, a jock.*

"I know her," the girl says. She does not stop playing. "Why?"

"You seen her lately?"

"Why?"

"Are you her guardian or what?"

"I am the guardian of all girls who don't want to be bothered."

"Funny."

I sit down in one of the nearby chairs. Cross one leg over the other. Listen to this girl play a while longer. And she really can. Like, close your eyes and you might be at some concert hall in New York City. It is funny the amount of talent every person around you has. Sometimes completely unknown. Most folks only notice if it involves a ball in some way.

She gets to the end of the song, and I see her peek up at me from over the top of the piano. "You're still here?"

"Have you seen Hannah?"

"If you want to talk to me about her, you're gonna have to answer my question first." She sounds like some wicked witch guarding a bridge. Like, *If the truth you wanna see, first you must answer my riddles three.*

"Fine."

"Why do you want to know where Hannah went?"

"Because I haven't seen her in a while."

"Do you miss her?"

"Are you making fun of me?"

She picks up another tune. Slow and sad. Like a private eye detective film. "No," she says. "Genuinely curious."

I swallow, and there is a lump in my throat. "I miss her."

The music rises in intensity. Her fingers thumping heavy on the keys. The sound like howling wind. Like rain. Like walking under an umbrella during a thunderstorm. After a while, she says, "She changed schools after what happened. I haven't seen her since."

The bell rings.

The girl closes the piano. She gives me a half frown, half smile that says, *Sorry.* Then she leaves the room.

FINE, GREAT
MODERN BASEBALL

It's weird how I spent my whole childhood wishing I was done with school. And now that I'm at the end, it's like the whole thing is going too fast. I'm staring right at senior prom. At graduation. At my last baseball game at the high school level. And here's the kicker on the baseball one: We get to keep playing all the way to the state championship, so long as we keep winning. So. That's pressure. It all could end in heartbreak.

I try and not dwell on it. Because I still have games to win. Pitches to throw. Teammates to not let down. But bad news: It's impossible to tune out. Maybe being a good pitcher is not about tuning out the world. Maybe it's doing what needs to be done regardless of what else is going on.

Maybe that's everything. Work. Relationships. Life.

You show up. You sling pitches. You win. You lose. You keep showing up.

But what do you do when the one person you'd like to show up for told you to lose her number and now you can't find her?

To make it to state, we have to play through our conference and regional tournaments. Which, no problem. We are big fish in a small pond. We win conference with no problems. But get in a hairy situation against Danville in the regional tournament. Coach Rodriguez thought we could get past them without me. To give my arm a break. But we end up in the top of their lineup with two runners on with three innings left. Coach Rodriguez brings me in to close. And I go ahead and sit the rest of their crew. Boom. Conference and regional champs. Up next: state tournament.

On the way home, Adam reaches up and plops an envelope in my lap. It's got the University of Arkansas seal on it. "What's this?" I ask.

"Open it," Beth says.

I tear the fold open with a finger and pull out the letter. I read it. Then read it again. "They want me to come up for a visit."

"They wanna offer," Adam says.

"Maybe."

Pops was always telling me Division I baseball was complete nonsense. He'd say, "All the good'uns go straight outta high school." And I believed him. So I am reading this with some kind of disappointment. Like, *Guess I'm not as good as I thought.* Must be a million other pitchers in this country with better arms than me. Kids who can throw knuckleballs probably.

"What's wrong?" Beth asks. And it's so shocking to me that a grown person bothered asking.

I say, "I'm not sure how to explain it."

"Try," Beth says.

"It's just something Pops always said about going pro right out of high school."

Adam says, "Crawford, I know your heart is set on entering the draft, and I know folks are always saying we should follow our hearts, but our hearts are dirty liars sometimes. Sometimes, they repeat back to us the things that have been poured into them the most."

That gets me thinking.

I lie awake that night in my little shared room with Big Time, listening to him snore. My heart is telling me to go and find Hannah. But if Adam is right, and our hearts can be dirty little liars, does that mean mine is lying to me *right now*?

Hard to say.

Naturally, like the uncaged idiot I am, I drive out to her house in Jerusalem on Saturday hoping for some clue where she's gone. I drive all the way up to the porch and stand on wobbly legs near where Shotgun died. Down the sloping hill and across the highway, Cope Field looks even further along than it did back when I spoke to the news media. And it looks like they changed the sign out front, too. But I don't have the heart to walk down there and look at it. They probably added Pops' first name to the thing, just to make it extra clear who their hero is, even after everything.

I look out over the place, feeling sad and sick at the same time. Then I turn around and look up at Hannah's house. And I can tell, without even bothering to walk up to the front door, there's not a single soul still living there. The grass is growed up. The windows dark. No cars

Cope Field

parked out front. In my mind, I can still see Shotgun lying there. The wild look in his eyes. The blood on his lips. The way he said without speaking, *Please don't let me die.*

But we did.

We did let him die.

I go over it in my mind. Could I have done something? Could he have been saved?

The answer is no.

My logical brain *knows* the answer is no.

But it don't feel that way.

Not in my heart.

Shotgun's place is now a soulless husk. And the only soul it ever truly had that I know about belonged to a girl who liked punk rock and for a little while liked me, too. I connect my phone to the truck via Bluetooth and put on Hannah's punk music. I lower the tailgate and sit there, gazing across Cope Field, thinking of the hours I spent there with her. Think about paint splattered on her nose and cheeks. Her fingers tucking a strand of loose hair behind her ear. Me sweeping so furiously, getting dirt on her shoes.

The truck.

The mud.

The rain.

Our kiss.

LOVE LOVE LOVE
THE MOUNTAIN GOATS

On the way to school, Big Time is on silent mode. And I hate it. Because it makes me worried he is getting sucked into the *be quiet* trap I got sucked into. Things have gotten a little better between us. But I can tell he is still hurting. And I can tell he is burying it just like I would have.

I keep looking over at him while I'm driving. Finally, he's like, "Why you keep staring at me?"

"Just 'cause," I say.

"Just 'cause why?"

I laugh. "No reason, Sut. I like you, that's all."

Big Time rolls his eyes, puts his attention on something out the side window. "You have done lost your mind."

Hannah had this trick to getting me to talk called *never shutting up*. She asked questions. So many questions. Maybe Hannah's trick will work on him, too. She said, *I'll take loud and honest over strong and silent any day.*

Well.

Here goes.

"How are you feelin' about everything, Big Time?" I say. To start things out easy.

He looks at me, looking all the world like a teenager rather than like the eight-year-old he is, waves a hand dismissively, and says, "I don't feel nothing."

"We all feel something."

"Not me." He reaches over and turns on the stereo, cranks it up loud. Which, I still have it connected to my phone and tuned in to that punk rock playlist Hannah gave me. *Crawdaddy's Musical Education.* He claps his hands over his ears and looks at me like, *Oh God, not this again.*

And I can't help but laugh.

This song is pure noise. The drums going completely haywire. The guitar sounding like someone is just going to work on the strings with a hammer. And the singer barking out God even knows what over and over. Like, no melody. Just this guy screaming. This sweltering insanity coming from my speakers. Big Time shaking his head like, *Dear God, no.* And me cackling, refusing to let him turn it off, slapping his hand away from the control knob. It's bonkers. I love it.

We round the corner to his school, and all his little buddies are outside. I roll the windows down. Drive slow. Big Time is like, "If you ever loved me, you won't."

I turn into the school drop-off line. We are bumping.

But I let him hit the knob.

Everything goes silent, except the truck engine, the sounds of kids playing on the playground. Big Time sits with his hand clutched over his chest, like a church woman with her pearls. Like, *Well, I never.*

A few of his buddies wait for him under the awning. He says, "You are just about the worst."

"I'm the best. You love me."

"Debatable."

I roll slow though the line, so he can't get out. Not quite yet.

"Will you stop the car?"

"Sutton."

"Stop the truck. I want out."

"Sutton..."

"What, Craw?"

I stop the truck. His eyes lock with mine. "I love you. You know that."

He cracks the door open and slips outside. Before he leaves, he says, "I know, Craw."

Prom is next week. So is the state tournament. Therefore, so is that punk show I was gonna see with Hannah. Here's a bonkers thing maybe somebody can explain to me: If we make it to the state finals, it's on Saturday afternoon in Little Rock. Prom is that night. Meaning, if you are doing both of these things, you gotta go all the way to Little Rock, play an entire baseball game, then come back home with enough time to get dolled up for prom. Tell me: Which smooth-brained idiot planned that one?

Not that it matters. I have not asked anyone to go. Because who cares? All my baseball buddies got dates. Luis gives me a hard time every practice. Saying stuff like, "My guy, we have secured a keg for after prom. You need to be there. Craw, you might even get laid."

Luis was asked by a senior. And good for him.

But listen.

If I am going to two-pump chump my first time having sex, it's going to at least be with a person who loves me.

No and thank you to parties. And no and thank you to prom.

But I guess a few of my buddies want to be *helpful*. LeAnne Wilson's date backed out and she has always had a thing for me, apparently, so they have her ask me. She walks up during English class and puts a folded-up note on the corner of my desk. LeAnne is pretty. Like, it is insane to me her date backed out. But she is pretty in the normal way. Not like Hannah, who is pretty on her own terms.

The note says: PROM?

I spend the rest of the period trying to avoid eye contact. In the hall, she bounces up beside me. "Did you get my note?"

Like, *No duh. You handed it straight to me.*

"Do you wanna go?"

"I don't got a suit or nothing."

"Who cares?"

"It's formal."

"Buy one then. Come on, Craw. I'm sure you can figure it out. Aren't you supposed to be rich or something?"

I stop right in the middle of the hall. Take a deep breath. Clear up my brain space a bit.

"Actually," I say. "I'm going to this punk show in Little Rock. I told someone I'd go with them, so I can't get out of it."

I don't know why I said it. But it came out. And as it hangs in the air between us, it starts to feel less like a lie and more like a confession. If there is one place on this earth I might luck into seeing Hannah again, it's there. Right in that moment, I make up my mind. I'm going to that show.

LeAnne looks confused. "A punk show?"

"You know. The music?"

"Isn't that, like... old people music?" She folds her arms across her chest and rolls her eyes. "That's fucking lame, Craw."

I smile a little. Can't help it. Once upon a time, I'd have done everything in my power *not* to appear lame in front of a girl like LeAnne.

"Are you making fun of me?" she asks.

"LeAnne," I say. "I really am not."

EXISTENTIALISM ON PROM NIGHT
STRAYLIGHT RUN

If this were a movie, the state championship game would be huge and dramatic.

And it was.

In a stupid baseball kinda way.

Like, there was this moment in the third inning where they manufactured a little offense against me. A bunt. A dropped third strike. And then I was staring down their best batter with two runners on. And, yeah. Drama. But not like movie drama. In a movie, I guess I'd have got two strikes on the guy. Then he woulda hit a couple fouls until he had a 3-2 count. Then I woulda been like, *Aw jeez, aw heck, how am I gonna get past this guy?* Then I'd remember. The Goddamn knuckleball.

But fact is, I had no time to master that kind of thing.

Also, I struck him out in three pitches. Heater, curve, slider. Took a chop at all three like a moron. From there, it was smooth sailing. We won 3-1. School's first state championship since Pops. And now they got this media room set up. Like what you see when the pros get interviewed. Newspapers and TV journalists from all over the state waiting for us in that room. Already, I do not want to go in there. Because I know what's coming.

Questions about Pops.

We get to the door. Coach Rodriguez looks back at me. And he pauses. "Are you okay?"

I'm thinking about what Adam said to me a while back. How I don't owe them anything. Maybe it's bad to keep things buried deep, but there's some good, too, from discerning who is worth talking to. These media folks ain't it. "Coach, I do not want to go in there."

Coach Rodriguez looks into the room. At all the journos waiting with their dumb little recorders. "Craw, you won that game for us. They'll want to speak with you. You're a star. You know that right?"

"They'll ask about him," I say.

Coach Rodriguez nods slow. Then he hollers at an assistant coach over my shoulder. "Bring Luis out here. He can do the presser with me." Coach touches my shoulder. He smiles softly. Real kindness in his eyes. He says, "You're my hero, Craw. Not your Pops. *You.*"

I start to tear up. "Shut up," I say.

But I hug him.

Right there where all the media folks can see.

After the game, there's a mad dash back to Quiet County for prom.

Not me, though.

I say hello to Adam and Beth in the parking lot. I hug Big Time. Then I get down at eye level with him and tell him I love him again. That he blows my mind how smart he is. How funny. And how even when things get terrible, he finds a way to keep a smile on his face. And he tries his damnedest to get a smile on mine, too. Beth don't even correct me for the bad language.

And maybe it's the excitement of the state championship. Or maybe I got through to him in the car. Or maybe it's just time. Just plain old passing of time. But there's something of the old Big Time in his expression. A little mischief in that grin.

"You're going soft..." he says. "But maybe soft is good." Once again channeling some grandpappy ancestor with wisdom unheard.

I put my hands on either side of his head. Then I stretch out his mullet. Give the curls a yank and turn him loose.

"I love you, too, Craw," he says. "Sorry I didn't say it before. But it's true."

"I never doubted it."

Then, it's time to go. I promise them I'll be safe, and I'll be back as soon as the show is over. Beth asks me like six times if I'm sure I'm happy to miss prom. It's like, *I don't care about prom.*

It's a short drive to the venue. A marquee out front says MORONS, ALL OF YOU with BLOODY SOCIALISTS. Which might be the funniest names for bands I ever heard in my life. There's some punky looking kids already walking in. A whole fleet of them. Dressed in black with spiky jackets with patches all over them. Battle jackets, Hannah called them. These folks come outta the woodwork, I guess.

I buy a ticket. Head inside. Maybe a hundred folks in there. I lean up against the wall. Still in my dirty baseball uniform. Feeling out of place. Feeling the way Hannah musta felt every day at school.

I keep my eye glued to the door. Waiting for her to walk in. Trying to work out what might happen next. Should I walk straight up to her and say hello? No. The first words outta my mouth should be *I am so damn sorry for what I done*. Next, I'll wax poetic about how I deserve every inch of distance she put between us. But the thing is.

The thing *is, Hannah.*

Damn it.

I fuckin' love you.

And I'm having this conversation in my head all by myself against the wall of some punk band concert I do not even want to see, imagining how she might respond. How she might grin and hug me and maybe even *kiss* me. Like, *I love you, too*. And those words will be like pressing down the last piece of a puzzle. That little satisfying *snap*. All the interlocking pieces snug together. And even though my life is a mess right now, that one thing... that one simple little thing... would somehow make it right.

The band takes the stage. They fly straight into chaos. The lead singer screaming "Proud Boys fuck off!" over and over with no discernable melody while hammering his guitar like an absolute maniac. The drummer looks insane back there, crashing the cymbals and shaking his head back and forth and up and down so fast his entire face is a blur. It's like, is this supposed to be music? I reckon that is half the point. And the crowd seems to agree. Because they are just full-on slamming into each other. Kicking their legs and hands. Throwing fists.

Meanwhile I'm back here like the no-fun police in my cute little baseball uniform. Scanning the crowd. Not seeing Hannah. And getting a little desperate about it. Like, this is not my scene. And it's obvious. And if Hannah isn't even here, I should leave.

The band finishes screaming. Which transitions into more screaming. This time without instruments. A smoke machine fills the room with fog. The drummer crashes four times on the high-hat yelling, "One, two, three, four," and they fly into another number, the

Cope Field

words to which I cannot rightfully discern. All the dancing bodies move in and through the fog. Like monsters in a horror movie.

The room goes dark, except for the flash of a strobe. Like frozen milliseconds of time.

A girl dances out of the smoke. Her back toward me. Pink hair flying around her head. Turning. Turning. Almost facing me. Hope rising in my chest. It could be her.

It could be!

But then she disappears. Gone in the blackness of the strobe and the smoke and the dancing bodies.

It probably wasn't her anyway.

There are at least twelve girls here with pink hair. And who even knows what color Hannah's hair is nowadays anyway.

I could leave. But there's still hope inside me.

And I am not one to leave behind hope.

The girl appears again. Smiling. Laughing. And her face. Her beautiful face. She turns toward me.

It *is* Hannah.

She moves around the room. Bouncing and bopping to the music. And it is so good to see that she is happy I almost cry. Her eyes seem to land on me for a second. My heart flutters in my chest. My hand almost goes into the air.

Hi, Hannah.

But her eyes don't stay long. They move right past me. Around the crowd.

The music changes tempo. She starts rocking her head up and down. Then she spins back toward the band and throws up devil horns on her right hand. Another girl appears beside her, swaying back and forth. Long black hair. Purple eyeshadow so deep it makes her eyes pop from all the way across the room. She pulls Hannah close. The gap between them disappearing. Then wraps her arms around her neck and kisses her on the mouth.

They break away. Hannah's smile is the same one I saw when I kissed her on Cope Field the night I lost my mind. The kind of smile I thought maybe you could only give to one person in your whole life.

But I was wrong.

Hannah is happy.

And who am I to mess that up?

Happy moments are fleeting. But they are precious. And how terrible would it be to fall out of the sky, appear from nowhere like some monster, and ruin Hannah's night? No and thank you. If she can find happiness here, then she should have it. Even if it's not with me.

I watch the two of them dance for a little longer.

Think about Hannah crawling through my window.

Kissing me.

Holding me in her arms.

Me. The strong, silent type. Strongly silencing my way straight out of the relationship. I wanted to tell her all my secrets. Knowing somewhere deep down they ought not have been secrets between us to begin with.

But I never could.

I walk along the wall toward the door. A bouncer outside says, "Leaving already?"

I shrug. "It's not my thing."

He laughs. But he don't know a whole world is ending inside me.

It's an hour drive on the interstate, then another hour through the bottoms between the Ouachitas and the Ozarks. I get gas in a town called Manning, then head up into the mountains. One more stop at a diner in Samson for some grub. I sit there, chewing on a burger, listening to the old folks talk. A sign says *Home of the War Eagles*, and I wonder if we've ever played them in baseball.

I am not happy.

That's what it is.

Something way down inside me is broken. And I got no clue how to fix it.

"You okay, sweetheart?" the waitress says. I jump, nearly spilling my coffee. Which I don't like but ordered anyway to help me stay awake for the drive home. She laughs and says sorry. Then she says, "Can I warm up your cup?"

I blink at her.

"Your coffee. You want more to drink?"

I see my own face in the liquid. See Pops' face.

Then I start to cry.

In front of God and everybody.

And this woman. This waitress. This absolute gem of a human being. She sits down in the booth across from me. She takes both my hands. And she just holds them.

VINDICATED
DASHBOARD CONFESSIONAL

Adam rolls into our room early to wake us. But we're both already up. Both beyond shook, you might say. Because today is the first hearing in the case against Pops. Big Time woke me up at 4 a.m., asking what was going to happen. And all I could tell him was a lot of *I don't know*s.

Beth cooks us some eggs and bacon. We sit around the table. Adam offers up his prayers to God, like always. Adding in for God to be with us boys today. Which I guess I am glad about. Because most of the time I feel like I done something wrong. Like God is mad at me, has spun the whole wheel of the universe against me.

It's either that, or He don't exist at all.

But if He's up there, I will take all the help I can get today.

We pack up our stuff. Drive to town. Help Adam out of the van. Then Big Time pushes him to the courthouse, slapping my hand away when I try to help. Adam says, "Whatever happens, it's going to be okay."

We stop in the hallway outside the courtroom. A lawyer or some other dude in a nice suit walks through, and the door swings open far enough I can see Pops sitting on the far side of the room, wearing an orange jumpsuit. He's got his hair slicked back. And he looks tired. Like he isn't sleeping good. Smaller, too. Like he isn't eating much, either.

There is a policeman nearby, plus some other folks I don't recognize. Donna Melton sits on the other side of the room, one leg hitched over the other. This time she's wearing all black. Brawner sits beside her, his badge gleaming on his hip.

Big Time freezes by the door. And I'm not much better. I can't hardly get my feet to take a step forward.

Beth turns to face us. "Boys," she says. "We can leave right now.

There's no reason for you to be here for this. We only came because you said you wanted to be here."

I glance at Big Time. He nods slow.

"We do want to be here," I say.

Beth shakes her head. "Okay. But if you want to leave, you just let me know. We will walk out right in the middle. I don't care one bit about making a scene."

I take a step forward. Squeeze past Adam and cross the threshold. Big Time follows behind. We find seats, me and Big Time on either side of Beth, Adam close by in the aisle. I lean toward Beth. Whisper, "Thank you."

She looks confused. Mouths, "For what?"

"Everything."

I'm not sure what happens at a pretrial hearing. But as it gets going, I start to realize we really aren't needed. Nobody is asking us questions. We're sitting in the crowd, which feels a lot like sitting in church. The Judge—not Brucie Boy, thank God—asks Pops all kinds of questions. Pops gives little one-word answers. He don't look at us except one time. He turns around in his chair and puts eyes on me. When I meet his gaze, he quickly turns away.

Big Time swaps spots with Beth to be beside me. He sits there wringing his little hands together. Then he puts his head on my shoulder. And I know the anxiety he's got wriggling around inside because I got it, too.

The judge tells everyone no one is on trial today.

"The purpose of this hearing is to go over evidence and determine if the state has a case to charge Mr. Cope with first-degree murder, among other charges, at the prosecutor's recommendation," he says.

Then he reads the charges. Which include the whole murdering Shotgun business. But then go on to include things like endangering the welfare of a minor, battery, and aggravated assault. All these charges just having to do with how he treated me and Big Time. Pops listens. I can't see his face. Can't tell what kind of expression he is wearing. But he doesn't move one bit. He stares straight ahead at the judge and listens.

When the judge is done reading the charges, there is a pause. The sound of papers shuffling. People whispering to each other.

"If I may, Your Honor," Pops says. "I'd like to go ahead and enter a guilty plea to all charges."

The whole courtroom reacts. Some gasp. Others start talking. The judge bangs his gavel to get folks to be quiet. Then he leans forward from the bench and says, "Mr. Cope, you are innocent until presumed guilty. And you also have the right to a lawyer. If you cannot afford a lawyer, the state can provide one for you."

"I can afford a lawyer."

"Then I advise you to think hard before entering any kind of plea."

"I have thought hard already. All I do lately is think hard."

There's a pause. I realize I am sitting up straight. Leaning forward. Trying to get a look at Pops' face.

"May we approach the bench?" one of the prosecutors says.

And he and the other lawyers walk up and talk in whispers.

Then they sit down.

"Mr. Cope. Your children are in the room," the Judge says.

"I know."

"If you enter a guilty plea, you will lose custody of them. Forever."

Only then does he turn and look back at us. Tears streak down his cheeks. He says, "Your Honor. I never deserved them boys." Cries hard into his hands for a second. Then he regains control and continues. "I am saying what I am saying because I never deserved them. But there's something else, Your Honor."

My heart thunders in my chest. Like a hundred million fans at a World Series baseball game. The whole room is silent, waiting to hear what Hunter Cope, the man who sat down Sammy Sosa and Mark McGwire during the home-run race, the best baseball player to ever come out of Quiet County, is going to say next.

"I want to confess to killing my wife, Eliza Cope, and recruiting Samuel Ledbetter, who was my drug dealer, to help me hide the body." He pauses, struggles to speak. "He was the only person I knew vile enough to help me. I shot and killed him after he made a child abuse report against me over a dispute we had over drugs. He threatened me by saying he would tell the police what I done to my wife. So when I got to his house and saw Crawford there..."

He stops for a long time, tears streaking down his face. His lower lip trembles. He lifts one hand in the air, gesturing to nothing. It hangs there pointlessly while he sobs. Finally, he finishes his statement. "I snapped. Seeing him there with my boy, I snapped."

Cope Field

There is silence in the courtroom.

Then the judge says, "Mr. Cope. What reason did you have to kill your wife?"

He shakes his head. Won't look at anybody.

For a long time, we all listen to him cry. And my cheeks are wet, too.

"She tried to make me a better person," he says finally. "She forgave me when she outta not have. She loved me relentlessly. Foolishly. And I thanked her with violence."

Brawner nods to a police officer, who walks to Pops and helps him to his feet. Pops does not resist the handcuffs as they snap around his wrists. He looks right at me. "There is a glade behind our house, right behind the practice facility. About a quarter mile. We buried her between twin birches what growed together at their tops. I wanted to give her someplace beautiful to rest. I did love your momma, boys. I was out of my mind when it happened. I been outta my mind ever since..."

I MISS YOU
BLINK-182

On the drive home, Big Time don't ask for pizza or nothing. He sits with his hands limp in his lap, his head against the car window. His eyes are hidden behind a new pair of professional rassler glasses he got from who knows where, but there is a frown on his face. And sometimes, I think I see him wipe away a teardrop or two.

It's all out there now.

And it hurts.

But it feels good, too. Like this can finally end.

I can finally go on. And so can Big Time. He just don't all the way know it yet.

Adam sits beside him. "Are y'all boys okay?" he asks.

"Not really," I tell him.

"That's okay, kiddo. That's okay." There's a long pause. "Can we do anything to help?"

"No."

What can be done? It's all already happened. The judge accepted Pops' guilty plea. Next, he'll be sentenced. And here is the thing: He asked for the maximum. Said that's what he deserved. Which is true. And I am glad for it. But it still hurts somewhere inside me. How can I hold space for two opposite feelings at the same time? And how can I still feel anything besides disgust toward the man who killed my momma? I am old enough to mull over these thoughts. Grind them down until I can swallow them. But Big Time . . . I wonder if he will ever be able to untangle that.

There are finally answers about Momma. Justice for her.

But none of that brings her back.

I need to get my mind off things in a bad way, so I take out my phone and start thumbing through it. End up opening my music app and looking at the playlist Hannah made me.

Crawdaddy's Musical Education.

I pop in my headphones and hit play. And Hannah's wild music fills my eardrums. Wild music. But it's her voice speaking to me through these angsty songs. I close my eyes and think about her face. Her anime T-shirts. Her battle jacket. The way she felt in my arms. The way she always wanted to know what I thought. And the way what I thought never phased her.

I listen through the whole playlist.

Then a new song starts playing. And I'm like, *What in the hell?* I look down at the screen. Added by Hannah Flores one week ago. The song is called "I Miss You."

Later that day, Adam rolls to my room. "Hey, Craw," he says.

"Hey."

"Why don't you and Big Time come in the yard and let me show you how to throw a knuckleball. Get your mind off things. You know?"

"What will we ever need a knuckleball for?"

"Because you're gonna go on to be big and famous."

I roll my eyes. "Come on."

"No, it's true. And one day, maybe five or six years from now, you'll be in a tight spot. Maybe it'll be in the World Series. And you'll need to get through a batter to win the game. And you'll think back in your memories and remember this one pitch you got, one you haven't shown anybody before. The knuckleball. And if God is good, I'll be at home watching on the television. And I'll say to everyone, 'I taught him that.'"

I tell him no thanks. Feel a little guilty. Because it's a nice idea. And I have no good reason to say no. But I am just too exhausted for baseball.

Later, Beth says she's done cooking for a bunch of starving boys, so we're going out for burgers. This draws a cheer from Adam and Big Time both. We load up, she drives us to town, and we sit around listening to Big Time tell jokes for an hour and a half.

Then she runs a few errands around town. Picking up groceries and some prescriptions for Adam. And the whole time Big Time is cutting up. He has us laughing so hard, my belly hurts. I am so glad to hear Big Time being himself a little bit. I got this warm feeling growing way down deep. And some part of me wants to keep that going.

"You want to play ball tonight after all?" I ask Adam.

And he says, "Hell yes."

By the time we get home, the sun is low in the sky. All orange-and-yellow fire sinking low into the mountains. I help Adam out of the van and roll him into the middle of the yard. Big Time leaves to fetch our gloves and a bucket of baseballs. Beth hooks up a little Bluetooth speaker to her phone and starts blasting country music.

I get tingles on my arms. Like electricity.

"Adam," I say.

"Hmm?"

"Why do you got a trunk full of Dad's memorabilia?"

"You saw that, huh?"

Big Time comes around the corner, struggling to carry everything. "Someone could help," he says.

"Naw, you got it," I tell him. And I really shouldn't tease him like this since he is still halfway mad at me. But one way to for sure reach Big Time's heart is with a little jokey joke.

"Truth is," Adam says to me, "I grew up a huge fan of your daddy's. Being from the same town and all. Had all that stuff in my office. But when we heard what happened . . ." He sighs. Chooses his words carefully. "Sometimes our heroes aren't heroes. And we gotta let them go. I was gonna sell that stuff. Donate the money to a nonprofit that works with victims of domestic violence. Plus . . . I just thought y'all wouldn't appreciate seeing it, once I was sure you were gonna get placed with us."

Big Time plops the bucket on the ground in front of us. His shades fall in the grass. "Goddamn," he says.

"Language," Beth says, coming down from the front porch and into the yard.

Big Time's cheeks turn red. But Beth laughs. Scruffs her hand through his mullet. Then he laughs, too.

Adam picks up a baseball. He shows me where to grip it. Walks me through the throwing motion. He says an off-tempo pitch can be a "real bitch" for a batter. Which gets Big Time laughing hard. And Beth saying, "Good grief, Adam." And me thinking: These two are alright. They got love in them. And that is about the only thing that really matters, isn't it?

PALE GREEN THINGS
THE MOUNTAIN GOATS

On the morning of my eighteenth birthday, Adam is waiting at the kitchen table with a letter in his hand. "Y'all got mail," he says the moment we walk in from the back room. I take it from him and read the return address. It's from an attorney. So I sit down, tear open the envelope, and read it immediately.

"It's from Pops," I say.

"I thought he ain't supposed to talk to us no more," Big Time says, sitting beside me.

"I mean, it's on his behalf from his attorney."

"And?"

"Be quiet. Let me read."

But I can't read. My hands start shaking.

Beth puts her hand on mine. Gives me a soft squeeze. "It's gonna be okay," she says.

And somehow, that gives me the strength I need to keep going. "It says . . . it says Pops is planning on selling the house. But I don't understand the rest. There's a whole lot of pages to this, and there's places it wants me to sign."

Beth goes over it with me for the next hour. Pops is going to sell the house, along with everything in it, all his baseball memorabilia and equipment and sentimental items from his playing days. Then he's gonna put all his money into a trust. The letter says he isn't saving *a single cent* for himself. Half is coming to me once everything is final, which is why my signature is needed. The other half will collect interest until Sutton turns eighteen. The letter also says we oughta go over there and fetch anything of *sentimental value we would like to keep*.

"Well," Adam says, a big smile breaking across his face. "You're rich, Crawford. Now what?"

After graduation, I went ahead and took custody over Big Time. Even though Adam and Beth were happy to keep him, and I think he would have done okay there. They even said to me he can stay, and I can come get him anytime I want. That even though I'm striking out on my own, they still think of me like a son.

It's like, *Damn.* I have not lived with these people that long.

But hearing them say that...

I don't know. Full-on tears.

But in my heart, I know it is best for us Cope boys to stick together. So we move out on a Saturday. Heading up to Fayetteville because I accepted that offer to play ball for Arkansas. And I want to get settled and figure out about Big Time's schooling before college classes start. Beth helps me load our stuff. Adam rolls around and gives directions. The whole time, he keeps breaking down and crying.

"I'm just gonna miss y'all," he says.

"We will visit," I tell him. And I mean it. They feel comfortable. Like a cozy sweater. Like family ought to feel. "Every holiday, if we are invited."

Adam rises up from the chair as far as he can. He ropes his arms around my neck and holds me tight. "Love you, Crawford," he whispers in my ear.

And those words burn. Feel good and bad at the same time. Good because I love him, too. Bad because it makes me think of Pops.

We finish loading my truck. Then I back down the driveway, leaving them standing on the front porch. Adam waving. Beth with her hands clutched in front of her. Big Time hangs out the window and yells, "Goodbye!"

And I watch Adam and Beth get smaller and smaller in the mirror as we drive away.

It feels like we are leaving Quiet County forever.

We aren't.

But it has that feeling to it.

I drive the long way down the bendy roads, through Hosanna, past the school, the baseball field, the diner where Pops liked to gossip and brag. I drive all the way out to Jerusalem. I stop in the road beside Hannah's old house, and we look down across the park. It's a little further along than it was before but still not all the way finished. I noticed they changed the wrought iron archway the last time I was here, but I didn't bother looking closer. It used to say COPE FIELD in big metal letters. But looking closer, I can see it says something completely different now.

"Can you read that?" I ask.

Big Time says he can't.

So I drive down into the newly paved parking lot to get close. Big Time peers up at the archway with his hands cupped around his eyes like binoculars, as if that will somehow help. But I can read it now. All this emotion swells up in my chest. I try to say something, but it rasps out. Half laugh. Half cry. I cannot believe they done this.

It says:

SUTTON-CRAWFORD FIELD

After that, we head up to Pops' old house because Donna called and said we oughta head over there and get anything we want to keep. When we pull into the driveway, there's a realtor sign out front. Says SOLD right across the top.

Sutton shifts in his seat. Looks uncomfortable. And I know why. This will be our first time in our house in a long while. And it feels a little bit like slipping back through time. Or walking into a hospital where you know someone you once loved has died.

"Hey," I say. His eyes cut to mine. He looks like he is on the verge of tears. "I'm here with you."

That gets a weak smile.

We get out of the truck and walk to the front porch. I still have my key, so I stick it in the lock, wiggle it, and open the door. And we stand there, staring into our old life. I reach down and take Sutton's hand. Give him a little squeeze. "You ready?" He takes off his visor glasses and hangs them on the front of his shirt. Then he gives me one quick nod, and we step into the house.

"The hell happened?" Sutton says.

I forgot how bad things got right before I left. Forgot Pops shoved me through a wall. That the couch flipped over with Pops on it. That the television came off the mantle.

We stand there looking at the mess a while. I am eager to put this all behind me. But at the same time transfixed by how terrible things had been. It's funny. But not haha funny. Things had been terrible for so long, and I always blamed myself. I always said it was me who escalated things, me who wasn't good enough, me who took things too far... but with a little distance, it's so obvious.

"Pops happened, Sut," I say, all the bad feelings coming back to me. "Pops happened."

That man bought us the world. But he charged us for it in ways we couldn't imagine.

Sutton says, "I'll get my stuff."

I head to my room and grab the PlayStation and a television. A few of my favorite pairs of Jordans. I leave the VR headset on my desk. I pack up some more clothes. Then I walk down the hallway to Pops' bedroom. It's filled with his own memorabilia. Photos of him on the hill. Baseball cards. Pictures of him with presidents, actors, and other people I don't recognize. I open the bedside table, start rifling through things. I'm looking for anything sentimental. The kind of thing that might still matter to Sutton and me even without Pops around.

But there's nothing.

This whole room is just a church built to Pops' baseball career.

I can't stay here long. So I hurry and finish with the bedside table. Then I walk to the closet and start yanking everything out of all the little cubbies and hiding spots and shelves, leaving it all in a pile around my feet.

Then I find what I'm looking for: a small photograph in a silver frame.

In my memories, it was always on Pops' bedside table.

Until it wasn't.

He couldn't stand looking at it, I guess.

I touch the glass.

Momma. In a field of tall grass. White sundress, blowing in the wind. Her auburn hair caught up in the sky. She looks at the camera over her shoulder. Maybe twenty years old in this photo. Barely older than me.

There is no meanness in her eyes.

And none could ever hope to land there.

We got one more stop.

And I have been meaning to make it for a while.

It's like typing Momma's name in that search engine. I gotta work up some kinda mega gumption within myself to do it. Because once I am there, I am not sure how I will react.

I walk out on the back deck, stare across the pool and up the hill toward the Baseball Dungeon. It's all woods behind there. But farther in, I know there is an open space. Pops would put feed out there sometimes, and I used to like to sit up there and watch the deer. I been up there a hundred times. Never knowing the truth about the place.

My whole life is like that, seems like.

Me and Big Time got so many memories here together. And not all of them are bad. I can remember Momma coming here the first time. Throwing her arms out and saying, *It's beautiful, Hunter.* Because she'd been scared about coming to Arkansas. Because all she knew about Arkansas was from things people said about it, which were not all true or nice.

She loved the big property. The trees. The mountains rolling in the distance. She loved the stars like you have never seen stars. And she loved him, too, it is strange to say. And me. And Sutton. And that is the bit that hurts the most, I reckon. To know there was a whole universe of love in this world meant for us.

And Pops stole it.

We felt that void our whole lives.

But we never knew it.

The good times shine heavy light on the bad times, make it all hurt a little worse in some strange way. It's like, *Pops, how could you throw all this away?*

Big Time and I walk up the hill toward the Baseball Dungeon. Then, we walk along the corrugated metal building until we come to the backside. We push through the trees and the brush out into the woods.

There, not even half a football field away from our house, we find the glade. In the middle stand twin birches, their white branches entangled, a blank space on the ground between them.

A blank space. Pale, green grass growing tall.

Momma's space.

We stand there a while, listening to the birds and the locusts. And I'm thinking about her being out here. Like *really* being out here. From this spot, I bet you she heard every crack of my baseball bat in the dungeon. Bet you she heard so much else I wish she never heard.

"What was she like?" Sutton says.

"I don't remember a lot."

"What do you remember?"

I think for a minute. I want my answer to be the right one. "When I think of Momma, I think about how strong she was. How she would stand up to Pops. He'd tear into me over some foolish thing. And there'd she be, saying, *He's just a boy.* And you know what? Sometimes Pops would listen to her. And sometimes, when I had a real bad night—a bad game, or even just a bad day at school—she would come into my room and sit on my bed. She'd say, *Tell me about it.* And I would. I'd tell her all about it. And she wouldn't say nothing about how I messed up my own life or how I could do better next time or how it was so important for me to be tough."

"Coulda used her a few times as of late."

I laugh. Because it is again one of those funny ways Sutton has of speaking where he sounds like some old farmer type sitting on his front porch dispersing wisdom to the young'ns. I say, "One thing is for sure, Sut. She loved you. And she loved me, too. And she didn't deserve what life gave her."

I am all the time thinking to myself how bad I got it. How I did not choose for things to be this way. And how unfair things have been to me. But the fact of the matter is I am still alive. I still got chances to make things different. But Momma don't. By no mistake of her own, she got stole from her all the moments she mighta had to be happy again.

Momma loved someone.

The *wrong* someone.

That's all.

Sutton sits down at the base of a tree. Then he lies down across the spot where she is buried.

He lies there for a long time.

I WANT TO SAVE YOU
SOMETHING CORPORATE

Not even a month into living in Fayetteville, a man walks up to me and Big Time at the Walmart. Smile on his face.

"Crawford Cope?" he says.

"That's me."

He sticks his hand in my face. I shake it. "I saw you were playing for Arkansas. I am a huge fan. Big fan of your dad's, too. And I can't wait to see what you're gonna do up there."

"Thanks."

The man says his name is Luke Roberts. He gets down with his hands on his knees to look Big Time in the eyes. "And this is the next generation?" he asks.

Big Time holds on to my hand. Which I've noticed he has done more and more since everything. Since we moved here. Since we both started seeing a counselor once per week. "This is my little brother, Sutton. We call him Big Time."

"Big Time! You don't get that kinda nickname for no reason. Listen, I coach this travel team. The Bombers. We got tryouts soon. You oughta have him come. I'm sure we could use him, if he's at all like you and your dad." He digs around in his pocket for a card. Then he writes a time and date on the back. We talk a little longer. Him super excited to see me. To hopefully see Big Time at the tryouts. Me just wanting this conversation to end.

When he is gone, I pay for our groceries. We walk out to the truck and load up.

"Well, how about it?" I say.

"How about what?"

"You wanna try out?"

Big Time shrugs. Looks a little embarrassed. Which is not at all like him. After a second, he says, "Can I tell you something, Craw?"

"What?"

"I... I don't really... wanna play baseball no more."

I wonder how long he's been kicking this idea around in his head. Scared to tell me. Maybe he's had it long enough he might coulda said something to Pops. Hell. Maybe he *did* say something to Pops. Lord. I wonder how that man would have reacted. Not good, I can tell you that. No matter what, I know whatever I say next will probably echo around Big Time's skull for the rest of his life. So I gotta choose those words careful.

I keep it chill. Like, *Who cares.* "Okay, bud. Do you got an idea what you might wanna do instead? I can see you as a comedian. Legit."

Big Time's shoulders relax. He smiles great big.

"Hell and yes," he says, his cheeks turning bright red. I swear to God, I have never seen him so happy. "I wanna be a YouTuber or some kinda famous person on TikTok. You know you can get paid just to be on the YouTube? I don't know how it works yet, but I aim to find out. I wanna go on there and talk about space but do it in a funny way where people laugh and learn stuff at the same time. I got like ten space jokes memorized already."

"Dang, boy."

"You wanna hear one?"

"Sure do."

"What kind of music do planets sing?"

I don't say nothing, waiting for the punch line. He nudges me. "You gotta say, 'What kind?'"

"What kind then?"

"Neptunes."

I laugh. "You made that up?"

"I got it from a book. But I'm writing my own, too." He bounces in his seat, so excited to be talking about something he loves. I have never seen him act this way about baseball. Not one time. Not even after hitting the homers what earned him his nickname. I want to pull him across the car and hug him tight.

So I do. "I love you, kid."

And to my surprise, Big Time says it back. He lays his head on my shoulder. My hand on the back of his head. We breathe together.

"It's been... a lot," he whispers.

I pull away far enough to look him in the eyes. "I know. But hey. No matter what, we got each other. You can always, always talk to me. You know that, right?"

Sutton's smile is soft and sweet. "I know, bubba. I know."

I'LL CATCH YOU
THE GET UP KIDS

We have a little club scrimmage tonight. Red versus White. Us versus us. I'm on the red team. Batting last in the lineup. Pitching cleanup. They got the stadium rocking with music. A few fans scattered around to watch. Not a lot, but more than I am used to playing in front of. I stand in the middle of the field, looking around, wondering what it's like to play when this place is full. When their cheers can be heard from blocks away. When every mistake and success you have on the field has a hundred thousand eyes watching.

And aw, hell. I just remembered. These games go on the television, too. And on ESPN sometimes. And those *SportsCenter* guys even sometimes talk about them.

That's a million eyes at least.

Makes me feel a little pukey. I scan the crowd until I find Big Time, sitting alone near the visitor's side dugout, his feet kicked up on the seat in front of him. Since it's his first chance to see me in an Arkansas uniform, I brought him with me. It calms my heart a little to see him there now.

One of my teammates, a senior, I think, comes up and slaps my ass. Which might seem weird, unless you ever been around a sports team before. Then he slings an arm around my shoulder and looks out over the crowd. "Freaking out yet?"

"A little."

"You wanna know what helps me?"

"What?"

"I pretend there's nobody out there. Nobody except my dad."

My eyes sting with tears when he says that. But I don't cry. It's getting easier not to cry.

"You're gonna do great," he says. "Believe it. Manifest it."

I stare out across the crowd. Watch a daddy and his son walking

Cope Field

down the aisle. The kid's hands full of ballpark food. He's got a huge smile on his face. And it strikes me that on first glance, he's happy. Like I was. But who knows, really? Who knows what his life is like.

I look over by the visitor's dugout again, hoping maybe I can say hello to Big Time before this thing gets started.

But there's a girl sitting next to him.

Pink hair. Black shirt with some jagged white logo on it. Big Time is talking up a storm, and this girl is laughing with her whole body.

Hannah.

Without thinking, I slip from under my teammate's arm and run toward her. She comes down the steps until there is nothing between us but the low wall that separates the stands from the field, and Big Time follows. He hops the wall, which he is for sure not supposed to do, and stands in the grass beside me, his hands on his hips.

"Look, Crawdaddy," he says, grinning. "I'm a big, bad college baseball player like you."

Hannah laughs. So do I. And then we get quiet. Because we have not really spoken in a long, long time. And it's awkward in a way I wish it wasn't. So I stand there like an idiot, itching the back of my head.

"Hey, Crawdaddy," she says.

"Hey."

"Good to see you."

Mmm. Still awkward as hell. Things with Hannah were never awkward. But things change, I guess. I know that as well as anybody. "What are you doing here?"

"Am I not allowed?"

"You are. Of course you are."

"I'm here on scholarship."

"Scholarship?" I'm a little surprised. The Hannah I knew told me she'd never get out of Quiet County. It wasn't even worth trying. But here she is, on scholarship. Better than that... she's on scholarship at the same school as me.

"Someone I know told me I deserved better than Quiet County. Told me not to get trapped. Turns out, one mediocre semester wasn't enough to tank all my scholarship opportunities."

"You came to my scrimmage," I say.

She smiles, her cheeks reddening. "I didn't have anything else to do."

There is something different about her. More calm. I don't want to say she is dressed normally. Like, there is still an edge. But it's toned down. Before, it was nothing *but* edge. Now she looks like she might ask you where you want to sit at a fancy restaurant. But if you give her sass, she might also cut you with a knife.

"I'm... I'm real glad to see you," I say.

"You are?"

I look at the grass between my feet. In my periphery, I can see Big Time inching his way closer to the baseline. He thinks I don't notice. I point at him, then I point to a spot of grass right next to me. He scowls, but he obeys, looking a bit like the world's saddest puppy. I look back up at Hannah. "I miss you. I've missed you from the second you walked away from me."

"I saw what you said on the news."

"Yeah... sorry about that. How have you been since everything?"

"You know, I'm good. I'm really good. Ever since Shotgun died, my life has gotten exponentially better. Isn't that sad? To be a person who dies and it makes the world you left behind a better place?"

I nod. Knowing exactly how she feels. Pops isn't dead. But he might as well be.

She tells me she went to live with her mom's sister after everything went down. She thought about texting me to let me know. But she thought she ought to get her own situation sorted first. "You know, focus on growth or some shit."

Then Hannah looks me in the eye and smiles. "And Crawford Cope, strongest king of the strong, silent types, finally broke his silence. And he did it to tell the entire world—" She stops. Shrugs. "What was it you said again?"

The question hangs heavy in the air. A little comical because the press box is playing wacky baseball organ music. I wait for the music to stop, my cheeks turning bright red. I've been practicing saying what I think, but damn it if it is not still hard as hell. She gives me a look like, *Well?*

"Just what I said. What you already heard."

"Still can't tell me?"

"No, I can."

She folds her arms across her chest. Waits for me to go on. I feel Big Time's little fingers slip into my hand. He nudges me. Whispers, "Go on, Crawdaddy. Tell this girl you love her."

Hannah laughs, her hand over her mouth.

I just about start crying.

Cope Field

"I love ya, Hannah. That's all. I know that don't mean much. And I know I messed up. But it's true. I love you now, and I always will. Even if we aren't ever together again."

A coach yells my name from across the field, and Big Time turns me loose and immediately scrambles back over the wall and into the stands. I look at the coach and nod to let him know I heard him. It's time to start. "Hannah—"

"You have to go."

"Yeah..."

I start to turn away. But she stops me. Her hand on my wrist.

"Crawford," she says, this look in her eyes like, *He's stupid, but he's cute, so I'll walk him there.* "I added that song to our playlist. Did you see it?"

"I did."

"I came to your baseball game on the express hope that I would get to see you."

"Oh."

"So aren't you going to ask for my number? If I'm doing anything after this? If we can get together sometime? For coffee maybe? A movie? Anything? You know, since you love me and everything?"

Heat rises to my cheeks. "I wasn't sure I deserved you."

Hannah laughs. She grabs the front of my jersey and pulls me close. Slides her hands around the back of my neck. She smells like flowers. Like rain. Like everything good in this world you want to keep but know you can't.

"You know, Crawford," she whispers. "Sometimes, I don't think any of us deserve a single thing that happens to us."

So I kiss her.

Because damn right, I kiss her.

Coach is yelling behind me. The whole stadium waiting for this thing to start. Wacky organ music blaring. The smell of popcorn. Hot dogs. The entire afternoon hanging on the prospect of baseball.

But me?

I got more important things.

Acknowledgments

Cope Field began on a hot summer afternoon as I watched my son play baseball. By this point, I'd been involved in youth sports long enough to know that some parents take it too seriously. But on this day, my son (age eight at the time) forgot to tag up and cost the team two outs. The coach became so irate he threw his hat on the ground and stomped it, and that day, my son left the ballpark with the part of him that loved baseball stomped out, too. He hasn't played since that season ended.

That planted a small seed in my brain.

In my years covering sports for the local newspaper, I have seen countless "star" players move through different high school programs. They seem like they have it all. They're charming, good-looking kids with a knack for throwing strikes, hitting nukes, or both.

But I knew that underneath that, at least for some of them, there was likely a parent who thought it was their job to push them into being a sports phenom. The funny thing is, none of these individuals have gone on to play professional sports. Few played at the collegiate level, and even fewer played Division I sports.

There are lessons to be learned from playing sports.

Sure.

But there are a lot of bad ideas being pushed around, too. You can learn a lot of the same good lessons from chess. Or band. Or from being an average player on a high school team.

Another thing I learned: Sometimes accolades and privilege can hide trauma and abuse. It's easy to see the kid in the big house with the rich parents and think they have it easy. But monsters lurk everywhere.

No book exists as the sole work of the author. *Cope Field* is no exception. This book would be nowhere near as good as it is without the dedication, vision, and story smarts of my editor, Meg Gaertner, who helped guide me into making this book the very best version of itself possible.

I have made so many writer friends and connections since my debut, *Strong Like You*, came out in 2024. I'd like to thank Jess Gutierrez (*A Product of Genetics (and Day Drinking)*), fellow Arkansan and hilarious writer. She was there every step of the way to encourage me, talk me down from the ledge, and remind me to enjoy this crazy experience. Also, Freya Finch (*Rise*), a fantastic writer who cheered me on from the moment she picked up *Strong Like You* and is just generally an awesome and kind person. Shaun Hamill (*A Cosmology of Monsters, The Dissonance*), who remarkably continues to be a friend after I cyberstalked him. We even got to do an event together! Also, huge shout-outs to Matteo L. Cerilli (*Lockjaw*) and Jeff Wooten (*Kill Call*).

Also, so many thank-yous to my wife, Melissa, who smiled wider than I did to see me doing this author thing. Thank you to my kids, Greg, Kaylee, Jeffrey, and Henry, who continue to inspire me. Thank you to Joshua Wilson and James Briscoe, who are the very definition of good friends. Thank you to James Ruiz and Sofia Robleda for help with the Spanish sections of this book. Thank you to Jeff Phillips, prosecuting attorney of the Fifth Judicial District, for answering some questions I had about court procedures. If I goofed anything up, it's on me—not him. Thank you to my agent, Shari Maurer. None of this would be happening (again) without her.

And last of all, thank you to all the book clubs, librarians, teachers, and readers who have supported me since *Strong Like You* came out. I hope you all love *Cope Field* as much as I do.

About the Author

T. L. Simpson is an award-winning journalist and novelist living in Arkansas. He is currently the editor of his hometown paper, *The Courier*. His fiction draws from his experiences growing up in the Ozarks, covering both sports and crime. Simpson lives in the Arkansas River Valley, between the Ozark and Ouachita Mountains, with his wife and four children. His debut contemporary YA novel, *Strong Like You*, released in 2024.

Also by T.L. Simpson

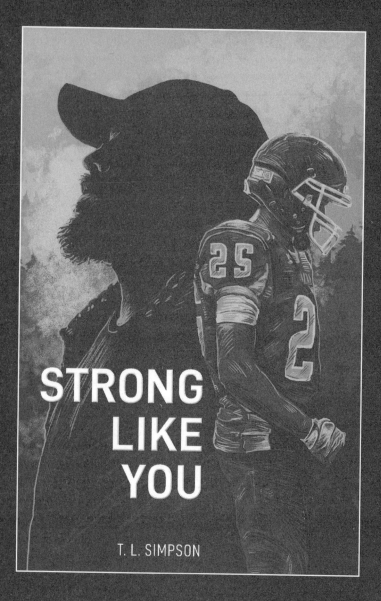

A 2025 YALSA Best Fiction for Young Adults Selection

A 2025 Indiana Read Aloud Selection

A 2025 TAYSHAS Top 10 Reading List Selection

**2024 Moonbeam Awards Silver Medalist
(Young Adult – General)**

I haven't cried one time since you disappeared. Not even at football practice when Paton Roper told the whole team you were probably dead. He said, "You know how sometimes a dog gets sick or bites somebody and you have to put it down?"
Somebody said, "Yep."
"That's probably what happened to Walker's daddy."

Walker Lauderdale hasn't cried once since his daddy went missing. And even though everyone says he's dead, Walker won't give up hope. He knows his father is out there, somewhere, cutting a wild trail through the Ozarks like always. But when a relative threatens to kick Walker and his momma out of the family home, Walker realizes he has no choice but to look for his daddy—a search that leads him straight to a drug-addled and dangerous man named Lukas Fisher. While attempting to balance life as a normal fifteen-year-old boy and star player on the football team, Walker begins a desperate search across the hills of the Ozarks for the man who, for better or worse, taught him everything he knows about strength.